PENGUIN BOOKS

The Girl Who Died

The Girl Who Died

RAGNAR JÓNASSON

Translated from the Icelandic
by Victoria Cribb

PENGUIN BOOKS

PENGUIN BOOKS

UK | USA | Canada | Ireland | Australia
India | New Zealand | South Africa

Penguin Books is part of the Penguin Random House group of companies
whose addresses can be found at global.penguinrandomhouse.com

Penguin
Random House
UK

First published in Iceland with the title *Þorpið* by Veröld Publishing 2018
First published in Great Britain by Michael Joseph 2021
Published in Penguin Books 2021

001

Typeset by Jouve (UK), Milton Keynes
Printed and bound in Great Britain by Clays Ltd, Elcograf S.p.A.

The authorized representative in the EEA is Penguin Random House Ireland,
Morrison Chambers, 32 Nassau Street, Dublin D02 YH68

A CIP catalogue record for this book is available from the British Library

ISBN: 978–1–405–94254–6

www.greenpenguin.co.uk

MIX
Paper from
responsible sources
FSC® C018179

Penguin Random House is committed to a
sustainable future for our business, our readers
and our planet. This book is made from Forest
Stewardship Council® certified paper.

To Dad

Lullaby, my little Thrá,
may you sweetly sleep,
dreaming of the sunny lands
beyond the ocean deep.

– Thorsteinn Th. Thorsteinsson
(1879–1955)

ICELAND

Skálar

Reykjavik

N

| 0 | | 50 | | 100 miles |
| 0 | 50 | 100 | 150 km |

Author's Note

This story takes place in the village of Skálar in the mid-1980s. In fact, Skálar has been abandoned since the mid-1950s, but the setting is nevertheless borrowed from reality, though the buildings are my own invention. The characters too are fictitious and bear no resemblance to any past residents of Skálar. In spite of this, I have tried to give an accurate representation of the historical facts about the settlement, with the help of information from works including Fridrik G. Olgeirsson's *Langnesingasaga* (*A History of the People of Langanes*). I also refer to folk tales that are preserved in Sigfús Sigfússon's collection of Icelandic folk tales and legends. Any mistakes in the book are of course my responsibility.

Thanks are due to Haukur Eggertsson for showing me around the Langanes Peninsula and the ruins of Skálathorp during the writing of this book. I am also grateful to my father, Jónas Ragnarsson, prosecutor Hulda María Stefánsdóttir and Hannes Mar Árnason, whose family came from Skálar, for their help in reading the manuscript. Thank you as well to Helgi Ellert

Jóhannsson, who works as a doctor in London, for his advice on medical matters.

Towards the end of the book, I quote from the poem 'Sleep Song' by Davíd Stefánsson.

I also quote 'Lullaby' by Thorsteinn Th. Thorsteinsson, which was printed in the *Heimskringla* magazine in Winnipeg in 1910. Thorsteinn was born in Svarfadardalur in the north of Iceland in 1879 and died in Canada in 1955.

— Ragnar Jónasson

Una awoke with a jerk.

She opened her eyes but couldn't see a thing for the darkness pressing in all around her. For a panicky moment she couldn't work out where she was, though she had the feeling she was in a strange place, not in her own bed. She stiffened with fear. She was so cold. By the feel of it, she'd kicked the covers on to the floor, and the room was freezing.

She sat up slowly, experiencing a moment of dizziness, but the feeling soon passed as she remembered where she was.

In Skálar on the Langanes Peninsula. In the little attic flat. Alone.

And then she knew what it was that had woken her. Or thought she knew . . . It was hard to distinguish dream from reality with her senses still wandering in the vague borderland between sleep and waking.

She had heard something. What, though? As the memory gradually came back to her, she felt the skin prickling on her arms. It had been a high little voice – the voice of a young girl, she thought. Yes, now she could hear it again in her head: a young girl singing a lullaby.

Unable to bear it a moment longer, she got out of bed and blundered across the pitch-black room towards the light switch on the wall. Not for the first time she cursed the fact that she didn't have a reading lamp by her bed. Yet she felt a moment's reluctance to turn on the light, for fear of what the retreating shadows might reveal.

The high voice echoed eerily in her head, but she couldn't recall the words of the girl's song. It must have been a dream, however real it had seemed.

Suddenly there was a loud crack, followed by a tinkling sound and a stabbing pain in her foot that caused her to stumble and fall heavily to her knees. What the hell?

She bit back a scream, only for it to dawn on her a second later that she had trodden on the wine glass she had left on the floor the previous evening. Fumbling for her foot, she found a shard of glass sticking out of it and felt something hot and wet oozing from the wound. Gingerly, she extracted the glass. The pain was excruciating.

It took all her willpower to force herself back on to her feet, then grope along the wall for the switch, but finally she found it and turned on the light. As the room sprang into view, she shot a glance around, half-expecting to see a small figure in there with her, while telling herself that she'd imagined the whole thing: the voice hadn't been real, the lullaby had been an illusion, a trick played on her by her sleeping mind.

Limping back to the bed, she sat down, drew up her foot and examined the cut, which, luckily, turned out not to be as deep as she'd feared. Now she had satisfied herself that she was alone in the room, she could feel her heartbeat slowing and returning to normal.

Then, in a flash, the words of the girl's song came back to her:

Lullaby, my little Thrá,
may you sweetly sleep . . .

A chill spread through her flesh.

PART ONE
Several Months Earlier

I

Teacher wanted at the edge of the world.

Una read the unusual heading again.

She was sitting at the kitchen table in her little flat in the west end of Reykjavík, where she'd been living for four years, after scraping together the money for a deposit through sheer determination. Her mother – the only family she had left – hadn't been able to lend her anything and Una had been forced, as always, to stand on her own two feet.

The kitchen had hardly changed since the day Una moved in. It was still shabby and old-fashioned, with yellow linoleum on the floor, faded tiles on the walls and garish red units, which, like the white Rafha cooker, were at least twenty years out of date. Nothing about the decor or furnishings said 1985.

Still, at least the coffee tasted good, with a drop of milk. Having picked up the caffeine habit at university, Una couldn't get through the day without it.

'I don't know, Sara,' she said, trying to smile at her best

friend, who was sitting across the table from her. There wasn't much to smile about these days. Una's pay as a supply teacher at a small school in the neighbouring town of Kópavogur was barely enough to cover her bills and she was never sure from one month to the next whether she would get enough work. Despite her strict economizing, it was always an effort to make her wages stretch until the next pay day. She was resigned to eating the cheapest fish on offer at least three times a week. Every time she found herself struggling to make ends meet towards the end of the month, she regretted not having finished her medical degree, though, if she were honest, she wouldn't have been any happier if she had. It had taken her three gruelling years to admit to herself that she'd only enrolled in medicine because it was what her father had wanted; she'd been trying to make his dream come true instead of pursuing her own. She could never have worked as a doctor – she just wasn't suited to the job; she had no passion for it. Three years of her life . . . She'd passed all her exams, done well even, but it wasn't enough. The spark wasn't there.

'Why not? Come on, Una – you're always moaning about having to struggle to get by. You love teaching. And you're the adventurous type.' Sara was bursting with optimism, as usual. She'd brought *Morgunbladid* round to Una's that Saturday morning with the sole purpose of showing her the advert, aware that Una couldn't afford a subscription to the paper herself. They were planning to meet up at Sara's place that evening to watch the live broadcast of a concert in aid of starving children in

Africa. Una couldn't wait: it was rare for Iceland's sole, state-run TV channel to offer anything that entertaining. And she loved music; loved dancing, going out and having fun – given half a chance, she thought wistfully.

'But it's so far away,' she protested. 'On the opposite side of the country. You couldn't get any further from Reykjavík if you tried.' She looked back at the job advert. 'Skálar? I've never even heard of the place.'

'It's a tiny village. A hamlet, really. Right at the end of the Langanes Peninsula. Look, they say they need a teacher for a very small class. There's free accommodation thrown in. You could save up all your pay, pretty much.' After a pause Sara added: 'I saw a report about the village on TV earlier this year. Only ten people live there.'

'What? Ten! Are you joking?'

'No. That's why the TV company sent a reporter there – because it's the smallest village in the country, or something like that. It stuck in my mind: only ten inhabitants, according to the latest census. The reporter seemed to think it was funny. I assume that means there can't be more than a couple of kids to teach.'

Una hadn't taken her friend's suggestion seriously at first, but maybe it wasn't such a mad idea after all; maybe it was the opportunity she'd been waiting for. It had never crossed her mind to move to the countryside. She was a Reykjavík girl through and through, having grown up on a post-war housing estate in the suburbs, in a little house that her doctor father had built more or less with his own two hands. She'd had a good childhood there, until the event that had shattered her life.

Until then, she'd been happy, if her memories were anything to go by; playing with her friends on the unpaved roads of the estate in the light summer evenings, watching the new houses springing up all around. Now she stopped to think about it, growing up in that self-contained community had been a bit like living in a village, if not a village of only ten souls. Her images of those vanished days were bathed in a soft glow of nostalgia; a time that could never be revisited.

She and her mother had moved away, and strangers lived in their house now: Una didn't care who they were – she had no intention of ever going back. But the thought of the tiny community at Skálar struck a sudden chord with her, as if it might offer a way of recapturing the happiness of her childhood. She so badly needed a change of scene.

'I suppose it wouldn't hurt to apply,' she said at last, without really meaning to. She had a sudden vision of making a new start. Of living by the sea, in the heart of nature. 'If it's on the Langanes Peninsula, I'm guessing it's by the sea?'

'Of course it is. The place is entirely dependent on the fishing. It sounds rather charming, don't you think? Living in such a remote spot, without actually being alone.'

A village of ten souls, where everyone knew each other – everyone except her, Una corrected herself. There was a sense in which she'd still be alone, wasn't there? She'd be an outsider. But perhaps this was what she had been yearning for: solitude without loneliness. A chance to drag herself out of this rut and escape the rat race in the city, where her wages mostly went on paying off her mortgage. Where she had no money to socialize, no man in her life, and the only friend she still had any real contact with was Sara.

'Oh, I don't know, Sara. We'd never see each other, or hardly ever.'

'Don't be silly,' her friend said affectionately. 'We'd just have to make more of an effort to visit one another.' Then: 'To be honest, that's why I hesitated a bit about showing you the advert. Because I don't want to lose you. But I still think it would be the ideal opportunity for you – for a year or so.'

Teacher wanted at the edge of the world. The honesty of the advertisement appealed to Una. There was no attempt to hide the fact that the job would be a challenge. She wondered how many people would apply. If she went for it, she might be the only one. And she had to admit that there wasn't much to hold her here in town. Of course, there was Sara, but, if she was honest, they weren't really as close as they used to be. Now that Sara had got herself a family – a husband and a child – she seemed to have less and less time to devote to their friendship. They'd met at sixth-form college, but over the years life had conspired to send them in different directions. Una had been kidding herself that this evening would be like it was in the old days, when they used to party late into the night. They'd watch the concert together, mix themselves some exotic cocktails, have a laugh. She had a sudden horrible suspicion that maybe Sara was trying to get rid of her by showing her this advertisement. Maybe she was secretly bored of their friendship.

Well, the truth was that Una wouldn't find it that hard to spend a winter on Langanes without seeing Sara. It was her mother she was more worried about missing. They were so close, after going through so much together, but her mother, a fit and healthy fifty-seven-year-old, had long ago found herself a new husband who she adored. No, Una had to face facts: her mother no longer needed her there every day.

'Anyway, let's leave it for now,' she said, closing *Morgunbladid*. 'Can I keep the paper?'

'Sure.' Sara stood up, her coffee cup empty. 'I've got to get going, but we're still seeing each other this evening, aren't we? It's going to be fun, just the two of us – a girls' night in. And you promise to think about it? About the job, I mean. I reckon it could be just the thing for you.'

And Una found herself thinking that maybe it was time to move on and meet new people. To do something spontaneous and exciting for once, without wasting too much time weighing up the pros and cons. 'All right, all right,' she said, smiling. 'I promise.'

II

It was an unusually fine August day, mild with not a breath of wind stirring the leaves, and even the odd glimpse of sun.

Una tended to find August rather depressing. It marked the end of the brief Icelandic summer, the point at which the first proper darkness began to creep back after weeks of light nights, but this year she felt different. She was standing on the steps outside the block of flats in Kópavogur where her mother lived with her stepfather. The building was so bleak and run-down that Una would never have dreamt of living there herself. She was much happier in her little place in the old west end, even though it was a basement flat. Now, however, it had been rented out to a young couple with a small child.

Una's mother had come outside with her after their morning coffee. The time had come to say goodbye, at least for a while.

'We'll come and visit you – you know that, darling. And it's only for a year, isn't it?'

'Only for the school year, Mum; only over the winter,' Una said, 'but you're both welcome any time.' She wasn't being entirely sincere. Her mother was welcome, but Una had never warmed to her new husband – well, she still thought of him as new, though he had entered their life quite a long time ago. She couldn't put her finger on it, but there was something about him she didn't like.

'Are you planning to stop for the night somewhere?' her mother asked. 'It's a terribly long way. It must be more than 700 kilometres! You must rest if you feel yourself getting sleepy. It's dangerous to drive if you're tired.'

'I know, Mum,' Una answered patiently. 'I'm breaking the journey in Akureyri.' Her mother's fussing could be a bit much at times. She needed to be able to breathe, to be allowed to stand on her own two feet. And what better opportunity would she have than this: the position of teacher in a village so small it hardly deserved the name? Only ten people. How on earth could such a tiny community survive?

It would certainly be interesting and also, she hoped, reinvigorating for body and soul. In the event, getting the job had been child's play. Several days after Sara had come round with the advertisement, Una had finally psyched herself up to ring the number provided. The phone had been answered by a woman – in her thirties, Una guessed – who lived in Skálar and apparently sat on the education committee of the local authority. 'I'm very pleased to hear you're interested,' the woman said. 'To tell the truth, no one else has called about the job.'

Una had explained that she was a qualified teacher with plenty of experience.

'But why do you want to move out here?' the woman had asked.

Una had been momentarily stumped for an answer. She had so many reasons: to escape from her monotonous life in town; to have a break from Sara, or rather, to let Sara get on with her own life for a while; to have a rest from her mother – and even more from her stepfather; to have a change of scene. But the real reason lay deeper.

'I just want to try living in the countryside,' she had told the woman after a pause. Although she hadn't been given the job then and there, she had known that she must be in with a good chance. Before ending the conversation, she had asked: 'How many children are there . . . for me to teach?'

'Just two, two girls. Seven and nine years old,' came the reply.

'Just two girls? And you need a teacher?'

'Yes, the fact is, we do. It's too far to drive them back and forth to the nearest school, especially in winter. They're lovely girls as well.'

And now the moment had come. Una was embarking on her adventure here in Kópavogur, at the crack of dawn: a winter in the countryside, right out at the end of the Langanes Peninsula, among strangers, with only two pupils. It still seemed faintly ridiculous that she was being hired to teach such a tiny class, as if it would hardly justify a full teacher's salary. But inside she was excited; there was something so appealing about the idea.

Salka, the woman she had spoken to on the phone, had come across as friendly and approachable. If all the locals were like her, perhaps the little village would welcome Una with open arms. And perhaps she would be so taken with the scenery and the people that she wouldn't want to leave after her contract was up . . .

She snapped out of her thoughts when her mother touched her arm and repeated her question, although Una had already answered it: 'You're sure it's only for one year?'

'Just for one winter, yes. I've no intention of living that far from Reykjavík for ever.' She smiled reassuringly at her mother.

'Well, Una. I feel as if the bird's finally flown the nest.'

'What nonsense, Mum. I flew the nest years ago.'

'Yes, darling, but you've never been far away. We've always been there for each other . . . I just hope it won't be too difficult for you, being alone up there, not being able to come and see me to talk about . . . well, about the past.'

Una had a sudden suspicion that her mother was in fact describing her own fears; that this parting might prove harder for her than Una had realized.

Una hugged her tight, and they stood there for a moment, neither of them saying a word.

There was nothing more to say.

He had never killed a man before.

Had never come close, despite his sinister reputation. It was a reputation designed to instil respect and fear, cultivated deliberately because he had a position to maintain. Plenty of people no doubt believed him capable of murder, and some probably thought he had already killed, given all the times he'd been forced to resort to violence. Although his appearance didn't necessarily suggest it, he was strong and knew how to fight.

And today he had finally done it; he had killed a man.

It had been a strange feeling. At first, all he had been aware of was the adrenaline pumping through his veins, telling him that from now on there was nothing he couldn't do. He'd proven capable of taking a life, of standing and watching as a man drew his last few breaths, savouring the power of knowing that at any moment he could have intervened to save him.

He had brought along the sawn-off shotgun. It was late, the evening was dark, wet and cold. He had battered violently at the door, knowing there was little risk that anyone would hear. The block of flats was hardly more than a construction site, the first half-completed building in a concrete jungle. No one else had moved in yet; there were no witnesses to his visit. His victim – who didn't deserve to be called a victim – had obviously realized what was happening and tried to defend himself. He had felt an urge to shoot him, but the purpose of the shotgun had only ever been to intimidate, not to kill. The fallout from a gunshot would be too messy.

Instead, he had spun the gun round and used the butt to knock the man senseless, then finished him off with his bare hands.

It hadn't been that hard. Not really. He had to do it; he had no choice.

Now the poor bastard was lying dead on his own living-room floor, and somehow the body would have to be removed and made to disappear. That was tonight's job.

He stood there motionless for a while, examining the lifeless corpse, and as he did so it came home to him that everything had changed; he had crossed a line, committed a deed that couldn't be undone. He would have to learn to live with it. From now on, he would always be a fugitive, because he had every intention of getting away with it. The alternative was unthinkable. There were people who knew about this visit, but they were on his side. They were the ones who had asked him to deal with the problem. He wasn't too worried about the police, as long as he managed to dispose of the body without a trace. The Icelandic CID didn't have much experience of real crimes. He would probably be interviewed, since he had links to the victim; he might even be a suspect for a while, but he could live with that. He just needed to make absolutely sure he didn't leave behind any incriminating evidence like fingerprints.

Luckily, there was no blood as it had been a clean blow, and it was dark – in fact, it was pretty much dark round the clock now, in late November. He just needed to get the body out to the car, then *find a good place to dump it. He had an idea or two about suitable places, but he would probably need one of his mates to give him a hand.*

It briefly crossed his mind to wonder if anyone would miss the dead man. Did he have parents who were still alive, or siblings, perhaps? He'd never had many friends, treacherous scum that he was. No, nobody would miss him.

At that moment the doorbell rang.

III

Una heaved a sigh of relief when, after two days' driving on bone-juddering roads, she finally reached the fishing village of Thórshöfn on the north-east coast, the gateway to the Langanes Peninsula and the last settlement of any size before Skálar. The place felt small and remote enough in its own right; nothing more than a handful of houses scattered along a curving sweep of black sand, a striking white-roofed church and a picturesque harbour with a few colourful fishing smacks. Finding a kiosk open, she stopped for a drink and a snack, and took the chance to consult the map again. From now on she would be travelling another thirty kilometres out along the mysterious Langanes Peninsula, a place so far away from Reykjavík that Una didn't know anyone who had actually visited it. To get to Skálar, she would have to drive almost as far as Fontur, the headland at the very end.

It was with a sinking feeling that she embarked on the final leg of her journey, as though she wasn't quite sure if she really wanted to reach her destination. She kept telling herself it wasn't too late to turn back. The sky was overcast, the sun hidden behind a seamless, grey layer of cloud that weighed heavily on her spirits. To make matters worse, her old yellow Toyota Starlet, which was fine for nipping around town, proved hopelessly inadequate when faced with the rough dirt road. The views didn't provide much compensation either: the treeless landscape was desolate and featureless, nothing but rocks and grass, though at one point early on she did pass a pretty country church, with walls clad in white corrugated iron, and a red roof. All she knew about Langanes was that a polar bear had come ashore there from the sea-ice during the Great Frost Winter of 1918 and almost killed a man. She'd heard the story from Sara: it was yet another piece of information her friend had picked up from the TV report about Skálar.

For the most part, the road hugged the coast, passing a succession of grey, stony beaches littered with great piles of bleached driftwood, which no one seemed interested in collecting. A few Whooper swans shone white here and there among the waves. But before long all Una's attention was focused on the road, which grew steadily worse until she became seriously alarmed. Although she did her best to swerve round the deepest potholes, in the end, inevitably, she drove straight into one, with a sickening lurch.

Switching off the engine, she sat there trembling for a moment, sure she must have got a puncture and bracing herself to have to change the wheel. But when she got out to inspect them the tyres looked fine. Flooded with relief, she paused to take a lungful of fresh, salty air and examined the map again to reassure herself that she was going the right way.

But when she started the engine and moved off again, she immediately noticed a strange clattering noise. Worried that it was the exhaust or gearbox, she drove on, never going above second gear, desperate not to break down on the final stretch. The landscape became hillier, cliffs reared up from the sea, and finally a long, narrow headland appeared in front of her, presumably the famous Fontur. Beyond it was nothing but the vast, empty ocean. When she reached a junction with a signpost pointing to Fontur on the left and Skálar on the right, she was aware again of that cold, sinking feeling. *I don't want to live here*, she thought. But there was no turning back now, especially with the car limping along and the clatter growing ever more worrying.

As she was approaching Skálar, fog rolled in without warning, blotting out the landscape and merging sea with sky. It felt like driving into an Impressionist painting, in which her destination kept receding as fast as she approached it; like entering a void in which time had ceased to have any meaning. Maybe, in a sense, this was true: maybe time was less important there; it mattered less what day it was, what hour it was, out here where people lived at one with nature.

When she finally reached it, the tiny hamlet of Skálar was wreathed in dense cloud. And now the feeling was more like being in a folk tale, an ominous, supernatural tale, set in a vague, shifting world. There was nothing solid, nothing real about her surroundings. Just as there had been nothing natural about her decision to turn her life upside down and promise to spend nearly a year out here, at the edge of the habitable world. But she must put a brave face on things: it wouldn't do to pay too much attention to first impressions.

She had passed a pinprick of light a little way back and remembered Sara saying the TV programme had mentioned a farm that counted as part of the village. And now she saw the dark shapes of houses looming through the billowing veils of grey vapour. If she hadn't known better, she would have thought it was a ghost town. But there were people living here, she knew that. She began to have a powerful sensation of being watched; that here and there eyes were peering through the gaps between the curtains, curious about the identity of this newcomer.

It was only an illusion created by the fog, Una told herself; just as it was the fog that was to blame for her impression that the place was deserted; that no one had lived here for decades. Of course that happened sometimes: whole villages vanished – the fish disappeared and the population upped sticks and left. Yet here ten stubborn souls had clung on, and she was about to increase their number by one. Now she had seen it for herself, she had no intention of settling here. One winter, she told herself, then she would head back down south, the richer for the experience, having used the time to get her life back on track.

She parked her car at the edge of the village, next to a handful of other vehicles. So there was life here after all.

The village itself could only be entered on foot. She had been given a clear description of Salka's house, in which she was to have the use of the attic flat: a handsome, white, two-storey building, she had been told, dating from the turn of the century. As luck would have it, the first building to meet her eyes was a house fitting this description, right next to the car park. It was set back a little from the sea. The dense cloud stirred in the breeze, shifting and parting to reveal a number of other houses clustered around the water's edge. To her right, she noticed a particularly imposing building, dominating the settlement from its position on a rise in the ground, and, down by the sea, she glimpsed an attractive old wooden church. She hadn't necessarily expected that, in a community this tiny.

Una got out of the car and went to stand in front of Salka's house, which had large windows in keeping with the period in which it was built. Now there was no question that she was being watched. The curtains in one of the downstairs windows moved, and she waited, expecting to see Salka herself appear in the gap, so she was rather taken aback when the face that appeared behind the glass was that of a little girl, of perhaps seven or eight years old, with long, pale hair.

Although Una could hardly make her out in the gloom, she felt sure the child was watching her.

It was 10 p.m. Should children be up this late?

Smiling, Una waved at the girl, but even as she raised her hand, the small figure vanished from sight behind the curtain.

Salka hadn't mentioned that she had a daughter.

Una walked slowly up to the front door, feeling a little chilled now. She couldn't see any doorbell, just a heavy, functional-looking copper-lion knocker. As she lifted it and brought it down, the noise echoed around the silent village, and only then did she notice how quiet it was here compared to Reykjavík. Apart from the lapping and sighing of waves from the shore, you could have heard a pin drop – until she shattered the hush with her knocking.

She stood and waited, feeling apprehensive about meeting Salka and about her stay here. Next minute, without warning, the heavens opened and the silence was dispelled by a sudden downpour. In the absence of any shelter, Una stood where she was, trying to ignore the rain, but she raised the knocker again just to be on the safe side. The blows sounded muffled this time, almost drowned out by the drumming of the rain.

Probably only a few seconds had passed between the rain beginning its assault on Una and the door opening, but in that brief interval she was completely soaked.

'Una? For goodness' sake, come in,' said the woman standing in the doorway. 'Just look at that! I didn't know it was supposed to rain this evening, let alone as heavily as this.'

She held out her hand once Una was under cover. 'Hello, I'm Salka, obviously. Nice to meet you.'

'Hello. You too,' Una replied, trying to stop her teeth from chattering. What a welcome – gloom, cold and rain. She hoped with all her heart that the place would look less bleak in the morning. At this moment all she wanted was to turn around and flee straight back to Reykjavík.

Inside, however, it was warm and homely. The entrance hall was unusually large and it was immediately apparent from the shoes and outdoor clothing that a child lived there. Salka appeared to be around thirty-five, as Una had guessed from their phone conversation. She had black hair and the expression on her thin face was hard to read. Una thought she was very pretty.

'Do take your things off,' Salka said. 'Just hang your coat up here for now. You can take it upstairs later. Would you like some coffee?'

'Oh, yes, please,' Una replied, trying to smile. It was too late to back out now, and the coffee was bound to raise her spirits, though it probably wasn't wise to drink it this late in the evening.

The sitting room opened off the hall. It was lined with shelves full of books and photographs; there were handsome wooden boards on the floor and ceiling, and paintings on the walls. Una could imagine the room looking much the same in the 1920s or '30s; it was like stepping into the past.

There was no sign of the little girl, though she had been standing behind the curtains downstairs.

'I didn't know you had a daughter,' Una said, taking a chair, as she didn't want to sit on the elegant old sofa in her wet clothes.

Seeing Salka's brows lift in surprise, Una explained: 'I saw her at the window just now. She was watching me.' She smiled.

'Really?' Salka said. 'I thought she'd gone to bed. She promised she would. But she's always up to mischief. Her name's Edda.' She called out in a low voice: 'Edda, love, are you awake?' There was no answer. 'She must have gone back to bed. It's difficult to maintain any sort of discipline here in the countryside. It's just her and me living in this house, and, as you know, there are only two children in the whole village, so they're treated like grown-ups and do as they like. Edda's seven; the other girl, Kolbrún, is nine.' Salka hovered, still on her feet. 'They have to play together, though, to be honest, if we lived in a bigger community I doubt they'd be friends. It's not just the age gap; they're very different types as well. Edda's outgoing and cheeky, always off somewhere, hardly ever home, helping herself to food at our neighbours' houses, even up at the farm. Everyone likes her, though I say so myself.' She dropped her voice slightly. 'Kolbrún's . . . a bit more reserved, not quite as sociable.'

Una got the feeling something wasn't being said.

'Anyway, I'll make that coffee.' Salka left the room.

Una stayed put, taking the opportunity to close her eyes for a moment and rest after the long, at times nerve-racking drive. Her task for the next few months would be to take charge of the education of these two girls, Edda and Kolbrún. And judging from Salka's description, which was bound to be partisan, Una guessed she would probably have an easier time with Edda, though of course she mustn't let herself think like that. Hopefully, the girls would help her adapt to her new circumstances.

The sound of Salka's voice made her jump – she must have nodded off.

'Do you take milk or sugar?'

'Just black, thanks,' Una replied, a little sheepish about being caught napping.

Salka handed her a cup, then sat down herself.

'Well, what do you think?' Salka asked. 'Based on what you've seen so far?' She smiled. 'I know you can't really say much since you've only just arrived, but one often gets a sense of a place straight away.'

Una paused to choose her words tactfully. The truth was, she was feeling rather demoralized. Maybe she was just exhausted from the drive and stressed about her car. She had to give the place a chance; it wouldn't do to start by being critical, so she replied: 'I really like what I've seen so far. Of course, it's quite remote and everything, but I'm optimistic that I'm going to enjoy it here. I'm sure the locals are a good bunch.'

Salka's reply was disconcertingly slow in coming, and, when she did speak, Una was almost sure it was against her better judgement: 'Yes. Yes, a . . . a good bunch of people.'

There was an odd note in her voice.

Una told herself firmly that she was reading too much into it. Changing the subject, she asked: 'How long have you and your daughter lived here?'

'A year and a half now. We're still newcomers, really. Everyone else in the village has lived here for decades. Some of them all their lives. It's an old, established community and no one moves here any more. That's why I'm so pleased you've come.' She smiled again.

'Yes, I'm quite excited about experiencing what it's like to live out here. It must be so relaxing; quite a change for me. It's good to get out of the hustle and bustle of the city – everyone's always rushing around in Reykjavík, life's a constant rat race.' *With me always bringing up the rear*, she wanted to add. In a place like this, money was bound to be less important; people wouldn't be as obsessed with owning the newest car, the latest TV, the best stereo or VCR. Una doubted there was even anywhere to rent videos.

'Yes,' Salka agreed, 'it's very quiet here, which is great if that's what you're after. If not, I expect it would be a difficult place to live. It suits me, though. I've got used to it, but then, I'm the quiet type. An old soul, as they say.'

'What do you do for a living? Sorry, I should probably know, but it didn't occur to me to ask before.' Una tried to suppress a yawn, finding it increasingly difficult to fight off her weariness. 'You're involved with the school, aren't you? Didn't you say you were on the local council?'

'Well, "school" is a bit of an exaggeration; we alternate between holding the classes here at my house and at Kol-brún's parents' house. The community's too small to justify having a separate school building. But yes, I'm on the council. It covers Skálar and the neighbouring district. I've been fighting for us to advertise for a proper teacher, someone with teacher training. The others thought it would be fine for us to carry on home-schooling, but I wasn't happy about that. We have a duty to provide the children with a proper education. They shouldn't be disadvantaged just because they live out here.'

'Then I suppose I have you to thank for the job.'

'Better wait and see if you want to thank me,' Salka said with a humorous arch of her eyebrow. 'Give it a week or two before you decide . . .'

'OK, you're on . . .' Una took a sip of coffee. 'By the way, are you sure it's all right for me to stay here? I can live somewhere else if that would be better; I mean, better for you and your daughter.'

'Oh no, it would be nice to have you here. The public sector pays your rent, which is great for me as it means a bit more money coming in every month. The house is too big for the two of us, but this is the first chance I've had to get a lodger. People aren't exactly queuing up to rent rooms in Skálar, as you can imagine.'

'So how come you and your daughter live here? Did you decide to move to Skálar because you were on the local council?'

Salka laughed. 'Not directly, no. I inherited this house from my mother. She grew up here but later moved to Reykjavík and it stood empty for years. It's such a beautiful house, though, that I decided to try living in it, so I sold up and moved out here with Edda. It's cost a small fortune to do it up, but I'm getting there, slowly.' After a moment, she added: 'As a matter of fact, I'm a writer.'

'Oh, really?' Una said, then immediately regretted it, thinking perhaps she should recognize Salka's name.

'Yes, it's three years since my last book, but I've got another one coming out fairly soon.'

'I'm sorry, I'm afraid I don't read much,' Una confessed, then worried that this might not sound very good coming from a teacher. 'That is, I don't read many novels.'

Salka laughed. 'Don't worry. I'll lend you one of mine, though, if you're interested.'

'Yes, thanks, that'd be great. Incidentally, what do the locals do? For a living, I mean?'

'Those who aren't writing books?'

'Exactly,' Una said. She found herself liking this woman, who evidently didn't take herself very seriously and was, moreover, an outsider too. Una was grateful that she wouldn't have to live alone, as she'd been doing that for far too long already. Maybe everything would turn out OK, after all. She must make an effort to think positively.

'There aren't many of us here, as you're aware.'

'Only ten people, I gather.'

Salka nodded. 'Ten, that's right. There's a bit of land above the village where a woman my age is trying to make a go of farming. It's going OK, from what I hear, but she's not very sociable, to be honest, so I don't know her that well. Everyone else is more or less dependent on the sea for their living – on the fishing, that is. The fishery owner with a capital "F", the big man of the village, lives in the only house that's nicer than mine.' She laughed, and Una reflected again that Salka seemed like the cheerful type; a woman who knew how to enjoy life. 'He's getting on for sixty and has been running fishing boats here for longer than the oldest folk can remember. Sadly, his wife's wheel-chair bound these days.'

'Is he well liked?' Una asked.

'You'll either love Guffi or loathe him. He's that sort of

type. Nothing in between. But he's very popular here. He's extremely generous, always doing his bit for our little community. And he's a devout Christian too and sponsors events at the church. Which reminds me, one of your jobs will be organizing the Christmas concert at the church this year, with the children.'

'What, both of them?' Una said with a grin.

Salka chuckled. 'Indeed.'

'I hope there'll be enough room in the church for the audience . . .'

Salka smiled. 'Joking apart, it's a lovely old wooden church. You probably noticed it when you arrived. The altarpiece is really special. It's hard to describe, but it's like a portrait of Christ and there's so much depth to the painting; it's as if he's there in the church, reaching out from the frame to his flock, enfolding us all in his embrace . . .'

'Are you religious yourself?' Una asked, then wished she hadn't, thinking her question might seem inappropriate.

Salka didn't look offended, though. 'No, not at all, actually. But I can still appreciate a good piece of art, especially when it's that striking.'

Una wasn't much of a churchgoer herself, though she had held on to her childhood beliefs; she'd certainly had great need of faith at times in her life.

Salka went on: 'But I warn you, you're expected to attend church. Almost everyone does, because they don't want to get on the wrong side of the boss – the fishery owner, I mean. His name's Gudfinnur, but everyone calls him Guffi.'

'It shouldn't be a problem for me to go along to services. Is there one every Sunday?'

'Are you kidding? We're lucky if we can get the vicar out here more than a couple of times a year. He can't face the journey. The poor man's getting on, and of course he doesn't live in the village. But he always holds a Christmas service, if the roads are open, though not on the twenty-fourth. Last year it wasn't until 28 December, if I remember right.'

Una was used to going to church at Christmas – it was the only time she ever went – and then always to Midnight Mass on the twenty-fourth, after the family – she and her parents in the old days; now just she, her mother and her stepfather – had eaten their gammon and opened their presents. It sounded as if her Christmas would be very different this year.

'And does the vicar come to the concert I'm supposed to be organizing?'

'Oh, no, that's just something we put on ourselves. It was properly festive last year. I took care of the music and the girls sang like angels and looked like them too, all dressed in white.'

'Are you a composer then? As well as an author?'

Una had sometimes wished she could write music or stories or poetry, or play an instrument, but her talents didn't lie in that direction. Although she had been a good student, she'd never been artistic. Her parents had been very down-to-earth people and her father, in particular, had never had much time for creative types. He had been a doctor who believed in science above all else, wouldn't stand for any mention of God in his house and used to describe artists as 'a plague on society', arguing that people ought to stick to the sciences and try to understand the world as it really was. He didn't even listen to music, just used to pore over his books all day – and certainly never bothered with fiction. 'It's a total waste of your time, reading trash like that,' he'd said. Una remembered that conversation well, though she'd only been about twelve at the time.

'A composer?' Salka shrugged. 'I wouldn't say that, but I'm not bad at several instruments. I play the piano quite well, though I say so myself, and I've been practising on the little organ in the church. I accompanied the children last Christmas.' She paused, then said: 'Actually, I have written a few bits and pieces, just little songs and that sort of thing.'

Una looked round the room again. It was certainly a cultured home, with all those books and paintings . . . All it lacked was a piano.

Salka seemed to read her mind: 'I've got an old upright piano in the dining room, through there . . .' She pointed. 'It belonged to my grandmother. We're a very musical family. It's an old Russian instrument – don't ask me how it ended up here, but it's still got a lovely sound. Maybe I'll play something for you one day. My daughter enjoys it too – I'm teaching her to play – and the other girl as well, though I have to say she displays more determination than talent.' After a brief silence, she continued: 'It's quite something, isn't it? For a tiny hamlet like this to have its own teacher and piano teacher for a class of two. Beat that if you can!'

Una grinned and nodded. 'But aren't I holding you up?' she asked. 'Don't you need to put your daughter to bed?'

'Oh, no, she puts herself to bed. Don't worry, I like talking. Just say when you're ready for bed yourself.'

'I'll stay and finish my coffee then, if that's OK,' Una said. Despite being tired, she was grateful for the company.

'I'd like that,' Salka said warmly.

'You were going to tell me about the other locals. Who else lives here?'

'Oh, yes, so I was. There are two couples; both the men work for Guffi on the boat. I gather they've been with him for years. I think they own shares in his fishing business and do quite well out of it. Like I said, he's generous, I'll give him that.'

'What sort of age are they?'

'One's in his late fifties like Guffi. That's Gunnar. His wife, Gudrún, runs the local Co-op, though it hardly deserves the name. Gunni and Gunna, you know.' She winked. They were two of the commonest names in Iceland. 'The Co-op's next door – the little concrete building. You may have noticed it when you arrived. It's only a small shop and sometimes the choice is a bit limited but, don't worry, no one has to go hungry here. Though I suppose it'll be quite a change for a city girl like you.'

'Oh, I'm sure I'll get used to it.'

'Yes, one can get used to anything.'

Una wasn't so sure about that but didn't like to argue.

'Then there's Kolbeinn and Inga, who are younger, both fortyish. They're the parents of your other pupil,

Kolbrún.' Salka hesitated, then said: 'Inga's quite like her daughter, to be honest – not particularly outgoing. She can be a bit gruff with people. Kolbeinn, on the other hand . . .' She let the sentence trail off. 'But they go to church with Guffi, of course.'

'I look forward to meeting this Guffi. What do you think of him?'

'I have a lot of time for him,' Salka replied. 'Like I said, his wife, Erika, is in a wheelchair, poor thing. She's quite a lot older than him too, ten years or so. I don't see her very often as she doesn't get out much, but apparently she used to be a librarian in Egilsstadir and that's where they met, before she moved out here with him. I don't know exactly what's wrong with her and don't like to ask. Perhaps it's just general fatigue and her age, but presumably the time will come when they'll have to move to a town where she can have access to better care.' Again she paused. 'But since Guffi's the loudest advocate for keeping the village going, it would be a difficult decision for them. Or for him, at least.'

Una finished her coffee. 'Is there a doctor anywhere nearby?'

'No, not here in the village. But there's a district doctor, of course, who's supposed to look after us when necessary. He visits from time to time, and people try not to get ill until he's expected.' She smiled.

A silence fell and after a while Salka resumed: 'Everything revolves around the sea here, Una. There are good fishing grounds just offshore, which is the only reason the village exists. If it weren't for the fish, I wouldn't be here writing books and you wouldn't be here to teach the children. We're totally dependent on the fish. And the weather – the wretched climate. The men need good conditions to be able to get out to the fishing grounds and home again safely. So here in the village we pray for the fish and the weather, as well as all the usual, everyday things . . .' The humorous note had left her voice and she sounded oddly serious. Una found herself wondering apprehensively what she had let herself in for. What would conditions be like in the depths of winter on this remote peninsula, thrust far out into the Arctic Ocean?

Bitterly cold, she guessed, with howling gales.

And all-enveloping darkness.

IV

'So, this is it,' Salka said, a hint of pride in her voice, once they were upstairs in the flat that was to be Una's new home.

Una derived a certain comfort from the fact that Salka seemed so pleased with her house and so at home in the village. Not that Salka was a true incomer, since her family had come from the village, but it certainly sounded as if the locals had welcomed her with open arms. Una hoped she would experience the same warmth herself.

'I described it as the upstairs but, as you can see, it's really more of an attic. I hope you're not too disappointed. Sometimes you have to play the role of estate agent and talk things up a bit. But I reckon it's not bad, though I say so myself.'

'Oh yes, it's great, really great.' They were standing in the living area, a combination of sitting room, dining room and kitchen, all rolled into one. The kitchen table stood by a large dormer window.

'You've got a good view of the sea from here,' Salka

pointed out, 'though of course you can't see anything now, in the fog. I used this kitchen myself for a couple of months when we first moved in, while I was renovating the kitchen downstairs. The fridge is in good condition and so's the cooker. Maybe we could take it in turns to cook for each other – from time to time, at least. I'm afraid I'm not very good in the kitchen. My daughter far prefers other people's cooking. I seem to have been born without any talents in that department, but I make up for it by playing the piano . . .'

'Sounds like a good exchange,' Una said. 'I know my way around a kitchen, and I bet you can get lovely fresh fish here?'

'You won't find better anywhere else. By the way, I stocked up the fridge with milk, cheese and some other bits and pieces for you, and there's bread in the cupboard.' Salka gestured to the right: 'Your bedroom's through there. It has a fairly large dormer window too, though no view of the sea, I'm afraid. I put clean sheets on the bed, and there's a washing machine downstairs that you're welcome to use, of course. There's a bathroom up here too. It's a bit dated, and there's only an old bathtub, but if you're careful you can have a shower in it. So, all in all, it's a pretty cosy set-up, I think; old-fashioned but homely.'

'I'm sure I'll be happy here. It's not much smaller than my flat in Reykjavík,' Una said, and it was true that there wasn't much difference in size. It was a pity her father hadn't left more money when he died, as life had always been a bit of a struggle for her and her mother. With his medical training he could have got a very well-paid job, but he would never hear of working in a hospital or GP's surgery. All he'd wanted was to stay within the university environment, doing research, trying to make the world a better place. He'd had neither the head for money nor any interest in making it.

'Of course, it's a cultural desert here,' Salka remarked. 'I must lend you some books – and maybe a painting too? Or did you bring that kind of thing with you from Reykjavík?'

'No, it didn't occur to me, so anything of that sort would be gratefully received.'

'There's a radio over by the sink. You can get Channel One on long wave but the quality's a bit up and down. You can never rely on the reception here, but the radio has an inbuilt cassette player, as you can see, and I've put some tapes in your bedroom, both pop and classical, and there are more downstairs. I mainly use the record player myself, so you're welcome to borrow as many tapes as you like.'

'Thanks. That's very kind. What about a TV?' Una asked hopefully.

'I'm afraid there's no reception here. I hope that won't be a problem. They're always working on it, or so they claim – it's a constant bone of contention – but nothing ever happens. It's hard to get them to prioritize such a tiny village, but I suppose it'll reach us eventually.'

'Oh . . . What about a video rental?'

Salka laughed. 'We're not in Reykjavík. There's no video rental here, though some people do have VCRs and their own tapes; Guffi for one, and no doubt some of the others too. You'll just have to come to an arrangement with them. I don't even own a television set, let alone a video recorder.'

'It doesn't matter.' Una had in fact brought her video machine with her, but it hadn't occurred to her to bring along a TV as well. She'd also grabbed some VHS tapes from the shelf at home, of programmes and films she'd recorded off the television, including the Live Aid concert she and Sara had watched together earlier that summer. She could happily watch that on repeat.

'One can get used to anything,' Salka repeated. 'Here are the keys. You can let yourself in and out of the flat by the back door, so you've got your own separate entrance, if you want it. Anyway, that's enough for now. I'll let you get to bed.'

V

Una lay in bed, staring at the darkness outside the window.

This was her home now; this was where she would be living for the next few months, sleeping in this bed, this room. The thought was rather daunting. Normally, she had no difficulty dropping off, but now she felt wide awake. Of course, she was tired and that was bound to affect her impressions of the place, but the truth was she didn't feel at ease, either in the village or in this house.

She had tried reading, but it hadn't helped and she had soon given up. After that she had lain there for a long time on her side, curled up under the warm duvet with her eyes closed, waiting for the sleep that stubbornly refused to come. She'd brought a box of red wine and several bottles of Campari with her from Reykjavík, and toyed with the idea of having a nightcap, but resisted the temptation. She wasn't sure what the locals would think about drinking. This had been a source of worry to her before she came here, as her image of country people was that they had stricter attitudes to alcohol than the citizens of Reykjavík did, and it wouldn't do her image as the local teacher any good if she was viewed as some kind of alcoholic. But what she did in the privacy of her own home was her affair.

The attic flat wasn't bad at all, she told herself firmly. It was small, with a sloping ceiling, but snug nonetheless, and although the house was old, it was in good condition and she had everything she needed up there: bedroom, living room, kitchen and bathroom. And it was possible to leave the house without having to go through Salka's rooms.

Perhaps that was what she needed to help herself unwind; to go outside, confront the darkness and fill her lungs with fresh air – that pure sea air that was supposed to be so healthy, far from the pollution in town. And if anywhere could be considered out 'in the sticks', it was surely this little village, located as far from the capital as you could get without dropping off the edge of Iceland.

She got out of bed, feeling dog-tired but not letting that get in the way of her plan. Once she'd stretched her legs a little she was bound to feel sleepy. Slipping out of her nightie, she pulled on jeans, a white jumper and her thick coat, then tiptoed out of the door and down the stairs, along the hall to the back door.

Una hesitated briefly, experiencing a moment's trepidation before she opened the door. It was her first night in a new place. All she needed, she told herself, was to breathe in the atmosphere and clear her head a little.

Outside she was met by the chill of a late-summer

night. There was a light breeze coming off the sea, which seemed to have blown away the fog. The rain had stopped and the little settlement was engulfed in darkness. It was past midnight of course, but only now did Una notice that there were no streetlights. Apart from the outside lights twinkling here and there on the houses, the surrounding blackness was almost complete.

Una found it oddly unsettling. Although not usually afraid of the dark, she felt suddenly vulnerable, as if anything could happen to her in the gloom. She started walking down towards the sea, passing the church and two houses, telling herself briskly that there was nothing to be afraid of. This was a peaceful little community and no one was going to jump out at her from a dark alleyway. The very idea was absurd. However unnerving the blackness might feel, she was unquestionably safer here, alone in the middle of the night, than she would have been in the brightly lit centre of Reykjavík.

Once down on the beach, Una was lulled by the tranquillity into a calmer frame of mind. She listened to the sighing of the unseen waves as she inhaled the briny smell of the sea and tried to persuade herself that she had made the right decision, that this move was going to change her life for the better.

After a minute or two, she turned up towards the building containing the Co-op, intending to walk there, then back to Salka's house next door. It was hard to see where she was going and she kept missing the gravel path and stumbling into long grass. If it hadn't been for the outside lights on a few of the houses, she wouldn't have been able to make out a thing. There seemed to be the odd derelict building here and there among the inhabited ones and she was unnerved by the empty doorways and windows, which formed gaping black holes in the walls.

A bird flew up out of a tussock right in front of her, giving her the shock of her life and making her gasp. Next moment she had almost collided with another person. Her heart lurched and in an instant of panic she thought she'd seen a ghost, though of course she didn't believe in ghosts. She recoiled, peering at the shadowy figure, which seemed unreal, as if the darkness had taken on material form.

'Sorry,' said a man's voice. 'Sorry, I didn't see you.'

She took another step backwards and, mastering her own voice, said: 'That's OK, I didn't see you either. I was just . . .' She was about to apologize and explain that she was just going for a walk when she checked the impulse. She didn't owe him an explanation and, anyway, it was obvious.

She strained her eyes in an effort to see the man. He turned a little and the outside light on one of the houses dimly picked out his face, revealing that he was thickly bearded and wearing a woollen cap over his hair. Although she could make out little more of his features than the gleam of his eyes, Una sensed that he didn't pose any threat. Once she'd recovered from her initial shock, she felt oddly as though she'd bumped into someone she knew, someone familiar and benign, though she couldn't work out what had created this impression.

'Anyway, I'm just on my way . . .' he said, a little awkwardly, making as if to turn back.

Acting fast, she held out her hand: 'My name's Una.'

'Yes, sorry.' He hesitated, then said: 'I'm Thór.' He shook her hand firmly. 'Er, who are you?'

'I'm the new teacher. I've just moved here from Reykjavík.'

In the faint illumination she saw that he was smiling, an attractive smile. She guessed that he was a little older than her, perhaps in his mid-thirties. Una had turned thirty that spring, and had meant to hold a party for her friends but never got round to it. She had kept finding reasons to postpone it, pleading lack of money and time, but perhaps the truth was that she didn't want to invite the girls round to her place. She had more or less stopped seeing them nowadays, except for Sara, of course. Nor was it a milestone she felt any particular desire to celebrate. Although she kept reminding herself that she was still young, it was a bit of a jolt to find herself entering her thirties.

'Yes, so I heard.' He still seemed reluctant to engage, as if he'd rather be somewhere else.

Now that she was standing still, the cold began to penetrate her coat, but she ignored it, eager to spin out the encounter as long as possible.

But before she could say anything in reply, he added: 'I don't really understand. Why on earth did you want to move to the back of beyond?'

'Why not? I was fed up with the city and wanted to try living in the countryside for a change.'

He was silent and she could sense his unspoken desire to get away. But eventually he replied: 'Living in the countryside's one thing, but living out *here* . . .'

'What about you?' she asked quickly. 'What brought you here?'

Again that hesitation, then he said: 'I work on the farm up the hill. Have you been there yet? I live in the guest-house and help out Hjördís, the woman who owns it.'

Una shook her head. 'No, I've literally just arrived this evening. I haven't had time to look around yet.'

'Well, to be honest, there's not a lot to see.'

'I was afraid of that,' she said ruefully, wondering why she should feel instinctively at ease with him, despite his obvious reluctance to engage with her. 'But I suppose I'll just have to stick it out because I've taken a job here for the whole winter.'

'Oh, it's not that bad,' he said, sounding a little embarrassed. 'And you'll have your teaching. That must be a great job.'

'Oh, well, it's not that bad,' she said, deliberately echoing what he had said in an attempt to be funny.

'I've always admired teachers.' His teeth gleamed again in a smile.

The way he said it, she wasn't sure if he was just being polite or if there was a hint of flirtation there. Now it was her turn to feel embarrassed.

'Anyway, I'd better get going,' she said.

'Sure. Good luck with settling in, Una. I hope you'll be happy here.'

'Thanks,' she said, and opened her mouth to add some

witty remark, but before she got a chance he was gone, striding away up the slope, presumably in the direction of the farm. She watched his vague outline retreating until he was swallowed up by the darkness.

Afterwards she found herself wondering, ridiculously, if he had been a figment of her imagination. There had been something so dreamlike, so unreal about this unlooked-for encounter. Her first thought had been that she'd met a ghost, and now the thought returned and she shivered, trying to push it away. It was absurd. He had been flesh and blood all right. She wished they could have talked for longer, but no doubt there would be other chances to get to know him. In a village this tiny it would be impossible to avoid him. She realized she was looking forward with genuine eagerness to their next encounter.

VI

She woke up drenched in sweat.

Could she be coming down with something? A fever after her long drive? Then it came back to her: she'd had a dream, or a nightmare, rather.

The girl in the white dress, who she had seen at the window, had appeared to her during the night. Salka's daughter, Edda . . . She couldn't quite remember her face, since the details had been vague and the dream was quickly fading from her consciousness; so intangible that it was more a sensation than a memory. The girl had been watching her through the window, just as she had earlier that evening, but this time Una had been on the inside and the girl had been outside in the darkness. She hadn't spoken, at least not that Una could recall, but the experience had been deeply unsettling. It had felt as if the girl was summoning Una with her silence, trying to lure her outside, compelling her to leave the house and come to her.

Even more disturbingly, Una had felt drawn to obey, as if she had actively wanted to go with the girl out into the night, into the unknown. It had been cold too; she had felt an icy chill during the night, although it was quite warm in her bedroom now.

Then the child had held up her hands with the palms facing outwards, as if to say: this far and no further. Una wondered if it had been a warning to leave the village; an omen that she should never have come there.

She got out of her sweat-soaked bed. It was still dim in her room but when she switched on the light she saw from the clock that it was morning, although few would be awake yet. She would have liked to have slept for a couple more hours as she needed to be on the ball for the first day of her new job, but she was unlikely to drop off again now.

She wondered if her dream had simply been a sign that she was tired from her journey and apprehensive about starting teaching, or whether it had been caused by something deeper in her consciousness; whether the fear that was always lurking inside her had reared up its head again.

It left her with an ominous sense of dread that she couldn't shake off.

VII

The tiredness was still there later that morning when Una entered the classroom, which wasn't really a classroom so much as the dining room in Kolbrún's house, which could be closed off with an old-fashioned sliding door to make an area where they could study undisturbed.

The two girls, Kolbrún and Edda, were both sitting waiting for her. When Una saw Edda, her first thought was that she looked quite different by daylight, her features much clearer and her whole demeanour brighter and more animated than it had appeared when seen through the window the evening before.

Una hadn't brought any textbooks along for this first lesson, having decided to use the time to get to know her two pupils instead. With the dream still impinging on her thoughts, she found it all the more important to start by lightening the atmosphere, in the hope that this would take the edge off her lingering sense of unease.

'Hello, girls. My name's Una. I've just moved here from Reykjavík and I'm going to be your teacher this winter.'

Edda nodded, but Kolbrún's face remained impassive.

'I've been so looking forward to coming here and teaching you that I even dreamt about you last night.' Una smiled. 'Well, about Edda, anyway, because I met her briefly yesterday.'

Edda frowned. 'You didn't meet me yesterday,' she said flatly.

Una smiled again. 'I didn't mean I literally met you, but I saw you when I arrived. You were standing at the down-stairs window, remember?'

'No. I didn't see you,' the girl insisted. 'I always go to bed early.'

'But your mother said . . .' Una stopped herself; there was no call to get off on the wrong foot by arguing with her pupil, though the girl was obviously lying.

'What are we going to learn today?' Kolbrún asked.

'I thought we'd just chat and get to know each other,' Una said.

She proceeded to tell them a bit about herself, then tried to encourage them to do the same. It proved much easier to persuade Edda to talk than Kolbrún. Edda was chatty and easy-going, like her mother, whereas Kolbrún said little, mostly answering questions with a monosyllabic 'yes' or 'no'.

Edda was quick to disappear at the end of the lesson, but Kolbrún remained sitting at the dining table, writing in her exercise book. She was tall for her age, with strong features and black hair, which she wore loose over her shoulders. Her expression was absorbed and she was bending over her book, lost in her own world. She had been scribbling on and off all morning, sometimes drawing, sometimes writing, as far as Una could see, though she had tried not to pry.

'Thanks for today, Kolbrún,' Una said, collecting up her things to leave. Of course, it was Kolbrún's home, but Una found it a slightly odd feeling to leave the classroom before her pupil. 'We'll get going properly tomorrow.'

Kolbrún didn't react.

'Were you happy with this morning's session?'

Kolbrún nodded without looking up, still focused on her exercise book.

'What are you writing? A story?'

After a pause, the girl muttered: 'Yes.'

'What's it about?'

This time the girl looked up and met Una's eye, and there was no mistaking her expression: *it was none of Una's business what her story was about.* Without a word, she lowered her gaze and carried on writing.

'Well, see you tomorrow, then,' Una said, with no expectation of a reply. She closed the door behind her and walked slowly across the hall, thinking. Just as she reached the front door, it opened.

'Hello, Una.' It was Kolbrún's mother, Inga.

Although Una had met her briefly that morning, she hadn't had a proper chance to speak to her yet. Inga had made a rather forbidding first impression, with her dour face and remote gaze. Like her daughter, she was tall with black hair.

'Have you finished already?' Inga glanced at the clock, her mouth turning down with disapproval, then asked:

'How did it go?' But it didn't sound as if she had any real interest in hearing.

'It was great,' Una replied, with a quick glance over her shoulder to make sure that the door was shut and Kolbrún couldn't hear. 'By the way, do the girls play together at all?'

The question seemed to take Inga by surprise. 'Play together? No, very little. Kolbrún prefers to spend her time with me and Kolbeinn. We're a very *close family*.' She stressed the last two words. 'I really can't imagine why Salka moved here with her daughter – a single mother bringing up a child like that.' Again, she radiated disapproval. She stood there, blocking the doorway, her arms folded across her chest. 'I must ask you to treat my daughter with respect. She's used to being talked to like an adult; to being trusted.'

'Of course,' Una said, rather taken aback by this conversation. 'I treat all children with respect.'

'I don't know what kind of children you were teaching in Reykjavík, but my Kolbrún is highly intelligent. She needs to be challenged in her schoolwork.' Inga tightened her lips, then added, as if compelled to: 'Kolbeinn and I – our *family* – are moving away soon. We're just looking for the right house.'

'Oh, that's good to hear,' Una said, then realized it could be taken the wrong way.

'Our house is on the market,' Inga went on. 'I'm not expecting it to sell, not immediately, but that's not a precondition for moving. Not for us,' she said, rather smugly.

'Well, anyway, thanks for letting us use your house for our lessons.'

Inga sniffed. 'What else are we supposed to do? Though of course they ought to pay us something for the trouble. But, like I said, the arrangement's only temporary, because we'll be leaving soon.' Although she didn't smile, her eyes held a glint of satisfaction at the thought.

She stepped aside. 'See you later, Una.'

VIII

The note was lying on the kitchen table in the attic when Una got home after her second day of teaching.

Would you come round and see me at five.
Gudfinnur

It made her feel distinctly on edge. Partly, it was the fact someone had entered her flat without her permission. Of course, it wasn't her house, or attic, but she still had a right to her privacy. And it occurred to her that Gudfinnur could have left it there himself; a complete stranger invading her space. It wouldn't seem quite so bad if it turned out that it was Salka who had popped upstairs with the note.

The message was clear: a full stop rather than a question mark. This was an order, not a request, and although Una was affronted by the high-handedness, she didn't dare disobey. There was no doubt about who ran the show in Skálar, and common sense told her it was better to avoid falling out with the big man.

Nevertheless, she made a brief detour on the way, as if asserting her independence, and scrambled down to the shore to breathe in the sea air and put herself in a better frame of mind for the coming encounter. The beach was covered in smooth, grey rocks, which were pleasing to the eye but difficult to walk on, and here and there she saw piles of bleached driftwood lying along the high-water mark. The truncated remains of an old concrete pier towered above her on one side, while beyond it she could see a modern jetty, but no sign of any boats. Sunlight flashed and danced on the gentle waves and the ocean stretched out in all its glory. To her right, a rocky headland reared out of the sea, and far away in the distance there was another long, blue line of land. Nearer at hand, on the other side of a small cove, rose an impressive line of sheer cliffs, with the white shapes of seabirds wheeling around them.

She picked her way along the beach until she was level with the fishery owner's house, which dominated the village from its eminence, then climbed back up from the shore, approached his front door, caught her breath, and knocked.

In the only glimpse she had so far caught of Guffi he had been wearing an old-fashioned fisherman's jersey and a woollen hat, so she had been half-expecting him to be similarly clad now. Disconcertingly, however, he was formally, if not very fashionably, dressed, in a blue shirt and checked suit. Instead of looking pleased to see her, he stood there unmoving, with the door half open, not saying a word.

Una was thrown by this reception. After all, he had

invited her to come round and see him. Unless someone was playing a trick on her? 'Hello, sorry,' she stammered, 'I . . . I got your message.'

'Yup, right,' he said gruffly, holding out his hand. 'Come in, then.'

She shook his hand. His clasp was warm but tight and he gripped her hand for so long that she wondered if he was ever going to let go. Finally, he did, and she followed him into the hall and down a set of stairs. The house was so gloomy inside that it was hard to see the furnishings in much detail, but Una had the feeling of going back in time. The present day seemed to have passed Skálar by in more ways than one.

'My office is down here,' Guffi said curtly, switching on the light in the passage.

His office, which was smaller than she'd expected, contained an old desk and a bookcase, and looked more like a study than a place where he conducted his business. A single leather armchair stood beside the bookcase. The only other chair was behind the desk.

'Sit down,' Guffi said. He was tall and very thickset, with a heavily lined face and eyes of flint.

When Una made to sit down in the armchair, however, he laid a heavy hand on her shoulder and steered her towards the office chair instead. She slipped out from under his grip and took a seat behind the desk, at the back, while he settled himself in the armchair, beside the only door to the windowless room. She had a disturbing sensation of being in a prison or cage, entirely at the mercy of this odd man.

'Nice to meet you,' she said, after an awkward silence, when it appeared that he wasn't going to say anything. 'You own the fishery here, don't you?'

'That's right,' he said, brusquely. He sat quite still, staring at her, without a hint of a smile on his face. Then went on: 'So you've come here to teach the children.'

Una nodded.

'Why did you want to move out here?'

She was momentarily tongue-tied, then said: 'It's . . . it's a beautiful place.' It sounded unconvincing even to her.

'How could you know that?' he said dismissively. 'Had you been here before?'

'What? No, actually, but . . . but . . .' She couldn't even claim to have seen any photos.

Gudfinnur interrupted: 'It isn't even a particularly picturesque spot for a village, I have to say. Or perhaps you think it is?'

'It's . . . it's all right. I've only just got here, you know.'

'And how long are you planning to stay, Una?'

Before she could answer, he ploughed on: 'I understand you have a teaching degree. I can't think why someone like you would want to kick your heels in a place like this. Nor do I understand why we should have to fork out for a professional teacher for two kids. Frankly, it seems like a disgraceful waste of money to me.'

Una nodded, though she didn't agree.

'It's Salka's fault, like so much else. She seems to be under the impression that she runs the place, though I don't know why she should think that.'

He sat there, solid and immovable, and Una was assailed again by the suffocating awareness that she couldn't leave until he decided to let her out.

'I believe she did you a disservice,' he continued, 'by tricking you into coming here.'

Una could feel the sweat breaking out on her body but tried to maintain her composure: 'Well, I suppose time will tell.' This came out more shakily than she would have liked.

'Oh, I think you can take my word for it. This isn't a suitable place for you, Una. It's not easy for outsiders to fit in here or to understand how our little community works.'

She nodded warily, unsure where the conversation was leading.

'If you ask me, you should think again, Una. It's not too late to change your mind, even though you've come here. We would understand. The isolation, being so far from anywhere, the darkness. You could hardly get any further from Reykjavík if you tried. And the house you're living in has a history. Not everyone feels comfortable there. You could pack up your bags and go home, and we'd manage. Just as we've been managing all these years.'

Although the last thing she wanted was to let him get away with threatening her like this, it did cross her mind that it might be best to abandon the whole idea. Clearly, she wasn't welcome here. On the other hand, there was nothing waiting for her back in Reykjavík. She had quit her old job and they had hired someone else to take her place for the winter, so financially, she had no real choice but to stay. And, besides, she thought, with sudden indignation, she had no intention of letting him bully her like this.

'Thanks for the advice,' she said, finally managing to suppress the tremor in her voice. 'I think I'll go now.' She stood up and walked steadily towards the door. Gudfinnur gave no sign of moving, but at the last minute he got to his feet and opened the door for her. He drew back his lips in a smile for the first time since she had met him, but his eyes remained stony. 'You can find your own way out, Una.'

IX

After this unpleasant encounter, Una took herself to the shop, partly as a distraction, partly because she needed to buy some food. She had tried to go the day before, only to find the Co-op shut.

The woman behind the counter, who looked to be in late middle age, greeted her with a broad smile. 'Welcome, Una.' At least there was no need to introduce yourself here. 'I'm Gunna . . . Gudrún, that is. It's nice to meet you.'

'Yes, hello, you too. I was just going to . . . to look around.'

'We stock everything here, pretty much.' Gudrún gave her another friendly smile. 'It's so nice to have young people come to the village. We don't get much fresh blood here, you know. It's always the same story: slowly but surely everyone's moving away. That's why it was so lovely when Salka moved here with her little girl, and now here you are. I gather we have Salka to thank for that too.'

Una nodded. 'Yes, I suppose . . .'

'Anyway, what can I do for you today?' Gudrún continued, barely pausing for breath. 'The freezer's over there in the corner. You can dig up all sorts of stuff in there. Then there's fresh fish on the counter ...' She pointed to the right, where there appeared to be a single fillet for sale. 'As for alcohol ...' She winked at Una. 'We keep that round the back. Because there's no *ríki* closer than Thórshöfn, we have a special licence to sell it.'

Una perked up at this. Thanks to Iceland's restrictive laws on the sale of alcohol, you could normally only buy drink from a small number of special state-licensed shops called *ríki* and she had been wondering if she would have to drive all the way to Thórshöfn, or even further afield, every time she wanted to replenish her supplies.

'Ooh, in that case, I think I'll have a bottle of red wine,' she said, although she still had the box she'd brought with her from Reykjavík, just to be on the safe side. 'What do you recommend?'

'Well, of course, I don't touch the stuff myself – my husband and I are strict teetotallers – but people say the French and Italian wines are the best. I've got both kinds.'

'Then I'll take one of each, please.'

Gudrún vanished round the back and reappeared with two bottles. 'Next time, you can just go in there and have a look for yourself, because I'm clueless about wine, as you can tell.'

'Thanks. Could I have two small bottles of Coke too, and a packet of liquorice? Oh, and that fillet of fish as well?'

'The haddock? Yes, of course. You're lucky to get the

last one. It usually sells up straight away, and if it doesn't, it goes in the freezer. We're used to freezing food here, as it's the only sensible thing to do. And do you know? I can't tell the difference; it always tastes fine to me.'

Una took out her chequebook and opened it.

'Oh, sorry, dear. I don't take cheques.'

'What? Ah. I . . . I don't have any cash on me, I'm afraid.'

'Don't you worry. I'll put it on the tab.' Gudrún smiled. 'But there's something you can do for me in return.'

'Oh, what's that?'

'Pop in for a coffee with me and Gunnar. How about tomorrow? Would three suit you?'

'Three? Er, yes, that should be fine.'

'Wonderful, Una dear. I'll look forward to it.'

X

'It's so nice of you to come round and see us.' Gudrún beamed at Una, then poured her coffee. The cup was genuine Danish seagull china, of the kind Una hadn't seen for donkey's years. An elderly aunt of hers in Reykjavík used to have a set. Come to think of it, Gudrún's sitting room might have been cut out of a magazine from twenty years ago. She and her husband, Gunnar, lived down by the sea in an old wooden house, which was handsome, though not as grand as Guffi's place.

The floor was covered in a curry-yellow carpet, the sofa upholstered in a rather threadbare scarlet fabric, there was wallpaper on the walls, and the rest of the furniture was clearly antique. Every available surface was cluttered with knick-knacks, most of which seemed to be birds made of wood or china.

From what Salka had told Una, Gunnar was not quite sixty, but the couple both looked at least ten years older, with plump, kindly, slightly careworn faces. Gunnar didn't look as if he could have many years left as a fisherman. Una's first thought when she saw him was that he must be starting to think about retirement.

Gudrún offered her milk and sugar, but Una declined both.

'People usually drink their coffee white with sugar here,' Gudrún remarked, though in a matter-of-fact rather than critical tone. 'But of course you city folk do things differently. It must be a big change for you, moving here?'

'I haven't had a chance to find out yet,' Una replied.

Gunnar was still hovering in the background. 'It's a good thing for the children to have a proper teacher,' he said, speaking for the first time. 'Inga's taken care of all their schooling up to now. Have you met her? She's Kolbeinn's wife.'

'Yes, but I haven't managed to have a proper chat with her yet – or with him either. She was, er . . .' Una let her words trail off, unwilling to find fault.

Gudrún saved her the trouble: 'She can be a bit short with people, can Inga. She's not very approachable, never has been. But they're good people at heart, and so's their little girl. Gunnar works with Kolbeinn, you know.'

'Yes, that's right,' Gunnar said, finally making up his mind to sit down on the sofa, uncomfortably close to Una. 'We may not fish on a very big scale, but we do make a decent living.'

'Kolbeinn's always on about quitting and moving away, though,' Gudrún chipped in, before he could say anything else. 'Of course, they're still relatively young, and they have a child to think of, so it can't be easy for them living here, though Gunnar and I are used to it. We're part of the surroundings, really.' She smiled.

'There's no sense throwing in the towel and leaving,' Gunnar said, sounding suddenly harsh. 'What would happen if all the young people left? The village would die – it would completely disappear. That would be a shame, a real shame, for a place with a history like this. I was born and raised here and it's never crossed my mind to leave – or Gunna's either. Has it, dear?'

'I should think not. You just have to put up with things and make the best of them,' Gudrún agreed. 'But I have to say, I do understand how they feel – as a young couple.'

Una began to wonder if Gunnar and Gudrún had forgotten she was there.

'Well, I don't. But I do know why Kolbeinn's always harping on about leaving. And you know too, don't you, Gunna?'

Gudrún nodded. 'Yes, you've told me before.'

'Yes, I've told you, but not Una.' Gunnar turned to her, so they were nose to nose on the sofa. 'The fact is, Guffi pays too well; we have it too good, Gunna and I, and Kolbeinn and Inga too. I have no need for all that money; it just goes straight into the bank. But Kolbeinn, he's always on about moving to Thórshöfn, or even down south to Reykjavík, claiming he has enough capital to set up his own company there.' Gunnar shook his head. 'Damn it, I don't know . . .'

Una sat on the sofa feeling awkward, unable to understand why they'd invited her round, since neither of them seemed remotely interested in her.

But Gudrún took advantage of the silence following Gunnar's tirade to say: 'Una, I gather you're going to organize the Christmas concert at the church?'

Una nodded, though all she knew about it was what Salka had told her the first evening.

'I'm delighted to hear it,' Gudrún said with sudden enthusiasm. 'It's an important occasion, especially for the children, and always has been. Of course, there used to be more of them in the old days, but that's the way it goes – everything changes, nothing stays the same. But I think I'm safe in saying that it's the high point of the Christmas celebrations here in the village. Don't you agree, Gunnar?'

Gunnar nodded and grunted.

'We always hold it in the evening. It's such a beautiful occasion, with the church all lit up by candles in the winter darkness, and everyone coming together. No one's allowed to sit at home on the last Sunday before Christmas.'

'Yes, I hear it's going to land on me this year,' Una said. 'Sorry, I didn't mean it like that. I gather it'll be my responsibility.'

'How old are you, dear, if you don't mind my asking?' Gudrún said. 'You look so young.'

'Thirty.'

'Goodness me, that's no age at all,' Gunnar broke in. 'You've never been here before, I take it?'

'To the village? No, I . . . well, to be honest, I didn't even know it existed.' She added, untruthfully: 'Though I might have heard of it.'

'It is a bit isolated,' Gudrún said, and sighed.

'A bit isolated? It was good enough for the American army, let me tell you,' Gunnar exclaimed, becoming agitated, 'and plenty of people lived here in the old days. It was quite a sizeable town at one time, I think I can safely say, although it was always referred to as Skálar Village.'

'Gunnar was born and brought up here,' Gudrún explained, although her husband had already told Una this. 'He has very strong ties to Skálar. The village grew up early this century when people moved here for the fishing. You've probably noticed the ruins of the old jetty? Though, of course, Guffi's invested in a new, improved one.'

Una nodded. 'How many people used to live here?' she asked, regretting that she hadn't read up on the history of the place beforehand.

Gudrún glanced at her husband. He frowned, then said importantly: 'Tch, over a hundred people, closer to a hundred and twenty at its height.'

'Seriously? Over a hundred people?'

'Believe it or not. And that's not all; the population used to double in summer with all the migrant fishworkers. It was a place in its own right, you know.'

'And you mentioned that the American army was here?' Una asked. It was the first she had heard of it.

'Yes, that was no joke. First it was the British. I remember them well, though I was only in my teens at the time. They were here for two years. Then the Americans arrived. They built a camp above the village. You can still see the ruins if you walk up the hill.'

Una hadn't yet explored the higher ground behind Skálar.

After a brief pause, Gunnar went on: 'They used to call it Camp Greely. There was a whole load of Quonset huts – it was a proper radar station, with a radio mast, a machine-gun nest and I don't know what else. They used to keep an eye on the air traffic in the area. I remember it so well – it was quite an adventure. Well, it was deadly serious, of course, but for me and my mates it was a real eye-opener. We used to spend as much time as we could hanging around up there, trying to take in the fact that the war had come all the way out to find us, in the remotest corner of the country. I reckon there were nearly fifty soldiers here at one time.'

Una stole a sidelong glance at Gunnar, seeing from the rapt look on his face that he was lost in his reminiscences, as if he'd travelled back forty years in time. Una could hardly imagine it: military barracks on the barren slopes above the village, dozens of armed American soldiers swarming all over the place, in the middle of a world war and yet so far removed from the fighting.

Gunnar hadn't finished: 'Guffi and I were best mates then, as now. We tried to make friends with the soldiers. I don't remember finding their presence at all threatening; for us it was just exciting. Of course, there was a bit of a language problem, as you can imagine, as we didn't speak a word of English, but we managed somehow and by the end we'd got quite good at making ourselves understood. It wasn't a bad school.'

'And what . . . what sort of relationship did the locals have with the soldiers?'

'Excellent, no problems at all. Us boys spent a lot of

time talking to them and they did their best to cause as little disruption as possible. It was an odd feeling for us to have a foreign army in the back garden all of a sudden. Unbelievable, really. But it can't have been easy for them either. Not everyone can cope with the winter here, with the cold and the dark. The storms can be something else: freezing winds, often blowing up a gale, and hardly a scrap of shelter to be found, and when you add snow to the mix, all hell breaks loose. As you'll discover. I don't really know how they stuck it out up there as it can't have been warm in those flimsy huts. But, like I said, they were very friendly. They gave us all kinds of goods, I remember; food, mainly – things we'd never seen before.'

Una opened her mouth to interrupt and change the subject, but Gunnar was oblivious to her, lost in his memories: 'They used to give us Christmas presents too, American toys that were quite unlike anything we'd ever seen before. I'll never forget them. But what I remember best of all was the time they held a movie show for us. I don't know what the film was, some black-and-white Hollywood feature, but it all seemed so exotic to us. None of us kids had ever been to the cinema before, so it didn't matter if we could hardly understand a word they said. It was all about the experience.'

'He's told me that story so often,' Gudrún told Una, with a smile of sympathy. 'Far too often. I know all his stories off by heart by now, as well he knows, but you're his latest victim.'

'That's all right,' Una replied. 'I enjoy hearing them. It makes me realize how little I know about this place.'

'I've got plenty more stories up my sleeve, don't you worry,' Gunnar assured her.

'They'll have to wait, dear,' Gudrún said. 'Now, Una, tell us about your plans for the concert. Have you made any arrangements yet? The children will sing, won't they? Have you chosen the carols?'

Give me a break, I've only just got here! Una thought. 'No, I haven't had a chance to start thinking about it yet,' she said aloud. 'I'm sure it would be a good idea to get the children to sing. "Christmas is Just Around the Corner"? That sort of thing?'

'"Christmas is Just Around the Corner"?' Gudrún made a face. 'That's hardly a proper carol. They need to learn some decent Christian hymns. And "Silent Night", of course, though, strictly speaking, that should only be sung on the twenty-fourth.'

'Like I said,' Una replied, 'I've hardly had a chance to think about the programme yet.'

'I've always been involved every year,' Gudrún said. 'I studied singing in Denmark when I was young. I could be persuaded to help out . . .'

'Oh, yes, please. I'd be very grateful.'

Gudrún brightened and the real purpose of this invitation to coffee finally became clear to Una.

'How about I come along to some of your classes and rehearse with the girls?' Gudrún suggested eagerly. 'I took them for singing practice a bit last year. Of course, I wouldn't expect to be paid; I'd offer my services for free. Gunnar and I have more than enough for our needs.'

Una thought for a moment, then decided to accept the

offer. What did she have to lose? It would make life easier for her, and it would do the children good to learn to sing. 'That would be great, really great. Perhaps we could start next week?'

'I like the sound of that,' Gudrún said. Gunnar was silent; with the change of subject he had withdrawn into his own thoughts.

'Are the girls good? At singing, I mean?'

'Edda is, yes. Kolbrún . . . well, I didn't feel she really made the effort last year. But of course we won't let her get away with that again. I don't think there's anything wrong with her voice. Children can generally sing, if they're made to practise,' she said, and her expression reminded Una ominously of the teacher she herself had once had.

A woman she hadn't got on with at all.

The doorbell rang again and this time the ringing was followed by knocking.

Shit, there was a light on in the sitting room. It was too late for him to turn it off now. The curtains weren't drawn either, which meant the visitor could walk round the corner, look in the window and see the dead man on the floor. Shit.

He had to act fast. Grabbing hold of the dead man's limp arms and recoiling slightly at the strange feel of them, he dragged the body with frantic haste across the sitting room and into the hall, where the lights were off and there were no windows. He didn't dare put his eye to the door's peephole for fear that the visitor might spot the movement inside and realize that someone was there. He pushed the sitting-room door to, without quite closing it, and positioned himself so that he would see if a face appeared at the window.

His heart pounding, he tried not to think about the body lying on the floor behind him, about the man he had murdered. He tried to breathe calmly. He'd had to do it; there had been no alternative. It was just that things were turning out differently from how he'd expected.

77

He caught a movement out of the corner of his eye. Someone was peering in through the window, looking for the man who was dead.

It was a woman, a young woman with black hair, as far as he could tell.

He hid in the shadowy hall, watching her as she pressed her face up against the glass. Was she the man's girlfriend? All of a sudden he felt a faint stirring of conscience; she would never see him again, perhaps never have any idea what had happened to him, especially if his plans for getting rid of the body worked out.

All he needed to do now was hang around and wait for the woman to leave. He just hoped she wouldn't do anything stupid, like ringing the police. It was bloody lucky he'd taken the precaution of parking a couple of streets away.

Once the coast was clear, he would lug the body out to his car and drive it to the lava-fields, under cover of night.

There was no alternative. There was too much at stake, too much money, and the men in charge were utterly ruthless. It wouldn't do to leave any loose ends that could upset everything. What did one or two lives matter, in the circumstances? Once he had taken care of this, he also had orders to deal with the other man who was planning to squeal.

So what if the bodies of two no-good pieces of shit went to their final resting place in the lava-fields? Few would miss them.

XI

Una had been planning to play it cool and let a bit of time pass before she engineered another meeting with Thór. Or, rather, she'd been hoping she might bump into him, but that still hadn't happened, even though she'd been in the village for three days now.

After the frustration of being talked at during coffee with Gudrún and Gunnar, she felt a simple longing to spend time with someone younger, someone she actually liked. There had been a spark between her and Thór during their encounter in the darkness, she could swear to it; some indefinable connection which convinced her they would hit it off. Not only was he close to her own age, but he had also come across as friendly.

In the end, she decided to take a walk up towards the farm, which was just out of sight of the village, over the brow of the hill. It was the first time since her arrival that Una had seen anything beyond the low, eroded slopes that formed a backdrop to the small area of grassy lowland on which Skálar lay. But as she breasted the rise, all she saw inland were more low, featureless hills. Immediately before her appeared the farmhouse, which was large, with a dilapidated air. Under the traditional red roof, the white walls were turning grey where the paint had flaked off to reveal the concrete underneath. In addition to the usual outbuildings, there was a smaller house, presumably the guesthouse Thór had mentioned. After a moment's reflection, Una decided it would be politer to knock at the door of the main house first.

As she stood there waiting, she had time to feel increasingly awkward before the door eventually opened to reveal a woman of about forty, with long dark hair and a wary expression, though she must presumably have had an inkling who Una was.

'Yes?' the woman said.

'Hello, I'm Una, the new teacher.'

'I know,' the woman replied. 'I'm Hjördís. I live here.'

'I wondered . . .' Una hesitated, feeling her face grow hot with embarrassment, as if she'd come round to ask after the popular boy at school. 'I was wondering if Thór was in.'

This time it was Hjördís's turn to hesitate. She stood there staring at Una, as if unsure how to react. Finally, she said: 'He's upstairs. I'll get him.'

She disappeared without inviting Una in, and Una wondered, belatedly, if there was something going on between Hjördís and Thór. Perhaps that was why she had reacted so oddly to Una's visit. It might also explain why Thór hadn't made any effort to get in touch since they'd met that first night. For a moment she considered turning and walking away. She lowered her head, closing her eyes briefly, then decided to tough it out. There was no point giving up straight away, before the battle had even begun.

'Hi,' she heard a voice say, and looked up quickly. There was the beard and the attractive twinkle in his eyes, but now she could also see his hair, thick, dark and tousled, which had been hidden by his woollen hat the other night. His manner was still rather diffident, as if he didn't know how to react to her, yet she felt instinctively that friendliness came more naturally to him than reserve.

'Oh, hi, sorry,' she said, stumbling over her words. 'Maybe I should have called first. I was just going for a walk and decided to drop by and say hello.'

'You're quite a one for walks, aren't you?' he said. 'Not that there's much scope for them in the village. You've hardly got started before you're out the other side.'

'Well, you've got to do something to keep the boredom at bay,' she countered. *Aren't you going to ask me in?* she thought, and wondered, if he did, whether he would invite her into the house or over to the guesthouse. Where did he actually sleep? And what was the nature of his relationship with Hjördís? Their eyes kept meeting, then skittering apart, embarrassed. Una could feel her cheeks going pink. She could have sworn he was feeling as shy as she was.

After a moment's hesitation, he said: 'Hang on, I'll grab my coat and walk along with you.' He ducked out of sight, then reappeared in the same thick anorak he had been wearing the first time they met.

'So, how are you finding life in the village?' he asked,

once he had joined her outside and closed the door behind him. They set off into the stiff breeze, hunching their shoulders and burying their hands in their pockets for warmth. 'How about heading up the hill, to the ruins of the Second World War air station?' he suggested.

'Sure,' she said. 'I'm slowly finding my feet, thanks. I had coffee with the old couple earlier – with Gudrún and, er, Gunnar, I mean.'

'Lucky you.' There was no mistaking the sarcasm in his voice. 'I tend to steer clear of them, but they make an amusing double act. Gunni and Gunna, we call them. They're rolling in it after all these years of sharing the proceeds from Guffi's fishing business, but they'll never leave. They wouldn't live anywhere else. Gunni hardly gets a word in edgeways when they're together. His wife definitely wears the trousers in that relationship.' After a pause, he added: 'Though, to be fair, she does let him bore on about . . .'

Una finished the sentence for him: 'Don't tell me – the history of Skálar?'

Thór laughed. 'Exactly! You obviously got the full treatment.'

'You could say that.'

'Did he tell you about the mine?'

'What? No, he didn't mention anything about mines.'

'One exploded by the seafront here during the war – I'm pretty sure it was in 1942. I've heard the stories about it and read up on the background a bit too. Gunni and Gunna's house was hit by the impact, all the windows blew in and I don't know what else. It was no joke, I can tell you.'

'Was anyone hurt?'

'No, thank God, there were no injuries, but several families moved away that same year, probably as a result. They must have thought things were getting too hot around here.'

They trudged on up the barren slope, ignoring the biting cold, with no sound but the wind in the grass. To their left was the vast, flat expanse of the sea, reaching away to the distant headlands, which were largely obscured by cloud.

'I met Guffi too . . .' Una said. 'He invited me round . . .' She didn't know how to put into words what had happened; the momentary suffocating fear of that encounter in Guffi's windowless, subterranean office. Thór was a complete stranger, in spite of the instinctive trust he inspired in her; the powerful sense that there was a thread, some affinity, between them. And perhaps an element of attraction too.

'Don't you like Guffi?' he asked.

'He was a bit offputting. Unfriendly, you know.' She decided not to say any more for the moment.

Thór laughed again. He had a captivating laugh; it had a warm, kindly ring to it. 'Is it a condition with you that everyone has to be full-on friendly the first time you meet them?' he asked, though it was clear he wasn't being serious.

'No. No, of course not, but . . .'

'Don't worry, I understand. The old boy can be a bit gruff, but his heart's in the right place. He didn't exactly welcome me with open arms either at first.'

Una couldn't tell if Thór really meant it or if he was just saying it to make her feel better. If so, it was kindly done. She changed the subject: 'Are you going to stay on here? I mean, have you moved here for good?'

There was a weighty pause before he answered. 'I've often asked myself the same question.'

He lapsed into silence again. They had reached the ruins now and he stopped. Una looked around, aware of an odd combination of claustrophobia and homesickness. She wondered what on earth she was doing here, so far away from everything and everyone familiar, and whether she would really be able to endure a whole winter in this place. All she could think of was that she might manage it if she was allowed to spend a little time with Thór now and then.

'I don't know,' he said at last, by which time she had almost forgotten her question. 'No, I'd rather not, Una, to tell the truth. It's a beautiful spot, and peaceful too. Peaceful and safe. But there's not a lot going on. Though, having said that, I don't have a bad life here. I read a lot. I never used to, but now I borrow loads of books from the library; all kinds of books, but non-fiction, mostly.'

'The library?'

'Yes, of course we haven't got one here in Skálar, but we can get books from Thórshöfn. Hjördís picks them up for me whenever she goes in.'

'You and Hjördís, how – er – how did you meet?'

Again there was a perceptible delay before he answered. 'I just saw the job advertised here and applied for it out of some kind of desire for adventure. I didn't know her at all.' He hesitated, then said: 'I expect there are stories doing the rounds about Hjördís and me, but I can assure you I only work for her.'

And with that he saved Una the problem of asking the question. Once again, their eyes met, then they hurriedly looked away.

As if to cover his embarrassment, he said: 'Anyway, here we are. Let me show you round the ruins. I need some excuse to offload all the information I've absorbed from those library books about Langanes.'

She'd been sleeping badly, and when she did finally drop off she tended to start awake again shortly afterwards, drenched in sweat.

Hannes had been missing without trace for a month and, immediately after his disappearance, his mate Hilmar had vanished too.

She was so frightened. She couldn't shake off the conviction that they were both dead; that they'd been murdered.

Of course she'd known that Hannes was mixing in bad company, and guessed that Hilmar was too, since they were both associated with the same crowd. But because she was — had been — in love with Hannes, she had tried not to ask too many questions.

The police had spoken to her and questioned her exhaustively. She'd told them she had gone round to Hannes's house the day he disappeared, and knocked on the door and peered through the window when he didn't answer, but hadn't seen anything. She got the feeling they didn't believe her.

She had also told them about his links to the underworld, explaining that she didn't know exactly what he had been mixed up in but that she could give the police some names. And now she was *frightened, terrified that these men would come after her in an attempt to shut her up.*

When she slept she dreamt of Hannes, but all her dreams were nightmares. A different sequence of events every night, but always ending in the same way, with Hannes dead, murdered by those men.

XII

The choice at Gudrún's branch of the Co-op was what you'd expect in the worst corner shop in Reykjavík, with prices to match. Some might have found it charming, romantic even, to live in an isolated hamlet like this, but Una was already fed up with having to forgo various luxuries that she had taken for granted in Reykjavík. It didn't help that the shop was only open between three and five in the afternoon, and not every day of the week either.

Of course, she could always knock on Gudrún and Gunnar's door, but Una was keen to avoid doing that, guessing that it would lead to her being roped in for coffee and a chat every time she bought something.

Apart from the inevitable fish, there was hardly any fresh produce available. Una had discovered that the villagers were largely reliant on their chest freezers when it came to cooking anything else.

She stood by the till, packing her shopping into a bag.

'Shall I put it on your tab again?' Gudrún smiled.

At that moment the bell over the shop door jingled.

Una turned hopefully, only to see Kolbrún's mother, Inga, walk in, accompanied by a man who must be her husband, Kolbeinn.

Kolbeinn smiled at Una, his gaze lingering on her as if he were sizing her up. Their daughter wasn't with them. Kolbeinn, although greying slightly at the temples, was a handsome man, tall, lean and muscular. It was easy to believe he had spent his whole life working at sea.

'Hello,' Inga said, in a colourless voice.

'Hello there,' Una replied.

'Hi, Una,' Kolbeinn said, his manner much friendlier, his eyes still fixed on her. 'We haven't met, but I'm Kolbeinn, Kolla's father. It's great to meet you at last.' He extended his hand and took hers in a firm grip that lasted a little longer than strictly necessary. 'Buying something exciting for supper?'

'Er . . . well . . .' A small bottle of Coke and a packet of liquorice would hardly count as exciting, but she had bought them as a little treat for herself, to be enjoyed that evening as she curled up in bed with a good book. She was learning to read herself to sleep since there was no TV on offer.

But Kolbeinn didn't wait for an answer: 'Everything going well with Kolla? She, er, she speaks highly of you.' Judging from his tone, this was something of an exaggeration. Kolbrún was so unforthcoming in lessons that Una didn't for a moment believe that the girl praised her teaching to her parents afterwards. Una was aware that she needed to concentrate on getting to know the child better and coax her into opening up a little. No doubt it would take time, but then she had the whole school year to achieve a transformation.

'Yes, your daughter's a credit to you,' Una replied, before hastily correcting herself: 'A credit to both of you, I mean.' For a moment, she had forgotten Inga's presence and felt as if she were talking only to Kolbeinn. His wife was standing there, a pale figure in her white winter coat, with her pallid complexion, melting into the background, not saying a word.

'She's special, Kolla is. I reckon it'll do her the world of good to have an experienced teacher like you. There's more chance she'll make something of herself. I don't think it's healthy for kids to live in a place like this. We're planning to move away sooner or later, maybe even go abroad. Perhaps spend a year in Denmark, something like that.'

'Sounds good,' Una said, a little shortly. She was feeling uncomfortable with Inga standing there silently watching, though at least Kolbeinn seemed like a nice guy.

'I can't spend my whole life at sea,' Kolbeinn continued. Then he added, humorously: 'I've eaten enough bloody fish to last me a lifetime. Breaded haddock, poached haddock, grilled haddock – God, I don't know how I've stood it for so long. I hope you're not having haddock for supper!' He patted her shoulder and smiled again. 'Anyway, see you soon.'

Una nodded. 'Nice to see you both.' She hurried out of the little shop, hugging her white plastic bag full of unhealthy treats. But when she was outside on the pavement she heard the bell jingle as the door opened behind her and, looking round, saw Kolbeinn standing there.

'Hey, Una,' he said casually. 'Maybe we should meet up some time and have a word about Kolla. The girl can be a bit shy. You need to approach her the right way. Could we find half an hour for a chat some time?'

'Er, half an hour? Yes, sure, of course.'

'Great. I'll see you, then.' He smiled.

XIII

Kolbeinn was sitting facing Una in Salka's sitting room, where she had just finished teaching. He had sent his daughter home, closing the door firmly behind her, and now he was looking at Una with that easy smile on his face. 'So, how do you like our village?'

She would rather have got straight down to business, as she never had much patience with small talk, and the purpose of the meeting was supposedly to discuss Kolbrún and her schoolwork.

When Una didn't immediately respond to his conversational gambit, Kolbeinn answered himself: 'It is a bit small, yes, I know. Crazy, really, even to think of living out here, but it's possible to make a go of it, especially when the pay's good.'

'I'm only on a teacher's salary.'

'You're not planning to stop here long, are you?'

'Just for the one winter, I think.'

'Oh, well, then you'll be fine.' He flashed his attractive smile again.

'Is Kolbrún good about doing her homework?' Una asked, trying to steer the conversation round to his daughter. 'Does she take an interest in it? She always seems well prepared when she comes to class.'

'Oh, yes. She's very hard-working. Always has been conscientious. The girl's quite clever, you know. But she's not very outgoing – she takes after her mother in that. They're both happiest when they're alone. That's why I'm not sure a community this small is good for her development. Of course, in some ways it's perfect: there's no pressure to make friends or fit in since there are only the two girls here and, well, they're mates. Sort of. At least, they get on OK. But the thing is, Kolbrún can get away with being withdrawn and antisocial here. But I'd prefer it if she was in a bigger community, a bigger class, where she would be forced out of her comfort zone. Do you know what I mean?'

Una nodded. She understood exactly what he was getting at. She hadn't been so different herself as a child; paralysed by shyness until she had eventually changed schools and found herself in a class of friendly kids, where she had begun to emerge from her shell a little. But not long after that the cataclysmic blow had fallen and she had reverted to type, shutting herself off from the other kids. She'd had to learn all over again how to make friends and trust people.

'Yes, I do. I'd thought maybe Kolbrún and Edda were friends outside school, but I gather that's not the case.'

'Well, there's not much we can do about it. We can

hardly force them to play together, and there's the age difference too, of course.' He got up and moved to a chair closer to Una, and lowered his voice confidingly: 'I just wanted to share this with you and let you know that she needs special attention. If you think of anything . . .' He laid a hand on Una's shoulder.

'Naturally, I'll keep an eye on the situation. Not all children develop at the same pace, as I've learned from experience, but then you don't usually have a chance to pay this much attention to individual kids. I have to say, it's one of the advantages of having such a tiny class.'

She was acutely conscious of his hand still resting on her shoulder.

'I'll try and meet you – you and Inga – from time to time to keep you updated,' she went on. 'I'll organize a formal parent–teacher meeting before Christmas. Your wife didn't want to come with you today?'

He shook his head. 'I'll take care of this.'

He removed his hand at last.

'Are you sleeping OK in Salka's house?' he asked casually.

The question confused Una. 'What? Er, yes. Why do you ask?'

'Oh, because the house has a reputation for being haunted. I thought you knew.'

'Er . . . No, I didn't, actually.'

'Salka was aware when she moved into the place, but she said she didn't believe in ghosts and I reckon that's what's kept her going. It all comes down to your attitude, I suppose. What do you think?' He smiled teasingly.

Despite her reluctance to hear any more, Una couldn't resist the temptation to ask: 'Why, what happened here?'

'A little girl died. Some time around 1930. People say she haunts the house and . . .' He paused dramatically: 'And they say the problem's worst up in your room. It used to be hers.'

'Seriously?' Una was shaken, in spite of herself.

'Yes, I've heard lots of stories from the old days about people staying there for one night, then never again. Of course, they're only stories, and not necessarily first hand, but I believe there's a grain of truth in them. I'm not saying I believe in ghosts, you know, but there's no doubt people have had some odd experiences there.'

'Like what?' Una could feel herself breaking out in a cold sweat.

'Oh, they see the girl. She appears in the room – dressed in white, of course.' He paused to let the impact of his words sink in. 'But you don't need to worry, I shouldn't think. Not if you haven't noticed anything.'

Far from having the desired effect, his words of comfort achieved the exact opposite. Una found herself remembering the dream in which Edda had appeared to her. And the girl she had seen in the window. *Had it definitely been Edda?*

He placed his hand on her shoulder again, edging even closer.

Next minute, his arm was sliding round her shoulders. She sat there rigid, not knowing how to react.

'I can go upstairs with you now and check, if you like,' he said, in a low voice.

She stood up so fast her chair almost fell over backwards. 'No, that's fine, thanks. I need to . . . I think it's best you go now.'

He rose unhurriedly to his feet, then smiled at her. 'Sure, I get the message. I'll see you around, Una.'

XIV

Una sat without moving for a long time after Kolbeinn had gone.

Although he hadn't said so in plain words, there was no doubt in her mind that he had been coming on to her. He had put his arm round her and angled for an invitation to go up to her bedroom. There was no way she could have misunderstood him, was there? He was a married man, for God's sake, and she was his daughter's teacher. It could hardly have been more inappropriate.

Eventually, she rose to her feet and put on her shoes and coat, desperate to get some air and clear her head. It was bitingly cold outside, even colder than it had been earlier, and the wind was gusting hard, but fortunately it wasn't raining yet. Someone had told her it didn't snow much in the village and at first this had sounded like good news – no chance of the roads becoming impassable or problems of that kind – but she had begun to realize that a bit of snow might not be a bad thing. Every day dawned darker and more depressing than the last, though it was still several weeks until the winter solstice. A snowfall would have brightened things up. In fact, it could have snowed to its heart's content, because she wasn't going anywhere. Even if she'd wanted to, she still hadn't got round to sorting out the worrying clattering noise in her car. She shivered, and it wasn't only because of the cold. Her encounter with Kolbeinn had become extremely uncomfortable by the end. How was she supposed to behave towards him next time they met? Would he try it on again? Should she simply act cool and pretend nothing had happened?

As if his pass at her hadn't been bad enough, there was the creepy story he had told of the girl who died. When Kolbeinn had hit on her, it had temporarily driven the story out of her head, but now it came back to her and she shivered. Was she really sleeping in a room where something terrible had happened? Or had Kolbeinn been pulling her leg? She would have to sleep there tonight, and not just tonight but all through the long, dark winter. Of course, she didn't believe in ghosts, and yet she couldn't help feeling a little spooked. She had heard so many folk tales over the years about unexplained forces, stories people had told each other down the centuries in this dark, forbidding country. And while she didn't really believe in anything like that, you could never be entirely sure . . .

Besides, the fact that a little girl had died up there was macabre enough on its own.

Perhaps she should ask Salka about it and seek reassurance from her that there was nothing to be afraid of.

They could have a good laugh over the silly story. Salka might be able to give her the lowdown on Kolbeinn too and tell her that he often behaved like this.

Una scrambled the last few feet down on to the rocky beach. There was no one about and yet she always felt a little twitchy there, as if curious eyes were watching her. She avoided looking in people's windows as she walked through the village because it was such a small place and the proximity to the other inhabitants could be uncomfortable. As a rule, she kept her eyes lowered, lost in her thoughts. Only when the sea appeared in front of her did she look up and marvel at its splendour. However grey and desolate it was at this time of year, however wild the waves that pounded the shore during the winter storms, the sea was the sole reason that anyone lived here.

There were times when she felt unwelcome in the village, as if she should have stayed in Reykjavík and never have ventured out here. It was hard to work out whether the feeling was real or caused by paranoia. Apart from Guffi, no one had said anything to her face, yet there was something offputting, hostile even, about the place and its inhabitants. The only person who had actively welcomed her was Salka – and her daughter, Edda, of course. But her other pupil, Kolbrún, remained sullen. And although Gudrún and Gunnar seemed friendly, it was obvious that Gudrún had her own agenda.

Then there was Thór, of course. She couldn't work him out, but hoped she would get a chance sooner or later.

Una stood there for a while, gazing unseeingly into the twilight, listening to the booming of the waves, wind-blown spray whipping her hair into a wet, salty tangle; her lungs scoured by the icy air. She hadn't suffered much from homesickness, until this evening. She had needed a change of scene for a number of reasons. And although Skálar was cold and lonely, and the locals struck her as being on the chilly side, she felt oddly safe here, as if nothing bad could happen to her. And that in itself was positive. Or at least she had felt safe, until her encounter with Kolbeinn.

The truth was that she didn't miss much from Reykjavík. None of her friends had bothered to get in touch since she moved. Her mother rang from time to time, but she was busy with her own life, and Una had discovered that she was quite content with being this far away from her mother, for the moment, at least. There was so much that remained unsaid between them, so many difficult memories, yet when they met their conversations were superficial, as if neither of them dared to open the doors to the abyss of the past and face up to the darkness and grief.

She had planned to sit down and have a chat with Salka but felt too restless to do so this evening. She wanted to be alone, to have a quiet, relaxing end to what had been a difficult day; cook a light meal in the kitchen upstairs or maybe just make herself some toast. Have a little drink; unwind by immersing herself in a book from Salka's library.

It had come as a pleasant surprise to discover how cosy it was to lose oneself in the world of fiction, forgetting time and place, helped along with a bottle of wine. Her evening stretched out before her, a vision of peace and calm.

She would sit down over a coffee with Salka another time and ask her about Kolbeinn, and also, if she got the chance, about the girl who was said to haunt the house.

Just not this evening.

XV

Una awoke with a jerk.

She opened her eyes but couldn't see a thing for the darkness pressing in all around her. For a panicky moment she couldn't work out where she was, though she had the feeling she was in a strange place, not in her own bed. She stiffened with fear. She was so cold. By the feel of it, she'd kicked the covers on to the floor, and the room was freezing.

She sat up slowly, experiencing a moment of dizziness, but the feeling soon passed as she remembered where she was.

In Skálar on the Langanes Peninsula. In the little attic flat. Alone.

And then she knew what it was that had woken her. Or thought she knew . . . It was hard to distinguish dream from reality with her senses still wandering in the vague borderland between sleep and waking.

She had heard something. What, though? As the memory gradually came back to her, she felt the skin prickling on her arms. It had been a high little voice – the voice of a young girl, she thought. Yes, now she could hear it again in her head: a young girl singing a haunting lullaby.

Unable to bear it a moment longer, she got out of bed and blundered across the pitch-black room towards the light switch on the wall. Not for the first time she cursed the fact that she didn't have a reading lamp by her bed. Yet she felt a moment's reluctance to turn on the light, for fear of what the retreating shadows might reveal.

The high voice echoed eerily in her head, but she couldn't recall the words of the girl's song. It must have been a dream, however real it had seemed.

Suddenly there was a loud crack, followed by a tinkling sound and a stabbing pain in her foot that caused her to stumble and fall heavily to her knees. What the hell?

She bit back a scream, only for it to dawn on her a second later that she had trodden on the wine glass she had left on the floor the previous evening. Fumbling for her foot, she found a shard of glass sticking out of it and felt something hot and wet oozing from the wound. Gingerly, she extracted the glass. The pain was excruciating.

It took all her willpower to force herself back on to her feet, then grope along the wall for the switch, but finally she found it and turned on the light. As the room sprang into view, she shot a glance around, half-expecting to see a small figure in there with her, while telling herself that she'd imagined the whole thing: the voice hadn't been real, the lullaby had been an illusion, a trick played on her by her sleeping mind.

Limping back to the bed, she sat down, drew up her

foot and examined the cut, which, luckily, turned out not to be as deep as she'd feared. Now she had satisfied herself that she was alone in the room, she could feel her heartbeat slowing and returning to normal.

Then, in a flash, the words of the girl's song came back to her:

> Lullaby, my little Thrá,
> may you sweetly sleep . . .

A chill spread through her flesh.

XVI

It had been a bad night.

After stumbling around in the dark and treading on the wine glass, Una had managed to dress the wound herself. She didn't think the cut was serious, although it had bled quite a lot at first. She had cleaned it with antiseptic, then closed it with a plaster. If she'd been in Reykjavík, she might have taken herself to hospital, but there was no doctor in the village and the last thing she'd wanted was to drag herself out in the middle of the night to drive thirty kilometres to Thórshöfn, only to be told that all it needed was a plaster. In the event, it had taken her ages to get back to sleep, and she hadn't been able to bring herself to turn out the light. She had finally dropped off towards morning and only just woken up now. It was unusually late for her, but fortunately it was a Saturday.

She glanced at the alarm clock to find that it was past 10 a.m., and the pale morning light was trying to force its way between the curtains – that fickle light which was quick to disappear at this time of year if it so much as clouded over. She could still remember the lullaby, or the first few lines of it, anyway, but by the light of day the night's events seemed quite different. Yet a hint of doubt remained in her mind: the little girl's voice had been so real, and Una was sure she had never heard the song before. Surely she couldn't have composed a lullaby in her sleep?

The very first night after being told Kolbeinn's ghost story, she had started hearing voices.

Damn it, she thought to herself, *it must have been my imagination.*

It was time to get up. She just hoped the cut would heal quickly. She would try to have a relaxing day and avoid going downstairs, even though Salka usually cooked a hot lunch on Saturdays. She wanted to allow herself the luxury of not doing anything at all, and hoped that the effects of her peculiar dream would wear off. She didn't want to go outside either, as the very last thing she wanted right now was to bump into Kolbeinn.

She got out of bed, taking care not to put any weight on her injured foot, and hobbled into the kitchen. Better start the day with some coffee. But even as she was making it, the high, eerie voice continued to echo in her head, singing that damned lullaby.

She sat in the dark, trying to make herself breathe evenly, calmly. She mustn't let her fear take control. If she did, she really would be lost in the darkness, in the fullest sense of the word. Fear was her greatest enemy right now, apart from the police, perhaps. The fear of being locked in, the fear of being deprived of her freedom, of not being able to breathe.

She still wasn't sure what had happened; it had all been so fast. Almost before she knew what was happening, she was sitting in prison, locked up in a windowless cell, no longer aware of the time, or even of what day it was. Everything had blurred together. She racked her brains to understand what could have led to her ending up incarcerated here, when she was completely innocent.

They had come to her little basement flat in the middle of the night and started banging on the door, and when she'd opened up, still half asleep, they'd almost dragged her outside in her nightclothes. They had clapped handcuffs on her, although she'd made no attempt to resist arrest since she was so confused that it had taken her a while to work out what was going on.

It was all connected to Hilmar and Hannes. She was supposed to have murdered them.

Murdered Hannes? The man she loved . . . And Hilmar? She had barely exchanged two words with him.

She had protested her innocence throughout, but the police thought differently. They insisted that she had taken part in the murders and helped dispose of the bodies in a fissure in the lava-field.

They could be horribly convincing, but she had to resist the intolerable pressure they were putting on her to confess. She knew better; they would never get her to admit to such terrible crimes when she'd had nothing to do with them.

It was so cold in the cell. She couldn't get warm, but worst of all was the feeling of claustrophobia, the fear of suffocation, of not being able to breathe. Sometimes she screamed at the top of her voice, but it made no difference. Perhaps it just made matters worse.

She huddled in the corner, in the pitch blackness, letting the time pass, trying not to fixate on the walls that were closing in on her, on the men who wanted to deprive her of her freedom. She told herself that she was still alive, still a young woman. She just had to get through this somehow.

It was all a terrible misunderstanding and the only question was how long it would take the police to realize this.

XVII

Una's attention was distracted by the lights which briefly swept across the room where she and Salka were sitting. They were unmistakeably the headlights of a car.

It was getting on for six on Saturday evening and, being the shortest day of the year, it had already been dark for three hours. The sun set noticeably earlier up here in the far north than Una had been used to in Reykjavík and, with Christmas nearly upon them, she found herself missing the lights and the festive atmosphere in the centre of town. Salka had taken out a few candles and other decorations in an attempt to dispel the gloom, but Una, who had long ago given up decorating her own flat at Christmas, was glad that she hadn't gone the whole hog: no tree, fussy knick-knacks or fairy lights. In fact, the only lights to grace the streets of the village so far were on Guffi's house: countless large, yellow bulbs, rather clumsily strung.

Salka hadn't mentioned any plans for the Christmas celebrations, but Una assumed she would be invited to eat supper with mother and daughter on the twenty-fourth, and thought she would probably accept. Given the choice, she would have preferred to spend the holiday alone upstairs with a glass or two of good red wine, but perhaps a bit of company would do her good.

This evening, however, Una's thoughts were preoccupied with the Christmas concert which was due to take place the following day. She had done her best to prepare for it, with staunch assistance from Gudrún. Or, rather, it would be truer to say that Gudrún had borne the brunt of the organization: she had chosen the carols, taken the rehearsals, selected the Christmas readings, baked the cakes to be served with coffee as refreshments, and overseen the decoration of the church. But Una's brooding over Gudrún's interference was interrupted by the novel sight of car headlights at this time in the evening. Most of the villagers went everywhere on foot since distances were short and few people had any business elsewhere, especially this close to Christmas.

Una and Salka both glanced over at the window.

'Is that a visitor?' Salka wondered aloud. 'I didn't know anyone was expecting guests.'

When she first arrived in Skálar, Una would have thought this was an odd thing to say, but by now she was aware that everyone knew everyone else's business. There were no secrets here.

Una heard the noise of a car, then suddenly all was quiet again: the engine had been switched off. 'They can't be coming to see us, can they?' she said.

'No, impossible.'

They waited in suspense. After a few moments, sure enough, there was a knock at the door.

Una and Salka both automatically shot to their feet, but Una hung back and let Salka go to the door before following.

There was a young man of about thirty standing on the doorstep, with hair so short he looked almost like a skinhead, wearing jeans, a white shirt or jumper and a leather jacket. For a moment he looked at Salka without speaking, then his gaze flickered to Una, who instinctively dropped her eyes.

'Sorry to bother you,' he said politely. 'I hope I'm in the right place. This is Skálar . . . ?'

'That's right,' Salka said curtly.

'I'm looking for a woman I know who lives here. Her name's Hjördís. I'm taking in the sights on Langanes and was hoping I could get a bed for the night at her place. I just knocked on your door because it's the first house I saw and I noticed that the lights were on . . .'

'Sorry, but she doesn't live here,' Salka said, with a quick glance at Una.

'No, right . . . then maybe I should, er . . .'

'She lives up at the farm. You need to turn round and take the track up the hill. You can't miss it.' Then she added, stressing the words: 'You can get back to the main road to Thórshöfn that way too, if you change your mind.'

The subtext was clear: *leave our village.*

'Right, yeah. Thanks very much.' He smiled, but Una thought she detected an underlying tension, perhaps even nervousness, in his manner.

Salka said goodbye and shut the door firmly.

'That was strange,' Una muttered.

Instead of answering, Salka went straight over to the phone in the hall. 'I'm just going to warn Hjördís.'

Una waited and watched. Perhaps she should have given Salka a chance to speak in private, but her curiosity got the better of her.

It seemed to take a while before Hjördís answered.

'Hello, it's Salka. There was a man here just now, a *stranger*, looking for you. He said he knew you and needed somewhere to stay. He's in a car, obviously, so he should be with you very shortly. He left us a minute or two ago.' Silence. 'No, I didn't ask his name . . . Yes, yes . . . No, I don't know what he wanted. That's all he said.'

Salka said goodbye and put down the receiver.

'That was strange,' Una repeated.

'It may seem as if we're being unnecessarily paranoid,' Salka said with a rather hollow laugh, 'but it's not that we don't like outsiders; we're just not used to having visitors here, especially in winter. The village isn't on the way any-where and people don't usually come out here in December without a very good reason. It's a bit livelier in summer; we do get the odd tourist then – Icelanders mostly – who find their way out to us, mainly to see the ruins from the war – the old radar station, you know. That provides a bit of welcome business for the village shop and brings some money into the local economy.'

Una nodded but was more interested in discussing the stranger.

'Do you think he was really sightseeing? At this time of year?'

Salka hesitated, then said: 'I suppose we should give him the benefit of the doubt. People do some odd things. But you have to be careful out here in winter, as there's not a lot of help available if anything goes wrong, except here and in Thórshöfn. There's literally nowhere else. He must be the adventurous type.' She smiled.

'Oh well, if he's staying over, he can always come along to the Christmas concert tomorrow,' Una said, only half joking.

'I don't think that would be very appropriate. It's not exactly open house. It's meant to be a private celebration for us locals. How's it going, by the way? Are the preparations on the right track?'

'I think so. Gudrún's been a great help, as you know. She's absolutely tireless.'

'You should watch it with Gudrún. Make sure she doesn't eat you alive. She does tend to take over. You have to be firm with her.'

'Oh, it's quite nice having someone to help out. And I'm sure she's done a good job. It should hopefully get people into the Christmas spirit.'

And that moment the phone rang.

'Hjördís again?' Una said, and waited for Salka to answer.

Salka shook her head, as a sign that it wasn't Hjördís on the line. 'Yes, she's here. Yes, I'll tell her. Yes, OK. Bye.'

'That was Gunna,' Salka said with a smile that contained more than a trace of sympathy. 'She wants you to go over to the church – right now. She says she's been waiting for you. Apparently, there's still a lot to do for tomorrow.'

XVIII

Salka had cooked haddock for supper. They had a tacit agreement that Una was welcome to eat with Salka and Edda, in return for taking turns in buying groceries for the kitchen downstairs. Nevertheless, she always made sure that she kept her own cupboards stocked up too, for when she wasn't in the mood for company.

Una had spent two long hours in the church, watching as Gudrún made the preparations for the concert. Although the event was nominally her responsibility, she herself didn't actually have any role in the proceedings. Gudrún had simply taken over, yet for some reason she liked to have Una at her beck and call. Perhaps to have someone to blame if everything went wrong, Una thought cynically. She smiled at the idea. What on earth could go wrong? Admittedly, it was one of the very few social occasions in the village calendar, but it wasn't that complicated, surely?

She sat down to a belated supper, in the mood for a

chat with Salka to distract her thoughts. Luckily, Edda wasn't there. No doubt she was over at one of their neighbours' houses. She often skipped out at mealtimes. Her absence would give Una a chance to discuss the two subjects she had been putting off raising with Salka. One was Kolbeinn, and the other the ghostly girl who supposedly haunted the attic flat . . .

'Everything ready for tomorrow?' Salka asked, filling Una's glass with water from the carafe. Una had learned that Salka never offered alcohol with supper.

'Yes, it looks like it,' Una replied. 'Gudrún knows exactly what she's doing. I just wish it would snow. Then everything would be perfect.'

'Unlikely, I should think.'

'Thanks for supper, by the way. This looks delicious,' Una said. She was grateful to Salka for providing her with a job and a roof over her head, but most of all for her warm welcome. She needed a friend.

'You haven't tasted it yet,' Salka said teasingly. 'Don't praise it too soon.'

Una took a mouthful. The haddock was a little overcooked for her taste, but she didn't let it show. 'About Kolbeinn . . .' she began, apropos of nothing.

Salka looked up. 'Yes?'

'Do you know him well?'

'Why do you ask?' Salka sounded wary.

'Oh, I was just wondering about him and his wife.'

Salka didn't say anything.

'He came round to see me recently,' Una went on. 'About Kolbrún.'

'Ah, I see . . . Is she OK?'

'What? Oh, yes. He just wanted to talk to me, as her teacher. Just a general chat, you know. But then . . . then he . . .'

Salka nodded. 'He can . . . come on a bit strong.'

'I got the feeling he was hitting on me. But I wasn't quite sure . . .'

Salka cut in: 'Oh, you can be sure, all right. It's not the first time and it certainly won't be the last.'

'Really? Are you aware of other times?'

'I certainly am . . .' Salka hesitated.

Sensing there was more to come, Una waited.

'He tried it on with me too,' Salka said at last. 'Shortly after I moved here. I think he was even quicker off the mark with me than he was with you.'

'Wow. He's got quite a nerve for a married man in such a tiny place.'

'I don't think he cares, to be honest.'

'How did he react when you turned him down? Did he try again?'

There was another lengthy silence.

'I didn't turn him down,' Salka answered at last. 'I was lonely and there aren't many other good-looking men around here, so . . .'

'Did you know he was married?'

'Yes, I did,' Salka answered, unabashed. 'Frankly, I felt that was his problem, not mine.' She smiled. 'It may sound a bit cynical to you, but there you go. And we were incredibly careful. For God's sake, don't tell anyone, though. I trust you.'

'Of course not,' Una assured her, not knowing what else to say.

'He told me his wife was involved with someone else, from outside Skálar; that it was a marriage in name only. And what do I know . . . ?'

'How . . . how did it end?'

'It didn't last long, just a few months. Then we both gradually lost interest. Maybe I thought better of it, if I'm being completely honest. It was uncomfortable knowing that his wife lived practically next door.'

This certainly wasn't what Una had been expecting to hear when she sat down to supper. Clearly, everyone had their secrets. 'By the way, I heard an interesting story about this house, something about a ghost . . . ?'

An odd expression flitted across Salka's face and Una sensed that the other woman didn't find it remotely amusing.

'Yes . . .' Salka paused. 'I wasn't necessarily going to bring it up. I try to avoid the subject, especially with you, as you're . . . well, as you're living in the flat upstairs. Most of the stories seem to relate to that part of the house.'

Una waited for her to go on.

'Have you noticed, er, anything out of the ordinary up there?'

'Why, should I have?' Una asked, feeling suddenly spooked. It was one thing to tell ghost stories for a laugh, but she had a horrible feeling that Salka might actually believe in the haunting.

'Well, it depends who you talk to, Una.'

'I did have a bad dream one night, but that was right

after my encounter with Kolbeinn, when he told me about the ghost.'

'Bloody Kolbeinn,' Salka said, with a sudden flash of anger. 'He never could keep his mouth shut.'

'I heard, or thought I heard, a little girl singing or reciting a poem. It woke me up and, to tell the truth, I was quite scared. It felt so real. But I'm pretty sure it was my imagination – just a dream or my mind playing tricks on me.' Yet Una was far from sure; it simply made her feel better to rationalize it away like this.

'Yes . . .' Salka said doubtfully, but didn't comment any further on Una's experience, and Una couldn't bring herself to ask if anyone else had heard something similar.

Eventually, Salka went on: 'I've heard various stories and I was aware of them before I moved here, because the house was in my family, as you know. The girl died in 1927 and her room was upstairs in the attic. That's to say' – she made a face – 'it was the room you're sleeping in now.'

As she said it, the high little voice started up again in Una's head, singing the same haunting refrain:

> Lullaby, my little Thrá,
> may you sweetly sleep . . .

She tried to banish it from her mind, watching Salka, focusing hard on what she was saying, but the voice seemed to grow in strength, becoming louder and louder, until Una was driven to her feet.

You could have warned me, Salka, she thought.

She sat down again, trying to control her trembling. 'What, er . . . what kind of stories? About people seeing or hearing her, you mean?'

'Honestly, I don't know how much I should repeat,' Salka said slowly. 'I don't want to frighten you, but, if you really want to know, I've heard various tales. There's one story I've heard many times. A woman lived upstairs over the summer and got on fine at first, but then she woke up one night – the midnight sun was shining outside – to see a girl, dressed in white, standing at the foot of her bed and staring at her. Apparently, the woman screamed and ran downstairs and out of the house and refused to set foot in it ever again.' At this point, Salka smiled, as if to lighten the tense atmosphere. 'Of course, people have to decide for themselves whether they believe in that sort of thing or not.'

'Oh, I don't know,' Una said, trying to laugh. 'I think stories like that get blown up over time, the more people repeat them. I expect details get added with every re-telling.'

'No doubt, but there's so much in this world that we don't understand. I'm sorry not to have mentioned it before you arrived, but it's the only free room in my house. If you want to leave – to move out, I mean – maybe we could see if there's anywhere else available in the village. I suppose there might be a room at Hjördís's place . . .'

'God, no!' Una intervened hastily. 'I'll just put up with it. At least I won't be lonely up there. She's never harmed anyone, has she?'

'Who, Hjördís?' Salka asked.

'No, the little girl.'

'Oh, right, of course. Sorry. I was thinking about Hjördís and wondering what happened with that man who knocked on our door. Whether she gave him a room for the night.'

'It seemed a bit weird,' Una commented. 'His story about sightseeing, at this time of year.'

'Yes, to put it mildly. Like I said earlier, we just don't get tourists out here in winter. Only the rare Icelander in summer, come to see the ruins.'

'Yes, I know,' Una replied, and was about to add that Thór had taken her up there and shown her round but then suddenly changed her mind, reluctant to draw attention to the fact she had gone to see him. 'I've read about it,' she said instead.

'First there were some British soldiers here, then the Americans took over. They called it Camp Greely. Apparently, they stayed here right to the end of the war. The army built the road up here and a radar station to monitor air traffic. I gather they were going to construct an air strip here too but then the war ended. Still, imagine how great it would have been to have an airport in our back yard. Perhaps there would be a few more people living here now if we had. There were army huts up on the hill, though they've all long since vanished, but you can still see the layout of the roads in the camp, or what remains of them – tarmac too. What a luxury.'

'Should we, er, maybe ring Hjördís and check?' Una asked, cutting short Salka's description. She was motivated more by curiosity than concern for Hjördís, and would have liked to go over and see for herself. She had an ulterior motive too, as it would give her an excuse to say hello to Thór, since she never ran into him in the village. But if, as she'd been assured, the Christmas carol concert was an event nobody missed, he was bound to show his face there. Una was determined to seize the chance to talk to him then and see if it led to anything.

'No, I don't think it would be a good idea to ring now,' Salka said. 'We'll see her tomorrow and hear the whole story then.'

'Yes, I assume she'll come along to church,' Una said, then added, unable to resist the temptation of saying his name: 'With Thór.'

Salka nodded, her thoughts obviously elsewhere. 'You asked about the girl upstairs,' she said eventually. 'No, she's never harmed anyone. So you needn't worry about that.'

'Have you seen her yourself?'

Salka smiled. 'Only in a picture.'

'A picture? What do you mean?'

'There's a photo of her. It's not dated but was probably taken the year she died. Would you like to see it?'

Una answered without stopping to think: 'Definitely.' Then immediately regretted it. It might be better not to give her imagination too much material to work with.

Salka got up and walked unhurriedly to the bookcase. Una admired the size of her library once again. There had been nothing like it in her own childhood home. Her parents had shown no interest in literature or culture of any kind, and the only books in the house had been on a shelf in her father's study. She remembered the room so well that when she closed her eyes she could still picture it in detail: the black office chair, the worn desk made of dark wood, the old radio set on which she used to listen to pop music from the American naval base at Keflavík. She used to shut herself in the study and turn on the radio, careful to keep the volume low. The soft lighting lent the room an air of enchantment and the black leather chair was so comfortable that Una used to sink into it and close her eyes, vanishing into a world of foreign music. The only illumination in the room had come from an old, green desk lamp that her father had been given by his father. In her memory, it had given the study a greenish glow. That's how it had looked the last time Una had seen it and that's how it would always remain in her memory, which was why there was no colour she now loathed more than green. None of her clothes were green and she had even gone so far as to throw away the only green jumper she had owned, unable to bear the thought of wearing it again.

'Here's the book,' Salka said casually, and Una snapped back to the present. 'And the photo. It's been kept in this book, always in the same place, for so many years that I hardly dare move it.' She opened the book, laid it on a side table and carefully picked up the photo, then came over to the dining table, where she handed it to Una.

The picture was clearly very old, worn and yellowing, dog-eared at the edges. There was the house – the photo had been taken from the road outside – and you could even see the light on in the window of the dining room, where they were sitting now. Upstairs, the dormer windows showed that the attic was there, just the same; in fact, the house didn't look as if it had changed at all in the intervening half-century. And there she was, the girl, standing on the steps up to the front door, wearing a dress that was white or at any rate a pale colour – it was impossible to tell since the picture was in black and white. She had pale hair and was staring straight into the camera lens, as if she were looking straight at Una and Salka.

Was this the girl she'd seen in her dream the other night? Even as she thought it, she smiled at her own foolishness.

The photograph was so old and the quality so poor that it was easy to imagine anything you liked. A faded image of a girl in a white dress. It was so indistinct that it could just as well be a picture of Edda.

And, quite apart from that, it had been a dream, that was all.

Nothing but a dream.

XIX

The old church was aglow with candles when Una walked in out of the cold.

This year, the last Sunday before Christmas fell on 22 December, only two days before Christmas Eve, which was the high point of the Icelandic celebrations. It was freezing hard outside – the mercury had plummeted without warning – and the weather was still and clear, the stars shining bright overhead. From outside, the church had looked wonderfully atmospheric, and the radiance of the candles streaming from the small windows reminded Una of an old Christmas decoration her mother had once owned – a simple white church with a light bulb inside to illuminate it during Advent. When Una was young, she had thought it a magical addition to their sitting room and every year she had looked forward to the moment when the church was brought out of the garage, where it was kept on a shelf in a battered box. Once the bulb had been tested, the family would gather for the ceremonial switching on of the light. The reminiscence had been enhanced by the passing of time, the glow no doubt brighter in memory than it had been in reality. Una hadn't seen the Christmas church for many years and didn't even know if her mother still kept it or had thrown it out. And she didn't care either. Christmas had bad associations for her nowadays.

It was quite hot inside the church, thanks to all the candles. There were too many to count, rows of them flickering on all the windowsills and other available surfaces, evidence of Gudrún's handiwork. She herself was standing by the altarpiece, looking very done up in a red dress. She came to meet Una, beaming from ear to ear.

'What do you think?' Her face shone with pride. Giving Una no time to answer, she went on: 'I've been baking as well. All the cakes are ready and waiting round the back. Did you bring anything?'

'It's ... It's great,' Una said, lost for a better word. In fact, it was dazzling, lending the church an air of enchantment, as if conjuring up the spirit of Christmas. Una took off her coat and hung it up in the porch. 'So pretty and welcoming. You should have called me. I could have helped. And, no, I'm afraid I didn't bring any cakes. Was I supposed to?'

'Oh no. I usually take care of that side of things myself. I just thought you might bring something as it was your job to organize the event, but of course it doesn't matter. It's just nice that you're here.' Again Gudrún smiled.

'Thanks for all your help,' Una said, insincerely. The warnings she had been given about Gudrún's tendency to muscle in and take over had been no lie, but, after all, why shouldn't she? Una had tried to do her bit, making feeble attempts to help Gudrún take the girls for singing practice, but teaching music had never been her forte. To be fair, though, she had quite enjoyed the rehearsals, which had mostly taken place during school hours. Edda was musical and might have a future as a singer, if she had access to better training than she would get here in the village. True, Kolbrún's voice wasn't as powerful. While her singing wasn't exactly false, it was obvious that music wasn't her strength and that she wasn't exactly throwing herself into it, heart and soul. It didn't really matter, though; the important thing was to take part, and there was no doubt the girls would look lovely. They had been encouraged to wear matching white dresses and Una was sure the audience couldn't help but be moved by the pure childish voices singing in this gorgeously festive setting.

'Wouldn't you like to cast your eye over the refreshments?' Gudrún asked. 'Of course, it's *your* concert, so do let me know if you feel something's missing and we'll try to sort it out – if possible.' She glanced at her elegant gold wristwatch, then shook her head. It was half past five, far too late to sort out any deficiencies now, given that the concert was supposed to begin at six.

Una followed Gudrún into the back room, where a table had been laid with all kinds of goodies, including a bowl of the cinnamon doughnut twists known as *kleinur*, a Swiss roll, pancakes, chocolate coconut balls, and finally a plate bearing a pile of *laufabraud* or leaf-bread, the delicate deep-fried wafers decorated with cut-out patterns without which an Icelandic Christmas would be incomplete. The effect was mouth-watering. There were drinks too: malt-brew, orange and Coke – nothing alcoholic. 'I'll put the coffee on later,' Gudrún said. 'You do think it'll be a success, don't you, Una dear?'

'I'm sure it will. You've put in a huge amount of work.'

'Oh, well, one has to fill one's time somehow. The shop's not exactly busy and Gunnar's always working, so this is my favourite time of the year – the concert most of all. It's all so lovely and Christmassy. Even the darkness seems cosy somehow, though it's so unrelenting here in winter, as you'll have noticed, because they never got round to installing streetlights and I don't suppose they ever will now. It's just a pity we don't get more snow. We have to put up with all the dreariness of winter without any snow to brighten things up.' She sighed. 'But you get used to it. You can get used to anything.'

'Are you two planning to stay on here?' Una asked. She hadn't meant to pry but suddenly felt a little sorry for the woman. It struck her that Gudrún wasn't as happy as she pretended to be.

'Oh, yes, there's no point moving. No point giving up now. It won't be long before Gunnar retires, and we've made ourselves so . . . so comfortable out here in the middle of nowhere. One can get used to anything in the end.' Yet there was a hint of sadness in her eyes as she repeated this mantra. 'Besides, I don't know who would organize the concert if I moved away.'

At that moment they heard a creak as the church door opened. 'Gunna dear?' called a voice.

'I'm back here, Gunnar.'

Gunnar was togged up in what was obviously his Sunday best: a grey suit, slightly too tight, a blue-checked shirt and a broad, stripy tie. He was visibly ill at ease in this get-up, clearly missing his usual overalls.

'How pretty you've made it, dear ... both of you, I mean,' he said. 'Hello, Una. Nice to see you. You must both have worked very hard. The whole village is looking forward to it, from what I hear.'

'Is everybody coming?' Una asked.

'Oh, yes, I think so,' Gudrún cut in. 'No one's ever missed it, as far as I can remember. People generally make the effort to come along, even if they're on their last legs.'

'Now you're exaggerating, dear,' Gunnar said. 'But it's a popular event. There's not much in the way of entertainments in Skálar. It was better when the army was here. Did I tell you about the film shows they used to hold up at Melar?' He was looking at Una eagerly, clearly longing to tell her again.

'Yes, you told me. It's a great story.'

'That was the life, Una, in those days. There were four of us boys here, me and Guffi, and our two mates, who've left now. Four best friends. Blood brothers, you could say. We used to look out for each other. That's why it's never entered my head to work for anyone but Guffi. The bonds you make in your youth never break. Though I expect you know all about that yourself.'

She didn't, in fact, though she wished she had friends she was that close to. Perhaps life was different nowadays and it was harder to form such close bonds in the city.

She hadn't exactly had a conventional upbringing either, for much of her childhood. None of these factors had helped. And perhaps she just wasn't very sociable by nature, in spite of having chosen to become a teacher.

Making her excuses, Una left Gudrún and Gunnar in the back room and took a seat in the front pew of the church. She hadn't needed to turn up this early since she had no particular task to perform. The couple carried on talking, the sound of their voices carrying into the nave, but Una tried to ignore it and savour the temporary respite of sitting there with nobody bothering her, enjoying the warmth of the candles. She raised her eyes to the altarpiece. Salka had described it as really special, saying it looked as though Christ was reaching out of the frame to embrace his congregation. It was certainly large, featuring a carefully executed oil painting of the Saviour against a wider background, but to Una's eyes it was no more than a pretty picture. It didn't speak to her in the way Salka had mentioned.

Closing her eyes, Una let her mind drift. She wanted a moment to compose herself before everyone arrived. She had been a little apprehensive, unsure if she would enjoy the evening, acutely conscious of feeling that she didn't belong among these people. But now she was determined not only to put a brave face on things but to have fun. She found herself wondering yet again if Thór would show up.

She jumped at the sound of the church door opening. She must have nodded off, though for how long she didn't know.

Turning her head, she saw Inga and Kolbeinn advancing up the aisle with Kolbrún drooping in tow. The girl looked as if she would rather have been anywhere else. She had on a black anorak over her white dress and wore a sulky expression. Kolbeinn shot a glance at Una, his face blank, as if he were seeing her for the first time. Their eyes met briefly, then he looked away and made some remark to his daughter. At the same moment Inga sent what could only be described as a venomous glare in Una's direction. Did she know her husband had tried to hit on her? Or did she suspect he had? If so, surely she should be angry with him, not Una?

Una averted her eyes and remained where she was, concentrating on the altarpiece, hoping the family wouldn't sit near her. Her wish was granted. When she eventually stole a glance over her shoulder, she saw that they had taken a seat in a pew two rows behind, as if deliberately avoiding her. 'Hello,' she heard Gudrún saying, 'how nice to see you. Kolbrún dear, are you all set?'

Una didn't catch the answer. No doubt the girl had just nodded, as uncommunicative as ever.

Peering round again, she saw that Gunnar had now emerged as well and was talking to Kolbeinn, while Gudrún was chatting to Inga. The conversations flowed together in a pleasant background murmur of voices and Una was struck once again by the melancholy thought that she didn't belong here. Everybody knew everybody else. Even Salka, who had only moved to the village relatively recently, had deep roots here. Una felt keenly aware of her position as the only real outsider, apart from Thór.

Again the church door opened. She heard from the greetings that Hjördís and Thór had arrived. Her heart beating a little faster, she curbed an impulse to look over her shoulder and kept her eyes lowered, trying to be unobtrusive.

'Hi, Una, sitting all alone?' Thór asked, and suddenly there he was, right next to her, smiling his shy smile. Next minute he was sliding into the pew beside her. 'It's . . . er, it's looking great. This must have taken a lot of organization.'

She hesitated, then said: 'Well, Gudrún and I did it together. She's had practice, so everything's gone very smoothly.'

'Are the girls as good as ever? I remember they did a lovely job last year.'

'Very good. They're both really promising kids.'

Hjördís joined them before Una could say anything else. 'Hello, I'll sit with you two. Best to be at the front.' She took a seat beside Thór. 'It all looks very festive, like every year.' They were both neatly dressed in clean clothes, though not in their party gear like Gunnar and Gudrún.

Una smiled. 'Yes, I gather it's the biggest event in Skálar's social calendar.' Then, realizing that her remark might come across as condescending, though she hadn't meant it that way, she said: 'I mean, a lot of effort has gone into it.'

Hjördís's rather hard face softened slightly. 'It's nice to see the church used, even if the vicar doesn't bother to show his face here that often.'

'Listen, while I remember,' Una said, 'some man knocked on our door yesterday. Salka gave him directions to your place. Who was he? Is he staying with you?'

'Oh, him. He's gone,' Hjördís replied. 'He only spent the one night with us. He was just someone who used to be at school with me. I hardly know him. The cheeky bugger scrounged a free bed for the night. He was asking about the history of the place, what it was like in the old days when the army was here, and so on. I did my best.' Her smile looked rather forced. 'But history's not my strong point, to be honest.'

'Do you do that sort of thing much – rent out rooms, I mean?' Una asked.

'Yes, every now and then, in summer mainly. There's not much else in the way of accommodation here in the village, but I've got plenty of room, and Thór's in the guesthouse, so the visitors don't get in his way.' After a moment, she elaborated: 'Running a farmstay is a way of earning a bit on the side, but this place is too far off the beaten track ever to be very popular. If it weren't for the old radar station, I don't suppose anyone would be interested in visiting us.' She sighed.

'Una, Una!' It was Gudrún calling. 'Could you come here a minute and give me a hand with these decorations?'

Una got up and went over. She wasn't sure if Gudrún really needed help or if the purpose was to make her feel involved by throwing her a last-minute sop.

Gudrún handed her a box of old Christmas decorations, a motley collection of little Santa Clauses and other odds and ends. 'Could you arrange these by the entrance?

She pointed to a small table by the door. 'I completely forgot. These are things that have collected in the church over the years and we always put them out during Advent.'

Things nobody wants, Una thought to herself, but smiled at Gudrún. 'Of course.'

She tried to arrange them tastefully but some of the Santa Clauses were so old and battered that they wouldn't stand up and none of the ornaments were in very good nick.

'Could someone help me with the door?'

Una recognized the loud, bass voice immediately. Guffi had materialized behind her, having entered the church quietly, though he was certainly making sure he was heard now. Ignoring him, she concentrated on arranging the ornaments. She had no desire to help him. Her visit to his house had left her feeling so intimidated that she had steered clear of him ever since. But his brooding presence seemed to hang over the village. Every time she walked past his house she felt as if hostile eyes were watching her, and from the way the locals talked about him, she felt as if he controlled everything.

'Una.' She felt a hard prod at her shoulder.

Swinging round, she saw him standing there, scowling. 'Una, give me a hand,' he demanded gruffly. 'I need someone to hold the door open for me.'

Only now did she notice the thin, pale woman in the wheelchair sitting outside in the cold; Guffi's wife, presumably. Una had never seen her before. She smiled tentatively at the woman, whose hollow-cheeked, heavily lined face creased in an answering smile. She looked exhausted.

Una held the door open while Guffi manoeuvred the wheelchair with difficulty through the narrow gap, then positioned his wife at the back of the church, behind the pews, which seemed to be the only practical solution. After this, he briefly disappeared. Una stood beside the woman, feeling awkward, then held out her hand: 'I'm Una.'

'Yes, I know, dear,' the woman replied in a low voice. 'I'm Erika.' Salka had mentioned that Erika must be at least ten years older than Guffi, but from her appearance the age gap could easily have been twenty.

Una waited for Erika to add something, or ask a question perhaps, but she just sat there in silence. Una didn't like to march off and abandon her, so she remained where she was, and was relieved when Guffi finally returned, carrying a chair, and sat down beside his wife. He didn't say a word to Una or give her so much as a glance.

She hurried away and slipped into the back room, where she stole a pancake from the refreshment table and sat down in a corner to think about her place in the village.

What on earth had she got herself into?

Guffi had made it clear almost from day one that she didn't belong here and now she couldn't help feeling that he was right. She sat there and ate the pancake, glad to be alone. The concert was due to begin in a few minutes, but all she wanted was to disappear. Everyone was there except Salka and Edda. The stranger hadn't shown up and hadn't turned out to be mysterious either. Perhaps deep down she had been hoping that he would do something to shake up life in the village.

She waited. At least she wasn't missing anything. The show couldn't begin without Salka and Edda, one to sing, the other to accompany the girls on the organ. Perhaps she should go out and sit down beside Thór again. It was so frustrating that Gudrún had called her away to deal with those stupid decorations. Although Una hadn't a clue what to say to Thór, sitting beside him had felt good. In fact, the prospect of seeing him had been the only reason she had been at all excited about this evening. No doubt there would be a chance to talk to him later – perhaps even to get him in private. Hjördís's presence was an inhibiting factor, though. Una had sensed, not for the first time, that the other woman took a possessive interest in Thór, despite his claim that they were just good friends.

She made up her mind to catch him, as soon as Hjördís took her eyes off him. The tradition was to hold an after-party in the church, where the villagers could socialize as they tucked into the refreshments Gudrún had provided. If the pancake Una had pinched was anything to go by, they were in for a treat.

She rose to her feet. Best go and reclaim her seat. Maybe she'd think of some witty remark to whisper in Thór's ear. Anyway, nothing could be more natural than for her, as the girls' teacher, to sit in the front row.

The programme consisted of three carols, each more beautiful than the last: first two traditional Icelandic songs, 'One Fine Night' and 'A Festival Entereth In', then 'Silent Night' as the finale.

As Una emerged into the nave, she almost collided with Salka and Edda. The little girl was looking lovely with her long fair hair hanging loose over a simple white dress, with a subtle decorative weave that glittered in the light of the candles. Edda smiled palely at Una, who suddenly had the disturbing feeling that she was looking at the girl in the old photograph. It must be an illusion created by the solemn atmosphere, the white dress, the blonde hair. They all combined to strike a chill into Una's flesh, making her shiver just as she had when she awoke in the night with that lullaby echoing in her ears. For an instant she stood quite still, and so did the child in front of her. Meeting her gaze, Una had a disorientating sense that she was looking into the eyes of the girl in the picture, as if her ghost had returned to the village, half a century later, wearing the same white dress.

Una closed her eyes for a moment, breaking the spell, then forced herself to greet the mother and daughter, looking only at Salka. 'Nice to see you,' she said weakly, then, drawing a deep breath: 'You must be excited. It's going to be a wonderful evening.' She tried to force her trembling lips into a smile: 'It's going to be absolutely wonderful.'

XX

Una had reclaimed her seat beside Thór and Hjördís. Twice she had been on the point of speaking to him, racking her brains for something interesting or clever to say, but both times she had changed her mind at the last minute and gone on staring down at the floor or up at the altarpiece. Thór and Hjördís sat in silence as well, exchanging no comments. Perhaps they had long ago run out of things to say to each other.

The keenly anticipated concert got off to a reasonably good start. Gudrún stood up unexpectedly at the beginning to say a few words. This should probably have been Una's job, but no one had mentioned anything about it to her, and, to be fair to Gudrún, she did at least thank Una for her generous help with the preparations.

Salka then played a beautiful piece on the organ, which was followed by a reading of the Christmas story from the Gospels, an honour which by custom fell to Guffi. He read the familiar text in a mumble, tripping over the words as if he had never seen them before and completely failing to capture the Christmas spirit.

And then at last it was the turn of the children's choir, as Gudrún liked to call it, though to Una's mind you couldn't really use the word 'choir' for two people. But perhaps in a community as small as Skálar, different rules applied.

Gudrún bobbed up again and this time invited Una to the front. Una shook her head, desperate to get out of the duty, but eventually let herself be persuaded and left her place, feeling the sweat break out on her forehead as she did so. She was used to standing in front of a group of children in the classroom, but not to public speaking on an occasion like this, especially not in the company of people with whom she had so little in common; where she didn't feel welcome.

After she had said a few, stumbling words, the girls walked slowly but confidently to the front, and Una threw them both an encouraging smile as she slipped back to her seat, though only Edda returned it. Kolbrún looked dour, as usual. Still, at least both girls seemed ready, and Una knew the audience wouldn't be too critical. In fact, the girls couldn't ask for a more sympathetic crowd. If their performance fell short in any way, no doubt the blame would be laid firmly at Una's door. As the first notes emerged a little false, she felt her heart beating faster and sent up a fervent prayer that all would go well.

The end of the first carol was greeted with thunderous applause, and the girls' performance of the second was as good as Una could have hoped for. The clapping resounded around the little church even louder than before, and now it was not only Edda and her mother who were smiling but also, wonder of all wonders, Kolbrún too. Perhaps all the child needed to bring her out of her shell was a little more encouragement and attention than she was used to getting. Remembering her encounter with Kolbeinn, Una reflected that Kolbrún's family life was bound to be overshadowed by the lack of affection in her parents' marriage. She felt a wave of pity for the girl.

The concert reached its height as Salka played the introduction to the final carol, 'Silent Night'. The girls stood poised, their faces radiating pride and pleasure in their own performance. Then they raised their voices again, and this time they sang as one, looking angelic in their white dresses, their voices perfectly in time, and even Kolbrún managed to avoid any false notes. It felt as if the holy season had truly arrived in the little church in its tiny village on the edge of the ocean, with the warm, soft glow of the candles, the solemnity of the audience, and the carol resonating in the silence.

Una found herself focusing on Edda. She knew she shouldn't have a favourite out of her two pupils, but in her heart of hearts she was much fonder of Edda, with whom she had developed more of a rapport, whereas Kolbrún remained something of an enigma.

Edda was looking curiously strained, but there was nothing wrong with her voice as it soared to the rafters:

> Glories stream from heaven afar
> Heavenly hosts sing . . .

Abruptly, Edda stopped singing and stared at the audience, straight into Una's eyes. She seemed to sway.

Kolbrún kept going a little longer:

. . . Alleluia . . .

Then she too fell silent and turned her head to look at her classmate. After that she just stood there, frozen into immobility.

Una was slow to react and for a moment it seemed as if no one else had realized that something was wrong. Then she leapt to her feet, but it was too late.

The little girl crumpled and fell with a heavy thud on to the floor in front of the altar.

Una's eyes rose for an instant to the painting of Christ gazing down from the altarpiece, and now, at last, she could see what Salka meant: it did look as though he were reaching out to his flock, spreading his arms, trying to save Edda.

Kolbrún screamed and ran, presumably into her parents' waiting embrace, leaving Una alone beside Edda.

The little girl was lying, deathly still, on the floor of the church.

PART TWO

I

All around Una there was a babble of voices.

Shouts.

Cries.

Salka was suddenly there at her side.

'Edda? Edda?' She shook her daughter, then lifted her up into a sitting position, where her body hung, limply unconscious. 'Edda?!' Salka shrieked.

Guffi now joined them and picked the little girl up in his arms. 'We need to open the doors, give her some fresh air. It's far too hot in here. All those bloody candles.' Holding the child very gently, he set off for the exit.

'What's happening? Edda, darling, Edda! Can you hear me . . . ?' The despair in Salka's voice was gut-wrenching.

Una still hadn't uttered a word. Her instinct had been to try to help the girl, though she had no idea what could be wrong with her. Of course, she knew a bit about first aid after her years studying medicine, but it was all more or less theoretical. Now she couldn't move, just stiffened up and stood there watching helplessly. Her mind was racing, the old Christmas memories rising up, the scenes she had tried so hard to forget. The only person who'd had the presence of mind to take action was Guffi. She didn't like him, hated him even, but at this moment she was placing all her faith in him, hoping against hope that he would be able to do something for the child.

Then there was that strange yellow colour. From close up, Una had thought there was a yellowish tinge to Edda's complexion. Perhaps it was her imagination, perhaps her eyes were deceiving her in the unfamiliar light of the candles.

Una watched as Guffi carried Edda quickly but carefully to the door. Kolbeinn held it open and little by little the church emptied until almost everyone was outside, and Una found herself following. Only Guffi's wife was left behind, alone in her wheelchair, forgotten in all the commotion.

'Shouldn't we put her down?' Kolbeinn asked.

'Somebody give me a coat,' Guffi said. Kolbeinn took his off and spread it on the ground, then Guffi laid the child carefully on top of it, and the two men bent over her. 'She's still breathing, just about,' Guffi said.

'Thank God,' Una heard a voice say behind her. It was Kolbeinn's wife, Inga.

Una looked round and saw Salka standing nearby, frozen in horror, watching what was going on without saying a word.

'Edda? Edda love?' Guffi said in a firm but kindly voice. He gave the child a wary nudge, then remarked to

Kolbeinn: 'She's such a strange colour. I don't understand what's happened.'

Her liver, Una thought, it must be her liver, but she couldn't stammer out a word. All she knew was that the girl needed urgent medical attention, but there was no doctor in the village and the nearest one was a long drive away in Thórshöfn.

'What's wrong with Edda, Daddy?' Kolbrún had come up beside her father.

'Go to your mum, sweetheart,' Kolbeinn told her, then asked quickly: 'Are *you* all right? How are you feeling?'

'Yes, Dad, I'm fine,' she said.

It was bitterly cold out there on the pavement in front of the church, but no one seemed to notice. As Edda lay on the ground in her white dress, enveloped in the icy darkness, the warmth of the candles seemed impossibly far away.

Una's teeth began to chatter with the cold, but all she could think about as she looked at the child's still figure was the old photo of the girl who had died more than half a century ago.

'We have to get her to a doctor,' Kolbeinn said with decision. 'Or straight to hospital.'

Guffi nodded and lifted up the unresponsive girl in his arms. 'Will you drive, Kolbeinn? With any luck we'll catch the doctor at home in Thórshöfn.'

'I'll go and fetch the car,' Kolbeinn said. 'Inga, you come home with me. You can call ahead to warn the doctor we're on our way. We need to be sure he's there.'

'I'm coming too! I've got to come too!' Salka cried out frantically.

'Of course you're coming with us, dear,' Guffi said.

'What's wrong with her?' Salka asked in a strangled voice. 'For God's sake, what's wrong with her?'

'It'll be all right, dear,' Guffi reassured her. 'It'll be all right.'

But there was no conviction in his voice.

II

At times during the proceedings, Una had felt oddly detached, as if watching a film rather than witnessing a real-life tragedy. The events of the evening had seemed so unreal after little Edda had fallen unconscious to the floor.

No one seemed to have a clue what was wrong with the child. And now Kolbeinn, Guffi and Salka had vanished into the night, in search of the doctor in Thórshöfn or, failing that, to undertake the long drive to the nearest hospital, which must be at least 200 kilometres away.

The little girl still hadn't regained consciousness by the time they set off. The villagers had stood there for a while, gazing after the red tail lights of the departing car, no one saying a word, until Gudrún finally broke the silence. No doubt she had learned the art, after all these years with Gunnar, of filling in gaps in the conversation.

'We can't do any more now,' she announced. 'Let's just pray that the dear child gets better. I'm sure Guffi will ring us when they get there. If anyone wants to wait in the church, of course they're welcome to.' She waited, watching the group. From their reactions, it was obvious that no one was going to take up her offer. 'Otherwise, Gunnar and I will just go and tidy up, blow out the candles and . . . and, well, put the refreshments in the freezer.' Gudrún bowed her head and went back inside the church, with Gunnar following a few paces behind, as usual.

Una looked around and briefly caught Thór's eye, but he immediately turned away and walked off with Hjördís in the direction of the farm. It came home to her with a sickening blow that she was quite alone in the world here, though she knew this was no time for self-pity. She should be thinking of Salka and Edda. Telling herself sternly to get a grip, she set off home.

Home . . .

Perhaps it was putting it a bit strongly to call the attic flat in Salka's house a home, but it was her refuge for now. She had made herself comfortable there. Although she hadn't brought many personal items from Reykjavík, she had made feeble attempts to put her stamp on the place. Salka didn't bother her when she was upstairs, never even knocked on the door; in fact, it was weeks since she had set foot in the attic flat. Edda would sometimes look in to ask Una a question, and from time to time they had played a game of chess together up there, but otherwise the flat was simultaneously Una's safe haven and a symbol of her loneliness.

As Una walked up to the front door, she became acutely aware of the quietness. The village was almost permanently wrapped in an all-encompassing hush, a stark reminder of how far they were from anywhere. And with no urban glow from a nearby town or distant lights of farms, there might as well have been no outside world. Perhaps what the few souls who chose to live here had in common was their preference for solitude. There was no sound of human activity, nothing but the faint sighing of the sea, but that didn't count as it did nothing to fill up the silence; all it did was echo her own thoughts.

The front door was unlocked, as usual.

No one's going to break in here, Salka had once remarked. *It's better to leave it unlocked so the ghosts can find their way out.*

She had smiled and Edda had asked: *What ghosts?* At the time, Una had been blithely unaware of the tales about the girl in the attic, and even now she only knew the barest outlines of the story. As soon as she got a chance, she wanted to find out more about the child who died. The pictures kept blurring together in her mind: the white-clad girl in the photograph and the memory of Edda in church, of her empty gaze before she collapsed on the floor.

Una turned on the lights downstairs. She was about to continue up to the attic when she paused, changing her mind, and began to wander through Salka's rooms, as if seeing them for the first time. Finding herself in front of the bookcase, she reached instinctively for the book in which the old photo was kept. But, at the last moment, she stopped. This wasn't the right time.

Instead, she went into Edda's bedroom, switched on the light and looked around. There were her dolls, her books, everything characteristically neat and tidy. Una had been in there before, not often but occasionally to talk or play with the little girl. And now she didn't even know if Edda was alive or dead. Feeling numb, she switched off the light, closed the door behind her and, after a moment's hesitation, warily entered Salka's bedroom. She had never been in there before and didn't know why she went in now. Purely out of curiosity, perhaps. She'd never had the house completely to herself before, as Salka had always been just around the corner. It was a welcoming room, small and cosy, just like a bedroom ought to be.

She had made up her mind to call her mother as soon as she got the chance. Maybe the lullaby in her dream was just a childhood memory and not some message from beyond the grave.

Una breathed in the atmosphere of Salka's room. A faint trace of her perfume lingered in the air. Contemplating her neatly made bed, she pictured herself lying down and sleeping there, just for tonight. No one could get to her there.

Trying to push these thoughts away, she made herself take a step backwards, out of the bedroom, but underneath she knew what was wrong.

She was afraid.

Afraid of the night that lay ahead, afraid of being all alone in the house; all alone in the world.

Her thoughts kept veering between these fears and her shock and bewilderment over what had happened to Edda. It had been such a horrifying sight. The little girl had always seemed so healthy and robust, had never missed a day of school, and then, out of the blue, *this*. Common sense told Una that it could have been a sudden illness – it must have been – and yet she felt an ominous foreboding that something else, much worse, lay behind it, though she couldn't put her finger on what. And she didn't want to pursue the thought any further.

She started climbing the stairs, slowly and steadily, leaving the light burning in the hall. She couldn't cope with darkness; not now, not when she was alone. She would have given anything to have someone there with her – Thór, preferably, though she supposed it was mere wishful thinking to imagine that he would have any interest in keeping her company. If only she had someone to hold her, to comfort her and tell her that everything would be all right.

Upstairs she hastily turned on the light, all the lights. Then she proceeded to check the rooms, carefully peering round every corner, a habit she'd adopted after the fateful night when she heard the lullaby. She had tried hard to convince herself that she wasn't frightened, that there was nothing to fear, but her behaviour betrayed her.

The feeling was so strong that she wasn't alone at night.

Her stock of Campari was finished, but she still had a couple of unopened wine bottles left. She had taken to drinking alone in the evenings in her solitude. If she'd been in Reykjavík, her alcohol intake would have been more varied. She used to go out for the odd low-alcohol beer in the city's pubs – proper beer was illegal in Iceland – but her preferred tipples were Campari and Martini. Here in Skálar, though, she didn't dare buy anything stronger than red wine from the little Co-op, for fear of what people would think.

The alcohol calmed her nerves and dulled her mind, but she wondered if it maybe had the effect of intensifying her fears at the same time. Still, the positive effects seemed to outweigh the negative ones.

She opened the window, though all this would do was let in the silence and the chill breath from the sea. Then she uncorked the bottle and poured herself a glass. She wished she could ring her mother, though they hadn't talked much in the intervening months. Anyway, what was she supposed to say to her? That she was afraid and lonely; that a little girl from the village had been rushed to hospital?

The first mouthful of wine was always the best; she took a big gulp and savoured the feeling as the alcohol filtered into her bloodstream. Then, finally, she took off her coat and her party clothes, got into her nightie and stole back downstairs to borrow a book from Salka's library.

Once again, it was as if the volume containing the old photograph were calling out to her, but she resisted the temptation and went instead to the other end of the shelf, eventually selecting a dog-eared whodunnit called *Murder on the Links* by Agatha Christie. Then, clutching the paperback like a talisman, she went back upstairs and climbed into bed with the book and her glass – making sure the bottle was within reach.

It was hard to concentrate on the story, but she did her best and the alcohol gradually had the desired effect. As she felt the drowsiness stealing over her, she hoped she would drop off soon, though she wasn't going to turn off the light.

She had no intention of sleeping in the dark, tonight of all nights.

But the instant her eyes closed she became uncomfortably aware of the noises in the old house: the creaking of the timbers, the hissing of the radiators, even her own breathing, which grew louder and louder until it destroyed any chance of sleep. She opened her eyes again and darted a quick look around, sensing another presence in the room.

Of course, there was nobody there.

The temperature was getting uncomfortably chilly, so she got out of bed, went into the other room and closed the window. Then she crawled back into bed, pulled up the duvet and tucked it tightly around herself to keep in the warmth. Finding that she was still wide awake, she picked up the paperback and her glass and made another attempt to read herself to sleep with the help of Agatha Christie and the wine. The book got off to a good start. Although it had been written more than half a century ago, it had stood the test of time. This was a house with a history, all right, with old books on the shelves and the spirit of the past in every corner.

It was hard to concentrate on the printed page as her thoughts kept returning to Edda and Salka. She was worried sick about the little girl and her heart went out to Salka. She pictured her driving through the night, jolting over the rough roads with her daughter's limp body in her arms. Had Inga got hold of the doctor in Thórshöfn or would they have to drive on for hours through the night to the nearest hospital? Una tried to send them kind thoughts. Perhaps she should have prayed for them, but it wasn't her style.

Her mind circled round again to her own plight. She was filled with dread at the thought that she might have to spend Christmas all alone in this big house. Her mother was planning to go abroad for the holidays with her husband, as Una had learned the last time they spoke on the phone. It didn't really surprise her. She and her mother had always spent Christmas together, but now at last her mother had a chance to celebrate in a warmer climate, without having to feel guilty about Una. It was ironic, then, that Una should feel a greater need than ever to return to her mother's warm embrace at this time of year, but, with her mother away, there was nothing in Reykjavík for her now.

After a long while she felt herself growing drowsy again. The tension left her body, the words on the page blurred together and her eyelids drooped.

III

Una woke up shivering. She was freezing. She must have kicked off her duvet in her sleep again but, even so, it was peculiarly cold in her room. Bracing herself, she got out of bed and checked the window in her bedroom, then the one in the sitting room, but both were firmly latched. Had there been a further drop in temperature outside?

The lights were still on and she meant to keep them that way. She glanced around, without really knowing why, then hurried back into bed and burrowed under her duvet as if hiding from something. She tried to get back to sleep, but her heart was still beating unnaturally fast.

IV

Una opened her eyes. She had been sound asleep with her head under the duvet. This time, she was sure she had been woken by the sound of the piano, by the faint notes of a tune she didn't recognize. Closing her eyes again, she concentrated on listening.

To say she was sick with terror would be an understatement.

She couldn't hear anything. But, just like the time she had been woken by the lullaby, the music had sounded uncannily real. So real that she kept expecting the sound to start up again any minute, convinced that someone was playing the old piano downstairs in the dining room, in the middle of the night, when Una was, or *should have been*, alone in the house.

Surely Salka couldn't have come home already? She felt the cold sweat prickling her skin. She couldn't get out of bed, couldn't make herself move, unless it was to flee outside into the darkness, away from the house and the village of Skálar for good. But the only option was to confront her fears, confront these horrible nightmares, by going downstairs to the dining room and reassuring herself once and for all that there was nobody there.

Salka had often practised in the evenings when Una was in the attic, so Una knew how well the sound carried between the floors; in that respect, her dream had been plausible. But she hadn't recognized the melody. As far as she could remember, it had been a simple tune of the kind a child might play. Perhaps it was something that Edda had played during one of her piano lessons with her mother.

Una emerged from under the duvet, climbed out of bed and braced herself with a deep breath.

There's nothing to be afraid of, she told herself, first in her head, then aloud.

'There's absolutely nothing to be afraid of.'

V

She opened the door to the landing, which was brightly lit, like the rest of the house. She had deliberately left all the lights blazing when she went to bed, something she would never have dreamt of doing if Salka had been home.

She walked downstairs, forcing herself to take it slowly, into the hall, then paused and waited for a few seconds, straining her ears. Against her common sense, she was half-expecting to hear something, a voice singing, the tinkling of the piano, that would freeze her blood. It was cold downstairs but for some reason not as cold as up in the attic. She stood there, shivering slightly, hearing nothing in the silent house apart from the ever-present creaking of the timbers, but even that was muted tonight as there was hardly any wind.

She stood there for a moment longer, staring at the door to the dining room, then shook her head and smiled at her own folly. How ridiculous to drag herself out of bed and come all the way downstairs just because of some nightmare.

Finding her courage, she put out her hand and opened the door, only to reel back in shock.

There was somebody in there.

A split second later she realized that it was her own reflection in the dining-room window, against the back-drop woven from the black night outside.

Still breathless and trembling from her reaction, she peered round the corner and saw the piano.

There was nobody there.

Of course there was nobody there.

But the piano was open.

Had it been open when she came home?

Surely Salka usually closed it?

Or did she . . . ?

Una wasn't sure, couldn't remember.

Feeling the cold clutching at her shrinking flesh, she dragged her eyes away from the piano and flinched again at the sight of her ghostly reflection in the glass.

Whirling round, she fled back upstairs to the attic.

VI

Christmas Eve was a bleak, lonely affair. It hadn't snowed, but then no one had expected it to.

News had finally come through from the hospital, though Una had probably been the last to hear it. Edda had died. The doctors could find no explanation for what had happened. She had been fit and healthy, and the only clue they had to go on was that her face had turned yellow, which seemed to indicate liver failure, as Una had suspected.

She had heard the news the day before from Gudrún at the Co-op, where she had gone to find out what was happening, since Salka still hadn't returned. Una hadn't shed any tears when Gudrún told her. She had just stumbled out of the shop, dazed with shock. The moment when Edda had collapsed in church kept playing over and over in her mind.

Desperately sorry though she felt for Salka, Una dreaded seeing her again. What could she possibly say to her? But perhaps she would be spared the ordeal as she doubted Salka would come back to the village. How would she be able to face living in the house after what had happened? Una was finding it hard enough herself. It was clear now that she would be spending Christmas alone there, and she didn't know how much longer she could cope with the solitude. Last night she had slept in her bedroom in the attic, with all the lights on. Although she had slept only fitfully, the nightmare hadn't returned.

The little girl in the white dress had left her in peace.

For the first time in many years, Una listened to the Christmas service on the radio at six o'clock. It seemed fitting somehow to hear something religious after what had happened, and, if the house was haunted, she told herself it wouldn't hurt to have God on her side. Besides, she had longed for the comforting babble of human voices; she'd had the radio on all day to drown out the silence, the eerie incidental noises in the house and the intrusive images of the two little girls who had died.

She hadn't cooked herself anything special for dinner as she wasn't in the mood to celebrate all on her own. Edda's death had cast a pall over the day. To make herself eat something, she had put some frozen chicken in the oven – at least it made a change from fish – and seasoned it with whatever she had to hand, then fried some potatoes to accompany it. Her mother would have told her off for this meal; when she was a child they'd always had a delicious gammon for Christmas dinner – until everything changed – but even after that her mother made an effort to cook something out of the ordinary, as long as it wasn't gammon.

The chicken had tasted all right, if a bit dry, but the last bottle of wine had made up for that. Once this one was gone, she would be completely out of booze. She would have to get hold of some more. She had been intending to stock up, within reason, of course, when she went to the shop the day before, but after Gudrún had broken the news about Edda, Una had felt it would be unseemly. She missed living in Reykjavík, where it was easier to be anonymous; where people couldn't watch your every move.

It was past eight o'clock and the bottle was half empty when Una gave in to the urge to ring Thór. She sat beside the phone for a long time, the radio's Christmas programme playing in the background. Then she selected the first digit of the phone number at the farm and turned the dial, before losing her nerve and hanging up again. What would he think? What would Hjördís think? The problem was that there was only one phone on the farm and the chances were that Hjördís would answer.

But Una had no alternative.

She couldn't cope with being alone, not this evening. Not this bloody evening – Christmas Eve, the worst evening of the year. Her mother should have known that, though of course she couldn't have foreseen the terrible tragedy in the church; but even in ordinary circumstances she should have realized that Una would want to come home and spend the twenty-fourth with her. But now Una was completely isolated, without even Salka and Edda for companionship. And she was *afraid*, so very afraid.

She had to talk to someone, or better still meet someone, but there weren't many to choose from in this godforsaken spot. It didn't even cross her mind to get in touch with Kolbeinn and Inga, and Guffi and his wife were out of the question. Gudrún and Gunnar would no doubt welcome her, but she had no particular desire to talk to them. They wouldn't listen to her, as they weren't really interested in hearing about her life; all they would want to talk about was Skálar, about the past, the church, the boat, the bloody fish . . . As for Hjördís, she remained an enigma. Una hadn't felt any interest in trying to get past her offputting manner.

She picked up the telephone receiver again, waited for the tone, then dialled with an unsteady hand and waited, telling herself it was actually, *possibly*, a question of life or death.

Some time passed before the phone was picked up and, inevitably, it was Hjördís at the other end of the line.

'Hello, Happy Christmas, it's Una here,' Una said in a small, diffident voice, immediately regretting the impulse to call.

The silence at the other end was crushing. Una could guess what it meant: *how dare you bother us on Christmas Eve?*

Una went on, trying to stop her voice from trembling: 'Could I speak to Thór?'

'Just a moment,' Hjördís said tonelessly.

'Hello, Happy Christmas!' Thór, in contrast, sounded friendly and not in the least put out by her call. 'It's good to hear from you.'

'Yes, er, yes, you too,' Una answered, flustered. 'I was just feeling a bit lonely, what with Salka not being around, you know. I just wondered how you were doing. And wanted to wish you a Happy Christmas.'

'I was thinking of you earlier,' he said. 'We should have invited you to dinner. It was very thoughtless of us. No one should be alone at Christmas.'

'Oh no, really, there was no need. I cooked chicken. It was . . . fine.'

Thór laughed and Una was surprised by what a relief it was to hear laughter again.

'We had ptarmigan,' he said. 'I always shoot a brace for Christmas. That's proper seasonal food. I'll bring over some leftovers for you.'

'Oh, er, great, it would be lovely to taste it, but only if you've got enough. I wouldn't want to deprive you of your dinner.'

'There's plenty left. I'll drop round in, say, ten minutes, if that's all right?'

She could hardly believe it. She hadn't even had to ask him to come, and she'd almost certainly have chickened out. Inviting a man round for an evening visit would have sounded bad enough, even if it hadn't been Christmas Eve. Yet, although she was attracted to him, her impulse had also been motivated by a craving for company, a chance to talk to someone who knew how to listen.

'That would be lovely,' she said, trying not to make her happiness too obvious. 'I look forward to it. I've got half a bottle of red wine to go with the ptarmigan.'

'Half? That won't do for Christmas. I'll bring one with me.'

She felt a flutter in her stomach at the thought, and it hit her that she hadn't only been afraid of being alone but also of the drink running out.

VII

Una had no idea where the evening might lead, but she wasn't getting her hopes up for anything other than some much-needed company.

She and Thór had taken a seat in the sitting room downstairs, among the old books and antique furniture. The chandelier threw a soft illumination over the scene, and Una had lit some candles as well. She didn't feel guilty about making herself at home down there since she knew Salka wouldn't be back any time soon and there was no need for her ever to know about Thór's visit.

'It's terrible news about Edda,' Thór said, once they were seated a polite distance apart on the sofa. The bottle of red he had brought with him was open on the coffee table and they had filled two of Salka's special crystal glasses. It had felt a shame not to use them, seeing as it was Christmas.

Una had laid the table too, helping herself to the contents of Salka's cupboards and taking out the best seagull china. The ptarmigan looked delicious and seemed very generous for leftovers. Clearly, Hjördís and Thór had done themselves proud.

'Yes, it still hasn't sunk in,' Una replied. 'And no one seems to have any idea what was wrong with her.'

'No, so I heard. You must have been quite close to her after teaching her and living in the same house all these months?'

'Yes, quite close, though it takes a bit longer to really get to know your pupils, even when there are only two of them.' Una smiled dully. 'She was a very open-hearted, lively little thing. Talented too.'

'Unlike Kolbrún, I imagine,' Thór remarked drily.

Una hesitated, reluctant to speak ill of a pupil. Choosing her words carefully, she replied: 'She's, well, a bit more reserved, a different type altogether. I have to admit I don't feel I know her at all, despite having taught her all autumn.' After a pause, she asked: 'Do you . . . do you think Salka will come back?'

Thór pondered a moment. 'I'm not sure, to be honest. She'd only moved here fairly recently, but on the other hand the village seems to exert a strong pull on people, and those with roots here stick together and look out for one another.' There was a faraway look in his eyes. 'It's almost like they don't let people leave, if you know what I mean?'

Una understood all right. Her thoughts immediately flew to Gunnar and Gudrún. It was obvious that Gudrún would have liked to live somewhere else but that Gunnar wouldn't hear of it. And then there were Kolbeinn and Inga, always on the point of leaving, of starting a new life somewhere else, but would they ever actually do it?

Eventually Una nodded. 'That just leaves us two, as the guests in the village.' She smiled and raised her eyes to his. 'The migrant workers.'

He looked away. 'I expect I'll be here longer than you,' he said. 'I don't really have anywhere else to go.'

'Oh, come on, you could work anywhere . . .' She broke off. She didn't want to come across as bossy or inquisitive. Perhaps there *was* something going on between him and Hjördís, or there had been once and he still had hopes of reigniting the embers . . .

'It's not such a bad place,' he said, sounding as if he felt he had to justify himself to her. 'We make jokes about it, you know? About living in the back of beyond, that sort of thing, but it's peaceful, there's a good atmosphere, nature on your doorstep, and it gives you time for your hobbies . . .'

A silence fell. Una didn't know how to fill it.

Thór saved her the trouble by saying: 'I'd like . . . actually, it's my ambition to study history one day.' She could tell from his voice that he was serious and, from the way he said it, she got the impression that he hadn't confided this dream to many other people. 'I'd probably write a dissertation about the war years here in Skálar. I've been giving it a bit of thought, making notes of various facts and stories I've come across. And I do a lot of reading about the 1940s, about what conditions were like in this area, and so on. I've even sat down with the old blokes here and made a tape-recording of them reminiscing about those days. It's important to preserve sources like that for posterity.'

His eyes were oddly bright, though whether from sorrow or happiness, Una couldn't tell. Both, perhaps.

'You should go for it,' she said. 'Go south to university in Reykjavík.' Then she realized that she didn't even know if he had finished his school exams.

'Ah, it's not quite that simple,' he said, so perhaps that was the problem. 'There's the cost and the hassle of having to find somewhere to live, giving up my job here, all that kind of thing.'

Although these sounded like excuses to her, she decided not to comment on the fact. 'You'll do it later, when the time's right,' she said instead, and smiled at him. 'But don't give up on the idea. Promise me that.'

'I promise,' he said, embarrassed.

She took a mouthful of wine; it was far better than the cheap bottle she had bought. Thór and Hjördís could obviously afford the more expensive stuff. She tried the ptarmigan. Its strong, gamey flavour wasn't what she was used to, but she said: 'Delicious food, really delicious. Thanks so much for rescuing my evening.'

He smiled but didn't say anything.

Una sensed that it was time to change the subject. Talking about his dream of studying history seemed to have left him depressed.

'Listen, Thór . . .'

He turned and looked at her, his eyes kind above his thick beard. She had never fancied men with facial hair, but it seemed Thór was the exception.

'There's something I'd like to ask you.'

'Fire away.'

'Have you heard any ghost stories about the village?'

'Ghost stories?' Thór smiled again, his warm, amiable smile. 'As far as I can tell, people have always told ghost stories about this area. But then, what do you expect from such an isolated spot? The most innocent things can appear sinister in the darkness and solitude, Una.'

She smiled at his tone, although she didn't find it amusing. 'I know all that. My stay here has been one long nightmare.'

He shifted closer to her on the sofa. 'Surely it can't have been that bad? I know what you're fishing for, though: the story of the girl in this house.'

She nodded.

'Where did you hear about it?'

'Kolbeinn told me.'

'Oh, Kolbeinn loves telling ghost stories, but you shouldn't take him too seriously. He likes to exaggerate. And . . . and that's not his only little quirk, from what I hear.'

Una nodded, but resisted the opening he had provided. She didn't want to ruin a wonderful evening by talking about Kolbeinn. 'So you don't think there's any truth in the tales?' she asked instead.

It took Thór a moment to answer: 'I wouldn't know. I've only heard the stories, like you. They're passed down the generations. But I've read a thing or two as well.'

'You're always reading.'

He laughed. 'It is ironic, really, because I never used to read anything. Reading makes you a better person.'

'As a teacher, I can hardly contradict you there,' Una

said. Then, unable to resist the temptation, she asked: 'What kind of stories?'

'Are you sure you want to hear them? I wouldn't want to be responsible for keeping you awake at night. It's bad enough that you've got a ghost upstairs in your flat.'

'Thór, don't joke about it, OK?'

'OK, OK.' He thought a minute, then said: 'Well, there's the "mare", of course.'

'The mare?'

'Yes, you know, the "nightmare" who supposedly rides you in your sleep and gives you bad dreams.'

Una nodded.

'There's a hair-raising story about the mare going for a man here in Skálar at the turn of the century. She attacked him and trampled him so mercilessly that he couldn't move. And it happened more than once.'

'Did he survive?'

'He bellowed some curse, from what I can remember, and after that it stopped.' Thór grinned, and it was evident from his manner that he took all this talk of the supernatural with a pinch of salt. 'Then there was the sea monster. That's quite a story.'

'Oh? Go on, tell me.'

'A monster with a great long tail once crawled out of the sea and attacked some poor farmer who lived here. He defended himself with an axe he happened to be carrying, but the fight lasted most of the night before the monster finally gave up.'

'So it all ended well?'

'Far from it,' Thór said gravely. 'Afterwards the farmer

became a leper!' He chuckled. 'You've got to laugh at these old tales.'

'You're not very receptive to that sort of thing, are you?' Una said. 'The down-to-earth type, I take it?'

His answer was a while in coming and, when it did, his manner was unusually grave. 'The thing is, as I've learned from bitter experience, the world is difficult, dangerous and unfair enough without needing to believe in ghosts and monsters.'

Una nodded again. This was a truth she knew only too well.

She couldn't remember exactly when she had started seeing the events, visualizing the murders of Hilmar and Hannes as if she had been there.

Hilmar, who she hardly knew, and Hannes, her boyfriend.

The police had described the circumstances in vivid detail, assuring her that she had been there, under the influence of drink and drugs. The reason she hadn't been able to remember at first, they explained, was that she had been drunk or high at the time.

But now she could remember, or thought she could, the deaths of both men, because the police had insisted that she could, and it was so much easier to do as she was told.

She couldn't bear the thought of being locked up in prison much longer. A confession would mean being convicted, of course, and yet she had gone ahead and confessed, because the uncertainty was even more unbearable, and solitary confinement worst of all.

Locked up alone in her cell, she had experienced a darkness of the soul like nothing else she had ever known.

The police had mentioned some dates, told her where she had been and what she had done, and in the end she had confessed.

She also remembered going round to Hannes's in the evening to look for him. She hadn't had a key as their relationship hadn't yet reached that stage, so she had knocked on the door and waited a while, then peered in the window before giving up and going away again. They'd had a date, but it wasn't the first time he'd let her down like that. She had told the cops this story, and at first they had believed her, but later they had told her that it hadn't happened, not then at any rate, because on the evening in question she had taken part in murdering Hannes. And not just Hannes but Hilmar too. Afterwards, their bodies had been disposed of in the lava-fields and she was supposed to tell the police where. That was the only thing the bastards didn't seem sure about.

The trouble was, she couldn't tell them because she couldn't remember anything except what they had ordered her to remember.

Deep down she had her doubts, but perhaps they were right. Perhaps she had drunk too much, taken too many drugs, blocked off the memories. And now here she was, sitting in solitary confinement, in her lightless cell, despite having confessed. They assured her it was only temporary; that the nightmare was ending, that it must feel so good to come clean and tell the truth.

The only problem was that she had been telling the truth all along, right from the beginning; the truth as it had appeared to her, and it was a long time before she had come round to seeing things through their eyes.

In spite of their assurances, she kept asking herself again and again: why would she have wanted to kill Hannes? And his friend too? The police couldn't give her any satisfactory explanation for that. They just said that the two men had been caught betraying their associates in a drug-smuggling ring. Since she had known that

Hannes was no angel, it wasn't that much of a stretch to believe that he had been involved in something dodgy.

But that she could have had anything to do with killing him . . . ? She would never have believed that — not until the police insisted she had.

VIII

'Have you seen her?' Thór asked.

They were still sitting on the sofa, on their second bottle now, and Una could feel the alcohol going to her head.

'Her who?' she asked, though she knew perfectly well what he meant.

'The girl in the attic, the girl who died?'

'Yes,' Una said. 'Or, I don't know, I feel as if I have . . . I've dreamt about her. And . . .'

He waited, not saying a word.

'She seemed so real and yet I can't really remember what she looked like. And it's possible . . . it's possible I saw her standing at the window on my first evening here. I assumed it was Edda, but I wasn't quite sure, and then Edda flatly denied that she'd been awake at the time.' It was an effort to talk about it, but Una didn't want to stop. There was a relief in being able to tell someone, to share the story with Thór and try to work out what had been her imagination and what hadn't; to establish what was within the bounds of possibility.

'And then I heard the piano playing in the middle of the night, after Edda . . . you know, after they'd gone and I was left alone in the house. It was uncanny – terrifying, really,' she said, feeling again the shiver down her spine, the horrifying certainty that she wasn't alone in the house. She couldn't bear the thought of being on her own there tonight. But with Thór at her side, it wouldn't be nearly so bad.

'Did she speak to you?' he asked, and from the way he said it Una sensed that he might be starting to believe; that he had temporarily muted the doubting voices in his head.

'She sang me a lullaby,' Una said. 'But the first time I sensed her presence the feeling was vaguer, more as if she was summoning me.' She immediately regretted saying this, knowing that Thór would ask her about it and that she might be tempted to tell him the whole story. She wasn't used to talking about it – the subject was too private and painful.

Perhaps it was the alcohol that had taken over and made the decision to let him come so close, or perhaps she had always intended to tell him about it this evening – *of course* this evening – because she knew it might just save her life.

IX

'Did you . . . did you know it was my birthday?' Una asked, letting the words filter in, then dissolve in the silence.

'Your birthday? What, today? Are you serious?'

She nodded.

'No, you're joking! On Christmas Eve?'

'Uhuh,' she said, trying to smile. 'A Christmas baby.'

'Seriously? Why didn't you say anything?'

'I don't celebrate it,' she said.

'Shouldn't you have been given some sort of Christmas-related name, like Natalía? Isn't that what usually happens when babies are born at this time of year?'

'No, I'm just Una.' She explained: 'It means "the happy one",' and didn't even try to hide the mockery in her voice.

'The happy one.' He smiled. 'Well, happy birthday, Una.'

'Thanks.'

Her mother had rung earlier that day from abroad to wish her a combined happy birthday and Christmas.

Their conversation had been brief, due to the cost of international phone calls – as a rule, her mother could hardly bring herself to make calls to other parts of Iceland – and the connection had been terrible too. But it wasn't as if they needed to say much; it had all been said before, in one way or another.

'Don't you do anything at all to mark the occasion?'

She shook her head, then said: 'Well, I did get a nice visit.'

'I'd have brought you a present if I'd known.'

'I don't want any presents, thanks. Like I said, I never celebrate my birthday. I don't really go in for Christmas either.' She hesitated, then said: 'It's not exactly my favourite day, not any more.'

'Any more?'

He had picked up on it, and now she knew she would have to tell him.

After a weighty silence, she said: 'It's linked to my dad.'

Thór nodded without speaking, as if he didn't want to interrupt her story.

'He was a doctor. Not in a hospital, though . . . not that kind of doctor. He wasn't interested in people, in patients, just in research. His friends from medical school all became specialists and bought themselves big houses and four-wheel drives, but Dad always lived in the same house; he wasn't interested in money. He was brilliant, absolutely brilliant at what he did, but all he wanted was to teach . . . Well, not even to teach, he couldn't be bothered with that. Like I said, he wasn't really interested in people.'

Again Thór nodded, but when Una showed no imme-
diate signs of breaking the silence, he remarked: 'You
never wanted to study medicine yourself?'

'Sure, I started a medical degree. Spent far too long on
it. I waded through a ton of textbooks and put in a huge
amount of effort but eventually I realized that I didn't
want to follow in his footsteps, I didn't want to be a doctor. The other students couldn't believe it when I dropped
out. I haven't stayed in touch with any of them.'

'Oh, so I'm guessing you showed potential, then?'

'Academically, yes. But I had no vocation. I became a
teacher instead.'

'Good for you, Una. You followed your heart.'

'Dad was forty when he died,' she continued, after a
while. 'I was only thirteen.'

She felt as if she had travelled back nearly twenty years,
to their old family home, where she had grown up as the
only child of loving parents.

'God, that's far too young,' Thór said, with genuine
kindness. 'I'm so sorry to hear that, Una.'

'He died today,' she said, 'on Christmas Eve. On my
birthday.' She felt a tear sliding down her cheek.

Thór moved a little closer and put a cautious arm
around her shoulders. 'That must have been tough. I
mean . . . it must have been devastating.'

Una didn't answer; she had to finish her story before
she lost her nerve.

'He killed himself,' she said. Turning to Thór, she saw
how taken aback he was.

'On your birthday?'

She nodded.

'Did you . . . was it you who found him?'

'Yes. He was sitting at his desk, where he used to spend every evening, his medical books spread out in front of him, his green desk lamp lighting up the gloom, and everything covered in blood.' Her voice threatened to give way and she broke off to compose herself. 'I never entered the room again. Afterwards, we moved into a tiny flat, because Dad didn't leave anything when he died except the mortgage on our house.'

'But . . . why . . . ?' Thór left the question unfinished.

'Why did he do it?'

He nodded.

'I don't know. Nobody does.' She was silent, then said: 'Why does anyone take their own life? On a day like that, too? Why would anyone want to kill himself on his daughter's birthday . . . on Christmas Eve? You can't imagine how often I've asked myself that, without finding any answers. He didn't leave a note, just . . . all of a sudden he wasn't there any more. The vicar they got me to talk to wanted to blame it on depression. *An invisible illness*, I remember him saying. *You can't see that people have it.* Perhaps he was right – no, I'm sure he was right. But I blamed myself for years and thought it must be my fault somehow, because he chose that day, of all days, to do it.'

'Of course it wasn't your fault,' Thór said.

He couldn't possibly know, but she appreciated his saying it.

'No, of course not, I know that now. But I didn't then. Mum and I don't talk about it any more, but I used to pester her with endless questions that she couldn't answer. And then I started to wonder . . . later, when I grew up . . . I started to wonder . . .'

Thór didn't say anything, just looked down at her face as he sat there with his arm around her.

She tried again: 'I wondered if the same thing might happen to me, you know? That one day I might just sink into depression and . . . and decide to end it all. I thought it might be hereditary.'

There was complete silence in the house. Una found herself thinking about the girl who had sung to her in the night, who might be summoning Una to join her . . . in eternity.

'I think that's why I moved here, Thór; to break up the monotony of my life. I'd begun to worry about what was happening to me in Reykjavík. I was afraid I might get some crazy idea one day, when I was alone at home. I suppose that's why I uprooted myself and came out here. But, to be honest, I don't know if it was such a good idea.'

X

It was getting late.

Una had shed a few tears into her wine after telling Thór her story. He had listened so attentively, so earnestly. Underneath that slightly rough appearance, that shaggy beard, he had a kind heart.

She had drunk far more than she ought to, she was well aware of that, but it didn't matter. Her behaviour was perfectly excusable, given that it was Christmas and her birthday too, and opening up the old wounds had been such a strain.

She knew it had done her good to tell someone about her father's suicide. It was a long time since she'd spoken about it. Her mother had sent her to a therapist for a while in the aftermath and she had been forced to open up to him about what she had felt on that traumatic day; about her grief and feelings of rejection . . . But it hadn't helped, not really.

She had been so taken up with her own problems that it hadn't occurred to her until towards the end of the evening to ask Thór about himself, but by the time she eventually got round to taking an interest in his early life, her questions sounded superficial, and he quickly ended the conversation.

'It's late, Una.' He smiled: 'And the wine's finished. Wow, did we really drink both bottles?' He held one of them upside down over his glass to show that there wasn't a drop left. *We*, he had said, though in truth she had drunk most of it.

'Listen, Thór, why don't you stay over? It's so late, as you said, and, er . . .' She was mortified to hear herself slurring. 'And, er, I'm a bit scared all alone in this big house. The girl – she keeps me awake sometimes . . .'

Again he smiled, but he didn't immediately answer.

'You know, I think it would be best if you tried to ignore the ghost,' he said at last, avoiding her question.

'That's easier said than done,' Una replied, a quiver in her voice, though whether it was from fear of the nightmares or because she was waiting for his answer, she wasn't sure.

There was an agonizing pause.

'About tonight, Una . . . I think it's best if I go home. For a number of reasons.'

She twisted her head to look up at him, but he wouldn't meet her eye.

'But this evening meant a lot to me. Honestly. It meant a lot to me.'

XI

New Year's Eve dawned bitterly cold. Una had started the day with a walk down to the shore, where an icy wind had blown in from the sea, piercing her flesh to the bone. She would have given anything for some snow, even just a faint dusting; New Year was inextricably linked to snow in her childhood memories; to her father poking fireworks into drifts before lighting the fuses. This year she didn't know if she'd get to see any fireworks at all. She hadn't ordered any from the shop herself and didn't know what the tradition was in the village.

Salka still hadn't come home, but Una had learned from Gudrún that Edda's funeral was to take place on 2 January in the town of Egilsstadir, where most of their relatives lived. No one had said anything to Una about attending and, although it didn't pay to mark yourself out as different in a place like this, she was reluctant to turn up to the funeral uninvited.

She had started spending more time downstairs, having grown bolder in Salka's absence. It was several days since she had last slept in the attic. Instead, she had been sleeping on Salka's sofa, making sure that she could easily remove all signs of her presence if her landlady came home unexpectedly. She felt guiltily as if she was trespassing, because she hadn't asked permission. And if Salka turned up in the middle of the night or early in the morning and found Una on the sofa, she had an excuse ready: she would claim it had been so cold in the attic that she had taken refuge downstairs, just this once.

At present she was sitting at the table in the downstairs kitchen, listening to the midday news on Salka's radio. It was surprising how quickly she had got used to having this big house all to herself. Her lunch consisted of toast and a bottle of Coke – a bad habit, but she had always had a sweet tooth. Besides, her supply of booze had run out yet again and she had resolved to get through New Year without replenishing her stocks. Thór had invited her to dinner at the farm. Sadly, Hjördís would be there too, but with any luck they would have something to drink to welcome in the New Year.

The radio news generally went in one ear and out the other in a pleasant murmur, and she was sitting, half listening to the announcer's deep tones reading the headlines, when she was brought up short by the first item of the main bulletin: 'The police are appealing for help in finding a missing man, Patrekur Kristjánsson, who was last sighted in Reykjavík, three days before Christmas. Patrekur is thirty-three years old, with close-cropped hair, and is believed to be wearing a black leather jacket and jeans. Anyone who has seen Patrekur is asked to contact the Reykjavík police.'

Una was so taken aback that she shot out of her chair, seeing again the man who had appeared at Salka's door three days before Christmas. Perhaps her mind was playing tricks on her – after all, she seemed to see apparitions in every corner these days – but the description matched. Of course, it could apply to any number of Icelanders, but she had such a clear memory of the man in the leather jacket.

She went straight to the phone in the hall, only to withdraw her hand at the last minute, realizing she didn't know the number of the Reykjavík police. It was one of those supposedly easy to remember five-digit numbers, but she'd never had to call the police before. She would have to look it up in the directory, but, on second thoughts, she told herself it might be better to see a photo of the missing man before she made the call. It wouldn't be a good idea to disturb the village during a holiday with a visit from the police, especially when she had no concrete information to report. What's more, it occurred to her that if the police came in search of this Patrekur, the trail would end at the farm with Hjördís and Thór. The very last thing she wanted was to get them – or him, anyway – into trouble.

The police were bound to have published a photo of the missing man in the papers. She assumed they came out on New Year's Eve, as it wasn't a holiday; in fact, she had a clear memory of reading *Morgunbladid* at home in the old days on 31 December. And although today's edition was unlikely to have reached the Co-op yet, no doubt it would turn up in the next few days.

Yes, it would be better to wait until she had seen his picture; better to be absolutely sure before doing anything drastic like involving the police.

XII

It was past one o'clock when Una nipped out to the Co-op to check if it was open. If anything, it was even colder than it had been that morning, and the wind was now gusting strongly. Her thick anorak provided little protection against the weather: just as well it was only a short step between the houses.

The shop was indeed open. The bell emitted its familiar jingle as Una stepped into the warmth. Gudrún looked up from her knitting and smiled at her.

'Una, dear. Are you after something for your New Year's Eve dinner?'

'Hello,' Una said cheerfully. In spite of Gudrún's bossiness over the concert, she was one of the only friendly faces in the village, and Una was grateful for that. 'I wasn't expecting you to be here today.'

'I'm always open until two on New Year's Eve, as well as on Christmas Eve. There's quite a . . . well, quite a holiday atmosphere, I always feel. Not much to do, but people often drop in for a chat and to buy last-minute things they've forgotten, like something for the gravy, or peas to have with dinner, that kind of thing.'

Una nodded. 'Actually, I just wanted to see which newspapers you had.'

'Oh? Any one in particular?'

'Today's *Morgunbladid*, if you have it.'

Gudrún laughed good-naturedly. 'Today's *Morgunbladid*? No, dear, no chance of that. We never get the papers the day they come out and, what with it being a holiday tomorrow, I'm not expecting deliveries until 2 January at the earliest.'

'Oh, OK. I thought as much, but I just wanted a quick look at it, just . . .'

'Was it something urgent, dear?'

'Well, I heard something on the lunchtime news. About a man who's gone missing.'

'Oh?' Gudrún said, stretching out the sound, her gaze narrowing almost with suspicion. 'Oh?' she repeated. 'Somebody you know?'

'What? No, nothing like that,' Una replied, wondering if she should tell Gudrún the truth, then decided that it couldn't do any harm. 'It's just that the description reminded me of the man who knocked on our door shortly before Christmas. It was quite strange. Did you hear about him?'

Gudrún shook her head. 'No, I didn't hear anything about that.'

'Well . . . Anyway, I wanted to see if there was a photo of him in the paper before I contacted the police.'

'The police?' Gudrún drew her brows together in a frown.

'Yes, or, I thought . . . you know, the police might want to know . . . that he was here, I mean. If it was him.'

'I find it very unlikely that it could have been him,' Gudrún said, her tone dismissive. 'What are the chances? I think you're letting your imagination run away with you.'

'I suppose you're probably right,' Una said, thinking about the ghostly girl. Perhaps her stay in this isolated place was having a peculiar effect on her mind, making her prey to delusions and diminishing her ability to think rationally.

She must be careful not to lose touch with reality.

'Was there anything else?' Gudrún asked, with a brusqueness that was unusual for her. She glanced at the clock on the wall. 'I'm closing in a minute.'

'But it's only a quarter past one,' Una muttered under her breath, then said more loudly: 'No, there's nothing I need . . . Not today.'

Gudrún nodded. 'Not even another bottle of wine?' she asked acidly, and Una shrank from the insinuation.

'No wine today, thanks anyway.' Una forced herself to smile. 'But could you possibly do me a favour?'

Gudrún waited without speaking.

'Could you keep back a copy of *Morgunbladid* for me when it arrives? Put one aside for me?'

'Put a copy aside? Of course, Una dear, of course.'

XIII

There it was again: that song, the same tune, same lullaby.

And this time she could see her distinctly. It wasn't Edda; it was the girl in the photo, wearing the same white dress, inside the house this time, standing there in the downstairs sitting room.

The girl paused in her song and a remote smile touched her lips, but her eyes were profoundly sad.

This time it wasn't fear Una felt so much as an overpowering sense of curiosity. She wanted to speak to the child and ask what had happened and why she kept appearing like this.

The girl finished her lullaby and stood there, quite still, staring into space, her eyes empty, then blinked once, and Una had a momentary confused impression that it might be Edda, but then the feeling passed. She had missed Edda's funeral. No one had reminded her about it or asked if she was coming, though she assumed most of the villagers had gone along.

Una waited without daring to breathe, she didn't

know what for, unless it was for the girl to speak or move. Perhaps she would sing the lullaby again; perhaps she just wanted to draw attention to herself so she wouldn't be forgotten . . . And then Una became aware of a mounting sense of dread, as if something ominous was brewing, something horrifying, that the girl couldn't comprehend . . .

Her stare was so unrelenting that Una couldn't take it any more.

She awoke with a gasp and opened her eyes to find herself wrapped in darkness. With part of her mind, she registered that she had kicked off the duvet. And then it came back to her that she was lying on the sofa down-stairs. She hadn't seen any need to leave the lights burning, as up to now she had been left in peace in Salka's rooms, but now a paralysing fear prevented her from getting up to switch on a lamp. Far from reassuring herself that she was alone in the house, she was convinced it would only confirm that she wasn't. The apparition hadn't felt like a dream at all; the girl's presence had been almost palpable. Una had been looking straight at her, though her eyes had been closed and she had been lying there in the limbo between sleep and waking. Yet, even through her fear, she was aware again of an overwhelming curiosity and knew instinctively that the girl didn't wish her any harm.

After this unsettling experience, sleep was the last thing on her mind. She wasn't sure she would be able to drop off again, even if she tried. Instead, she lay there, not moving a muscle, her heart thudding in her chest, until the cold got the better of her and she forced herself to reach down to the floor for the duvet, half-expecting someone to clutch at her hand. Snatching up the duvet, she spread it over herself again and waited for the warmth to steal back into her body.

She closed her eyes.

Listened.

Heard the incidental noises in the house, the roaring of the wind outside. A storm had blown up during the night and she was grateful, hoping that the noise of the weather would drown out the sound of anything else that might be lurking unseen in the darkness.

Una didn't know what time it was; it could have been anything from the middle of the night to just before dawn. There was no telling from the light at this time of year since the morning was as black as the night, and in this little village the new day wasn't heralded by the hum of traffic as it had been in her old home in the west of Reykjavík.

It had to be admitted too that the sitting-room sofa wasn't particularly comfortable. Maybe she should just go back upstairs to the attic, since it was clear that the downstairs rooms provided no protection from the haunting. But then an alternative occurred to her: she could sleep in Salka's bed. Her room had a comforting atmosphere and Salka didn't seem to have sensed the little girl.

But she didn't move, just lay there with her eyes closed and her mind racing, brooding over the fate of the little girl who had died more than half a century before. Una didn't even know her name, let alone how she had died, but it must be possible to find out since it was bound to be common knowledge in the village.

What happened? she wondered, or perhaps whispered aloud. *What on earth happened to you?* As she asked the question she had a disturbingly powerful sense of the girl's presence again, and was sure that if she opened her eyes she would see the small figure, vividly real, in her white dress.

Una tried hard to distract herself by thinking about something else, tried to relax . . .

XIV

She opened her eyes wide.

She could hear footsteps.

It was still dark; she couldn't have slept long, probably only dozed for a while, her mind still full of questions about the ghostly girl, and now . . .

A door creaked in the hall, sending a shiver of pure terror down Una's spine. She lay rigid, her eyes slowly adapting to the darkness, her breath caught in her throat, and heard them again – footsteps, coming nearer. She couldn't move, couldn't look round.

With a creak, the sitting-room door began to open – even though Una was still half drugged with sleep, she could tell it was really happening. She braced herself to hear the lullaby start up again, all her muscles taut with fear.

Light shone into the room from the hall.

'Una,' a voice said softly, and she almost jumped out of her skin.

She sat bolt upright on the sofa, jerking her head

around. How ridiculous to have believed, even for a second, that it was the ghost.

'Hello, Salka,' she said, embarrassed. 'Nice to . . . to see you. I . . . I'm so terribly sorry.'

Salka seemed to have aged years in a matter of days.

She lowered her head. 'Thanks,' she said quietly. Then asked, frowning in puzzlement: 'What are you doing down here, Una?'

'It . . . it was so cold upstairs. Sorry, I just crept down here during the night. I hope that's OK?'

'Of course. It's fine.' There was a brief pause, then Salka said: 'You didn't come to the funeral.'

'I . . . I didn't want to impose,' Una said, conscious of how feeble this sounded. 'You've all known each other so long. I wasn't sure I'd be welcome.' She immediately regretted her choice of words.

Salka nodded but didn't comment.

'Is it still night?' Una asked, pushing back the duvet and getting to her feet.

'It's nearly morning. I had a bad night, I just couldn't sleep, so I decided to drive home. To see if I could . . . could cope with being here for a while.' Salka's face was drawn; her eyes were dark with exhaustion.

'I understand,' Una said gently. 'I'll go upstairs now and let you get some rest.'

'I . . . I . . .' Salka stammered. 'Actually, I'm not sleepy. Would you mind sitting with me for a while? I'll make us some coffee.'

'Of course. Coffee sounds great right now. But why don't you rest while I make it?'

'No, don't worry, I'll do it,' Salka said. She disappeared into the kitchen.

Una took the duvet off the sofa, ran upstairs to the attic with it, and came straight down, still in her nightie.

The coffee dispelled the last vestiges of sleep. There was a lengthy silence that Una didn't like to break. She waited for Salka to make the first move.

'I wasn't sure if I'd come back,' Salka said at last. 'I wasn't sure if I could bear to come back here, to the village, to this house. But it's not like I have any other choice, and I think it would probably be a good idea to try to get back into some kind of routine.' Her words emerged, slow and halting, and it was plain that she was struggling to hold back the tears.

'Yes . . . I understand,' Una said inadequately.

'I don't know when I'll be able to start writing again, but it's not like I have much else to do here, and you have to begin somewhere. And if I do decide to move, I'll have to clear up, pack away her things . . .' Salka's voice broke, but after a brief, choked pause she went on doggedly: 'In spite of everything, it feels good to be here, at least for now – as if she's near, with her room next door, and everything just as it was.'

Silence fell again.

'Do they still not know what happened?' Una asked.

Salka shook her head. 'No, only that it was liver failure. It's impossible to understand.'

'I'm sorry I didn't come – to the funeral, I mean.'

'No need to apologize. It was a beautiful service. There were lots of people there.'

Una sipped the hot coffee, fighting back the urge to ask Salka about the girl in the attic. It was absolutely the wrong moment, yet she couldn't think of anything else to say, and, who knows, Salka might even welcome a chance to talk about something other than her tragic loss. 'Do you remember when we talked about the ghost?' she said.

Salka nodded.

'I feel like it's getting worse. Have you never noticed anything?'

'No,' Salka replied, but Una wasn't entirely persuaded by her tone.

'The whole thing's so strange. First it was like a bad dream, but now it feels more real, more tangible.'

Salka didn't react.

'What was her name?'

'What?'

'What was the girl's name?'

For a moment it seemed Salka wasn't going to answer, then she said: 'Thrá. I thought I'd told you.'

'No, I don't think so. It's an unusual name.'

'Yes, I suppose so . . .' Salka trailed off.

'I was wondering, do you by any chance know what happened?'

'What do you mean?'

'What happened to her?'

'She died.'

'Do you know how?'

'What does it matter?' Salka asked, glaring at Una, her voice abruptly sharpening. 'It was, what, nearly sixty years ago.'

'I was only wondering,' Una said awkwardly.

'I invited you to live here out of the goodness of my heart,' Salka said with sudden vehemence. 'You have no reason to stick your nose into my family's private history, Una.'

'No . . . no, of course not.'

Salka stood up. 'I'm going to bed. Maybe it would be best . . . maybe it would be best if we could find somewhere else for you to live before this evening.'

Without another word, she left the room.

They had told her that if she confessed, she would be released from solitary confinement immediately. So she had confessed. For a while she had even started to believe in her own guilt, but now the doubts were beginning to stir again. Nothing had changed; she was still confined in the cramped cell, alone in the world, utterly broken. The bastards hadn't kept any of their promises, but from time to time they dragged her off for further interviews, perhaps more out of habit than necessity now, because she couldn't tell them anything else. They repeated their former promises that this would soon be over; that she would be spared this torment once she had been charged and from then on the case would proceed in a conventional manner. She could live with that, she thought; it was the isolation that was killing her.

They told her about the two men who had been involved with her in the murders of Hannes and Hilmar, gave her a detailed description of how the three of them had dumped the bodies in the lava-fields. She could picture the scenes, exactly as they had been told to her; see herself taking part in the murders, then driving the bodies south along the coast, and helping to fling them into a fissure. Yet it seemed, from what she had been told, that their bodies still hadn't turned up.

They had even taken her out to the endless dark lava-fields of the Reykjanes Peninsula and asked her to point to the exact spot, but she couldn't because they had never told her where it was.

In spite of this, she had done her best to please them by pointing at random and trying to focus, to think. If it was all true, if she and her two associates had really murdered Hannes and Hilmar, she ought at least to be able to recognize some landmarks that would help the police to locate their bodies. Perhaps this was the last piece of the puzzle that they had been waiting for, the key that would finally put an end to her ordeal.

XV

As she made her way shakily from the sitting room up to the attic, Una felt as if the walls had come to life and were screaming at her, as if they were heaving in time to her own intakes of breath. She had no idea what had just happened. Why would Salka do this to her?

Naturally, Salka had gone through a terrible experience, so perhaps that was the explanation. Shock and grief had left her a bit unbalanced.

It hit Una with a sickening blow that now she really was alone and friendless in the village. Everyone was against her, and perhaps they had been all along. She had been thrown out on her ear; rendered homeless from one minute to the next. It felt as if the walls were pressing in on her and, when she reached the top of the stairs, she hardly recognized her little flat any more. She had been living there for more than four months, but had it ever really been *home*? And where was she to go now? Was there any reason for her to stay on in the village – with only one pupil – now that the only person who had wanted a teacher brought in from outside had turned against her?

Tired though she was after her bad night, Una immediately got busy, taking out her cases and her belongings. Either she could get in her car and go straight home to Reykjavík or she could knock on Thór's door and ask him for help. She would have liked to ring first, but that was out of the question as the phone was downstairs in Salka's part of the house and she had no intention of setting foot in there again.

Una tore her clothes out of the wardrobes and dumped them in a heap on the bed, in a state of high emotion. There was some food in the fridge; should she leave it behind? And several – actually rather a lot of – empty wine bottles that she hadn't yet got round to throwing away. It would probably be best to take them out to the car as well and dispose of them discreetly when she got back to Reykjavík. But for that she would need more plastic bags.

She lined up the empty bottles on the floor, almost without thinking what she was doing, then paused. She needed a bit more time to think before she took an irrevocable decision. She decided to venture out in the cold and walk up the hill to the farm. Thór and Hjördís must be up by now, since they would have to feed the sheep. After surveying her belongings, she sank down on a kitchen chair for a moment and drew a deep breath. Outside, the wind was raging, but inside the house there was no sound at all. There, in the midst of the quiet, she became aware of a peculiar sense of loss. It wasn't Edda she missed but the other girl who had died.

Thrá, where are you now?

Thrá.

It struck Una that Thrá was the only one in the village who had ever cared for her.

XVI

The morning was pitch black, with no grey rim on the horizon to suggest the approaching dawn. When the nights were at their longest like this, the winter darkness seemed heavier and more difficult to bear than anything Una had experienced in the city, the few lights in the village only serving to heighten the unrelieved murk beyond.

Defying the buffeting wind, which made it hard to snatch a breath between gusts, she battled up the slope to the farm, peering for the light of its windows through the inky blackness. As usual, the guesthouse showed no signs of life, so she headed to the main house. Only when she got there and was standing at the front door did she stop and wonder what she was going to say to Thór.

'You're becoming a regular visitor,' Hjördís said drily as she opened the door.

Una had been fervently hoping that Thór would get there first. 'What? Me?'

Hjördís nodded, her expression unreadable.

Una was stung by the unfairness of this. She wasn't a

'regular visitor' and it wasn't as if anything had happened yet between her and Thór, not really. She was struck by the paranoid fear that they all wanted to get rid of her, not just Salka. Maybe it would be simplest to do what they wanted and leave. The children could easily be home-schooled again, Una thought, then mentally corrected herself: 'the child', not 'children' – there was only one pupil left. But she wasn't accustomed to giving up. She'd always been the determined type, with a considerable amount of willpower, except, she admitted to herself, where drinking was concerned. Once she started, it was as if the alcohol sapped her of all her drive.

It had been the same when her father died; she had lost all her energy and her ability to concentrate and had fallen behind at school. Everyone had said they understood: the teachers, her mother, her friends. No one had dared criticize her.

'I'll fetch him,' Hjördís said shortly.

It was only too obvious that Una wasn't welcome here. It occurred to her to turn round and leave. She would go and finish packing, then get in her car and head back down south. To Reykjavík and home.

'Hi.'

She snapped out of her thoughts to see Thór standing at the door. In spite of her fears, the familiar smile was there, lurking behind his beard and eliciting an answering smile from her.

'You're up early,' he said. Then, apparently noticing her distress: 'Let's step outside. It's a while since we went for a walk up to the old air station, isn't it?'

She nodded. 'Yes, far too long.'

He already had his coat on, ready to go. Putting an arm round her shoulders, he gave her a quick hug, before letting go almost immediately, as if he didn't want to go too far. As if he wanted to keep a certain distance between them. 'Come on, then.'

Her spirits rose a little.

Neither of them spoke for several awkward minutes as they followed the same path up to the ruins as before, staggering from time to time as they were hit by powerful gusts of wind. These were no conditions to go for a walk in, but Una felt she could endure anything for the sake of having a chance to speak to Thór in private.

'Salka's back,' she blurted out at last. She hadn't meant to speak first but the silence between them was becoming oppressive. She had to break it somehow.

It was too dark for her to see his expression and, as usual, his voice gave nothing away: 'I wasn't expecting that – not this soon. In fact, I doubted she'd come back at all. I thought she'd want to make a new start somewhere else.'

'She may move away; she's not sure.'

'How did she seem? Was she bearing up OK?'

'Yes, fairly well, I think, in the circumstances. But our conversation was very strange. She wants . . .' Una broke off, her voice threatening to crack, then, controlling it, said: 'She wants me to move out.'

'She wants you to move out?' he repeated in a neutral tone. Una had been expecting a stronger reaction. 'And go where?'

'Either home or somewhere else in the village. I don't really know how to take it. Whether it was just something she said in the heat of the moment – after all, she must be shattered – or whether she's deadly serious. And . . .' She heaved a deep breath, the icy air filling her lungs.

Thór shot her a glance. 'You know it's thanks to Salka that you got the job here? She fought to get them to hire a proper teacher.'

'Do you think I'll be sent home?'

'It's a bit late now.'

'I'd like a chance to finish the school year, even though Kolbrún's the only pupil left.' For a moment Una allowed herself to think that her teaching this term would have been less of a trial if Edda had been the one to survive . . . Then, turning her mind away from this ignoble sentiment, she filled the awkward silence by putting the question that she had come here to ask: 'I hear that you and Hjördís have a spare room where you sometimes put up tourists . . .'

'Yes,' Thór said. 'Hjördís's farmstay.'

Una said quickly, before he had a chance to add anything else: 'You'd get some money for putting me up – not from me but from the local authority. Salka told me they pay her something.'

'That's not the issue,' Thór said, though Una guessed it probably would make a difference for them. Here in the village the fishermen clearly earned a decent wage, but for the others it must be a struggle. 'But, sure, of course we can sort something out. I'll have a word with Hjördís. We won't send you back to Reykjavík. Not yet, anyway.'

Although it was a relief to hear his answer, it occurred to Una that she wouldn't have minded having an excuse to give up and go home with her tail between her legs. No one would have blamed her, not after the tragedy before Christmas.

'But you need to understand . . .' Thór hesitated mid-sentence, which was unlike him. 'You need to understand that nothing can happen between the two of us. It's a long story, but it's just . . . We can't . . .'

'It's all right, I know,' she replied hurriedly, trying to keep her cool, though this unexpected development had thrown her a little. 'Because of Hjördís.' It was a shot in the dark.

'Yes, right,' Thór said, and left it at that. They walked on up the slope.

She felt mortified and was grateful that he couldn't see her cheeks burning in the dark. In an attempt to distract herself, she thought about the foreign soldiers who had huddled on this bleak, wind-blown hilltop during the Second World War, the elements and the isolation proving the worst enemies of all.

They went a bit further, battered by the blasts of wind, until Thór finally spoke again, raising his voice to be heard: 'Shall we turn back soon, Una?' As before, they were walking side by side. Although she couldn't see his face, his tone hinted that his wishes were quite different; that he'd rather have kept going. That, like her, he'd had quite enough of the village.

'Yes, sure, let's,' she said, deliberately sounding casual. 'It was good to get a blast of fresh air, though, even if it is freezing.' She hesitated, then spoke up again. 'By the way, you remember the man who came to see you the day before Edda died?' She hadn't intended to bring up the subject now but was seized by a sudden longing to discuss it with somebody, as it had been weighing on her mind.

'Yes,' Thór replied. 'What about him?'

'I . . . I heard on the news that a man's gone missing. His name's Patrekur – I can't remember his patronymic. Do you think it could have been the same man?'

'What made you think that? Patrekur? No, he was called something quite different. I've forgotten what, but I'd have remembered if it had been an unusual name like that.'

'There was a description of him. They said he was wearing a black leather jacket and jeans.'

Thór laughed. 'That would apply to half the men in the country.'

'And his age matched too, I thought – thirtyish. He had close-cropped hair as well, both the man they mentioned on the radio and the one who knocked on our door.'

'Again, that description would fit every other bloke of that age in the country. I think you're getting a bit carried away, Una. This place can do that to newcomers. Believe me, I remember it well. When I first moved here I was in a bad way for months. I kept seeing ghosts everywhere, hearing weird noises, getting confused by the wind and depressed by the darkness.' He relapsed into silence, and the whistling of the gale provided an appropriate accompaniment. 'But it gets better, Una. You aren't planning to stay with us for long, but I can assure you that everything improves when the sun comes back. The ghosts melt away with the shadows. Perhaps the old house *is* haunted, what do I know . . . ? But I have faith in the fact that things will seem better in the spring. And the missing man has nothing to do with us, though I can understand why you would think he might. So some poor sod's disappeared in Reykjavík. That kind of thing never affects us up here, however tempting it might be to imagine our little village making it into the news.'

He had turned round while he was talking, and Una followed suit. He had a point. She ought to be careful not to read too much into things.

'I expect you're right. When *Morgunbladid* finally arrives and I see a photo of him, I'll buy you a drink by way of apology. I feel a bit silly, to tell the truth.'

He laid a tentative hand on her shoulder as they walked. 'There's no reason why you should. And you don't owe me an apology. Skálar just takes some getting used to. And the village needs a bit of time to adjust to newcomers as well. This is a place with a soul, if I can put it like that.'

'Yes, I believe you're right. It does have a soul.' After a pause, she went on hopefully: 'There's a good atmosphere here, don't you think?'

'I'm not so sure about that,' Thór answered after a delay, an unaccustomed heaviness in his voice.

XVII

Salka was sitting at the kitchen table in the attic, waiting for Una, when she returned.

'Una, I'm sorry,' Salka said at once. 'I don't know what came over me earlier. I was so tired. I just don't know what I'm doing any more. I . . .'

'There's no need to say anything, Salka. I can't even imagine what you must be going through.'

'Well, anyway, the thing is, of course you can stay.' Salka's voice was gentle, almost sad. 'Really, I'd rather have you here. If I'm to go on living in this house, I couldn't cope with being alone. Could you bear to stay?'

'Of course.' Una smiled, feeling the weight falling from her shoulders. Her worries had been unnecessary, after all. And now there would be no need to accept Thór's kind offer. It would have been an uneasy cohabitation anyway, with the three of them living there.

'It'll be a comfort to know you're upstairs,' Salka said, and there was no mistaking her sincerity. Glancing around, she added: 'I see you've already started packing. I'm sorry. I can help you put everything back.'

'No problem. Honestly, it's not a problem.'

The question hung in the air: *Where were you intending to go?*

'You're welcome to help yourself to anything you like from the fridge downstairs,' Salka said, after a brief silence. 'I've got some wine too, in the sitting-room cupboard. You're welcome to take that, as I don't drink much myself.'

Only then did Una realize that all her empties were lined up on the kitchen floor. She blushed dark red, but, in an attempt at nonchalance, merely said: 'Thanks.'

XVIII

School wasn't due to start again until Twelfth Night, and Una had almost nothing to do in the meantime. All her wine was finished; a fact that chafed at her even more than the loneliness, though she couldn't bring herself to make inroads into Salka's supplies, despite the generous offer.

She would have dearly loved to talk to someone, but her mother was still abroad, so she couldn't ring her for a chat, and she hadn't been in touch with Sara for ages. She toyed with the idea of calling her but in the end decided against it, because it wasn't as if Sara had made any effort to contact her, even though she had Una's number. And despite all Sara's talk about coming to visit, she showed no signs of keeping her promise. That was a shame, as Una would have given anything to see a friendly face right now.

Una's time in Skálar had begun to feel like a prison sentence. She had let the day pass without going downstairs to see Salka, anxious not to intrude. She had also left Thór and Hjördís in peace, apart from ringing to let them know she wouldn't be requiring their guest room after all.

Una urgently needed to go to the Co-op to stock up on essentials. As well as basic food, she had a craving for Coke, something sugary, and a bottle of wine – just this once, as a treat. Above all, though, she wanted to pick up the New Year's Eve edition of *Morgunbladid* she'd ordered, in the hope of seeing a photo of the missing man.

Admittedly, Thór had been the voice of reason when he told her she was getting carried away. Of course it was nothing but an overactive imagination, and yet she couldn't stop thinking about the man and the brief news item on the radio. She *had* to be sure.

Since the papers generally arrived in the afternoon, she deliberately put off going to the shop until then. She would buy something for supper (and a bottle), then casually enquire after the paper Gudrún had promised to put aside for her.

The opening times at the shop were always a little irregular, but Una took a chance that Gudrún would be there at three, and she was right. What's more, Una managed to catch her alone, which meant she could buy the wine unobserved by any of the neighbours, though she had no reason to suppose that Gudrún was discreet about her fondness for the bottle.

'Oh, and I was going to pick up the paper too,' Una said finally, once she had filled a bag with groceries.

'The paper?'

'Yes, *Morgunbladid*, the New Year's Eve edition. You were going to keep a copy back for me.'

'Oh, yes, quite right, dear, I remember.' Gudrún smiled. There was a pause, then she said: 'The papers haven't arrived, unfortunately. It happens from time to time. After all, we are a bit out of the way.'

Una sighed. She'd been looking forward to settling the matter once and for all, so she could turn her mind to other, more practical, matters. 'Was it just *Morgunbladid* that failed to turn up or was it all of them?'

'None of the papers came today, dear. They're always sent in one batch; if one paper's missing, they all are. It can't be helped. Would you like tomorrow's paper? Assuming they deliver . . .'

'Er, yes, I suppose so.'

'It's always good to keep up with what's happening in the world and not let yourself get too isolated. I gather Salka doesn't even have a TV in the house. Gunni and I have had a television for several years, ever since we decided to get ourselves a video machine. It makes such a difference. We borrow tapes from the rental place in Thórshöfn; we have a special arrangement with them, of course. They can't expect us to bring the tapes back the next day, like everyone else. You should talk Salka into getting a TV and video, then you wouldn't be bored.'

Una nodded. She was actually getting used to doing without a television, but she reflected that watching a good film might take the edge off her loneliness.

'Gunni and I are glued to *Falcon Crest* these days. It's very good, I must say.'

'I haven't seen it.'

'Well, naturally, you'd be very welcome to borrow our

tapes once we've finished with them. Like I say, we have plenty of leeway about when we take them back.' It was kind of Gudrún to offer, though her generosity fell short of inviting Una round to watch.

'Thanks,' Una said, picking up her bag of groceries, ready to leave.

'How is Salka, by the way?' Gudrún asked with studied casualness as Una was on her way out of the door. Clearly she had no intention of letting such a good opportunity for gossip slip through her hands.

'She's doing OK, I think, in the circumstances,' Una replied, reluctant to give Gudrún too much grist for the rumour mill.

'It must be terribly hard for her. I can't believe she's come back,' Gudrún said, more to herself than Una. 'I wasn't expecting it. Not with all the memories here in the village, and especially in that house.'

'We haven't seen much of each other. She's downstairs and I'm up in my flat. We keep ourselves to ourselves most of the time.'

'Quite, yes. So she doesn't talk to you much, then?'

Worried that she'd already said more than she should, Una hastily changed the subject. 'Maybe you could help me, since you know so much about the history of this place. The ghost that's supposed to haunt Salka's house . . . ?'

Gudrún visibly brightened. 'Oh, you've heard the stories, have you?'

'You could say I've experienced it first hand.'

'Well I never! Don't say you've actually seen her?'

'Thrá, you mean?'

'Yes, Thrá.'

'I think so.'

'Well. Of course, I've heard plenty of stories. No one used to want to sleep up there in the old days, I can tell you. She haunted people in their dreams. They would wake up in the middle of the night, scared out of their wits, and pretty much run straight out of the house. That's why I found it a bit rich when Salka stuck you up there, and charged rent!' Gudrún laughed.

'Do you know what happened to her?'

'To Thrá?' An odd expression appeared on Gudrún's face.

'Yes.'

Gudrún didn't answer at once, then eventually said: 'I'm not old enough to remember.'

Una immediately got the impression that she was lying – and not for the first time. 'Strange about the papers,' she remarked.

'Sorry?'

'Strange they didn't arrive.'

'You get used to it, dear. It's not like living in the city. You just have to relax and go with the flow. Accept things as they are, adjust to the rhythm of nature and not chase every passing fad.'

Una nodded sceptically.

'How are you finding it here, Una?' Gudrún asked. 'Only a few more months and you'll be able to go home.'

Again, this made it sound like a prison sentence.

'I'm not so sure about that,' Una said, watching the other woman's reaction.

'Oh?' Gudrún raised her eyebrows.

'I mean, I'm not so sure I'll go home. I may stay on for another winter.'

'Has there been any discussion of that?' Gudrún's gaze was sharp.

'We'll see. Anyway, thanks for the offer of the videos. Maybe I'll borrow them some time when I've managed to sort out a TV.'

'Of course, dear. See you tomorrow.'

'Oh? Tomorrow?'

'Yes, there'll be a new *Morgunbladid* waiting for you. Let's just hope that one doesn't go astray as well.' Gudrún smiled.

XIX

'A village like this, Una; a village like this has a soul.' Salka was sitting at the dining table, sipping her evening coffee. She'd found some biscuits in the freezer and brought them out with the coffee.

She was a shadow of her former self, utterly unlike the Salka Una had first met. Her gaze was empty, her voice quieter, her face leached of all colour and her manner distracted.

'You have to adjust to the village, learn to fit in with it.' Salka had completely stopped smiling these days. 'People stick together here. You'll learn. We've all got family links to this place.' After a beat, she added: 'Except you, of course.'

Una didn't know what to say to her any more, didn't know if it was appropriate to mention Edda at all. It had been made clear that the distant past was off limits too, especially anything to do with Thrá.

'What, every single person?' Una queried, knowing that Salka's claim was an exaggeration.

'Guffi and Gunnar grew up here, of course. And Kolbeinn's late father was a friend of theirs. This house belonged to my grandparents, as you know. And, er . . . Hjördís inherited the farm from her grandparents. That's why I moved here, Una, to make a future home for me and Edda, among people who would accept me. It's so important to belong to a community, and that's what we've got here.'

'I think everyone would be happiest if I left,' Una remarked, taking herself by surprise. She hadn't intended to speak so bluntly. 'I mean . . .'

'I know what you mean, Una. And I think you're right, up to a point. It's not necessarily unkindly meant, but you have to learn about the place, the people. Try to be understanding.'

'I've always . . .' Una began, but Salka interrupted.

'Is the coffee OK? Not too strong?'

'What? Oh, no, it's fine.'

'Do you sense her? At night?' Salka asked abruptly. 'Do you see her?'

Against her will, Una recalled the image of Thrá and felt her flesh prickling. She was filled with trepidation at the thought of having to sleep in the attic. The question struck her as odd too, as if Salka had forgotten their previous conversation. She hesitated, then said: 'Well, yes, I think so, like I told you before, but of course . . .'

'I meant Edda,' Salka cut in sharply.

'Edda? I . . . no . . .' Una rose slowly to her feet, not wanting to know where this was going. 'Anyway, thanks so much for the coffee and biscuits. They were both delicious.'

'I had the idea I might be able to make contact with Edda here, in this house. There's something about this house . . .' Salka put down her cup and rose to her feet as well. 'I think I'll go to bed. Thanks for the chat, Una. I'll see you in the morning.'

'Yes, good night,' Una replied.

She went into the hall and lingered there until Salka had gone into her bedroom and finally closed her door, then seized the chance to make a phone call to Reykjavík.

'Hello.'

'Sara?' It was more than a month since the friends had last spoken.

'Yes, hi, is that Una?'

'Yes.'

'Do you know how late it is? Aren't you in the same time zone up there in Skálar?'

Only then did it occur to Una that she had no idea what time it was. The unchanging darkness outside made it hard to keep track.

'It's good to hear from you, anyway, Una. It's been ages,' Sara went on warmly. 'How was your Christmas?'

'Oh, fine,' Una said, her voice sounding unconvincing to her own ears.

'It's strange having you so far away,' Sara went on. 'I miss you. It was always so nice being able to pop round to yours for coffee.' It was her turn to sound unconvincing. 'How's it going with your tenants?'

'What? Oh, OK, you know,' Una said, though in reality she hadn't a clue. Her mother took care of that side of things. 'Listen, Sara,' she added. 'I wanted to check something. Have you by any chance got any back issues of *Morgunbladid*?'

'*Morgunbladid*?' Sara laughed. 'I didn't think you read it. I thought it was against your principles to read a conservative paper.'

In fact, the reason Una didn't have a subscription to *Morgunbladid*, or to any other newspaper, was lack of money, but there was no point going into all that again.

'Oh, the papers don't always reach us here and I just needed some information.'

'Sure, of course, no problem.'

'That man who went missing just before New Year, Patrekur something . . . Do you remember the story?'

'Yes, you couldn't miss it.'

'I need a picture of him.'

'What? You need a picture of him? What on earth for?'

'It's a long story.' Una added, rather pointedly: 'I'll tell you when you come and visit.'

'OK, I'll go and check. It was probably on the back page over New Year. I seem to remember that. Hang on a sec.'

There was silence at the other end. Una waited patiently. *What on earth for?* Sara had asked, and not without reason. Una wondered if she was letting herself get carried away. Could she have felt the need to invent some drama in an attempt to escape the dreary reality that confronted her up here in Skálar?

After a short while, she heard rustling at the other end of the line. 'Hi, found it.'

'Is there a photo of him?'

'Yes. He's got very short hair and looks quite muscular, and unsmiling – it's not a very good picture. He appears to be round about our age.'

That wasn't much help. Una needed to see the photo with her own eyes, if only to convince herself that everything was fine and the man's disappearance had nothing to do with the village.

'Could you send me the paper, Sara?' she asked after a moment.

There was a short delay, then Sara said: 'Sure, of course. I'll put it in the post to you tomorrow.'

'Thanks so much.'

'I don't understand why you want it, but of course I'll do it.'

'Aren't you going to come and visit me soon?'

'Yes, of course. But I'd need to check that my husband's happy to look after Rebekka by himself. And won't the roads be a bit dodgy at this time of year? Wouldn't it be better in the spring?'

'Yes,' Una replied tonelessly, 'it would be better in the spring.' Struck by a thought, she added: 'Actually, maybe it would be enough if you just cut out the news story with the photo. That's all I need. There's no need to send the whole paper.' It had crossed her mind that a bulky package containing a newspaper might attract attention, whereas a small envelope was more likely to pass under the radar. She tried to dismiss these suspicions as unworthy.

Could she be losing her mind?

Of course there was nothing to fear in this little community.

XX

It took Sara's letter four days to arrive. Una had tried to put it out of her mind in the meantime and get back into a routine, and a miserably cold Tuesday had heralded the first day of the new school term. Teaching had proved an uphill struggle. Kolbrún had never been a very responsive pupil; it was Edda who had generally kept up a conversation with Una during lessons, and now not only did her absence leave a gaping hole but Kolbrún seemed even less receptive than before.

The letter seemed to have passed unnoticed, though Una didn't receive post every day. She took it up to the attic, sat down at the kitchen table and opened it there, carefully, full of suspense, though really she was expecting the man in the picture to be someone she'd never seen before.

The cutting from *Morgunbladid* was folded together and Una waited a moment before opening it out.

And there he was, the man who had knocked on their door the day before Edda died . . .

Her heart lurched. There was no question at all, despite the poor quality of the photo. The man was still unaccounted for; she'd heard as much on last night's news. The case wasn't attracting much attention, though, and as far as she knew there had been no organized search for him.

Una stood up, leaving the cutting on the table. She had to decide on her next step. The man had asked after Hjördís, claiming to know her, and had apparently turned up at the farm. The question was, where had he gone after that? Hjördís and Thór should at least be able to give the police an important lead. Of course, it was absurd to think that they could have had anything to do with his disappearance. Una smiled at the thought. Completely absurd . . . She didn't want to get them into any sort of trouble, but she had to talk to the police. Sitting on this information was out of the question.

She didn't hurry downstairs to the phone, however. Not quite yet. The man had been missing for a couple of weeks at least; a few more minutes wouldn't make any difference. She needed to think. But she was sure she was doing the right thing. Confident in her own mind.

A knock at the door made her jump.

Salka appeared in the gap. Una was disconcerted by the way Salka had opened the door without waiting for an answer. Some instinct made Una slide the cutting under an old newspaper that was lying on the kitchen table. She couldn't explain her reaction to herself, except that at this moment she didn't trust anybody. Of course, it was a crazy way to think. She had to learn to resist such delusions if she was to survive the winter in the village.

Perhaps she should show Salka the picture so she could confirm that it was the same man and get her support for the decision to ring the police. After all, visits from the police weren't everyday events in Skálar and Una had a hunch that interference by the city girl would not be taken kindly.

'Sorry, am I bothering you?' Salka came right into the flat. She was unsmiling and her tone was flat but polite.

'No, that's OK,' Una replied.

'I was just wondering what you wanted to eat, if you'd like me to cook? It's hardly worth my while making something just for myself.'

'Yes . . . that would be great. I hadn't made any particular plans. Did you have something in mind?'

'Yes, I've got a haddock fillet in the fridge that should be enough for both of us.'

'Great, I'll see you downstairs in a bit, then.'

XXI

Supper was fine, if a little under-seasoned for Una's taste. Salka had cooked better fish that winter, but Una was grateful for the company, even if her landlady didn't have much to say.

'By the way, Salka . . .' she ventured, breaking a long silence. 'You remember the man who came here before Christmas – the one who knocked on our door, looking for Hjördís . . . ?' The secret was weighing heavily on her and, if she could trust anyone in the village, it was Salka.

Salka nodded. 'What about him?' she asked irritably. That didn't necessarily mean anything, though, as she seemed to be on edge most of the time these days.

'Well, the thing is, the man they reported missing in Reykjavík at New Year . . .' Una trailed off, waiting for a reaction.

'Reported missing? What?'

'Didn't you hear about it?'

'No, I haven't listened to the news much since . . . since . . .'

'No, of course not.'

'What's he got to do with the man who came here?' Salka asked.

'It was the same man,' Una stated flatly.

'What? The same man?'

'Yes, his name's Patrekur Kristjánsson. He hasn't been seen for more than two weeks.'

'You must be mistaken, Una. What could he possibly have been doing out here? Nobody comes here except . . .' Salka broke off in mid-sentence and Una had the feeling she had been about to say something hurtful.

'No, I'm telling you, it was him,' Una insisted. 'The moment I heard the description on the news I thought of him, I don't know why; he'd just been on my mind for some reason.' She left unsaid what she had been thinking; that maybe – just maybe – there had been some connection between the man's unexpected visit and Edda's sudden death.

'You can't claim that just from hearing a description.'

'I'm not. I've seen a photo of him. In the paper. In fact, I've got it upstairs.'

Salka looked disbelieving. 'Can I see it?'

Una nodded and, getting up from the table, ran upstairs to her kitchen and came straight back down.

'Did you cut it out of the paper?' Salka asked inconsequentially when she saw the photo.

'What? No, not exactly. But it is him, isn't it?' Una held out the picture.

Salka studied it for what felt like a long time without

saying a word, her brow furrowed. 'He was looking for Hjördís,' she said slowly.

Una wasn't sure whether this was a question or whether Salka was merely thinking aloud. Eventually she repeated: 'It is the same man, isn't it?' Although she was already convinced in her own mind, it would be good to have it confirmed by another witness.

Salka nodded. 'Yes, yes, you're right,' she said at last. 'But I just don't understand . . . can't understand . . . How long is it since the news came out?'

'It was at New Year. He's still missing, as far as I know.'

After another lengthy interval, Salka said: 'What a strange coincidence that he should have come here. Obviously, his disappearance can't have anything to do with us, though. It can't be linked to Skálar – or to Hjördís.'

'Of course not. But, you know, the information could help the police to pick up his trail.'

'We're not dragging the police out here,' Salka retorted, with unaccustomed firmness. 'It wouldn't serve any purpose.'

'Well, they might not need to come all the way out here, but I was just going to ring and let them know. Perhaps it's the missing piece they need –'

'I hope you're not implying that someone in the village was involved in his disappearance,' Salka interrupted, her voice harsh. 'That would be a slap in the face after the welcome we've given you. You've been treated kindly here.'

That was debatable. 'No, Salka, please don't get me

wrong, I'm not implying anything of the sort. I just wanted to help.'

Neither of them spoke for a while. Salka took a sip of the wine she had for once served with supper. Una had been grateful not to have to deplete her own limited supply. Perhaps the alcohol was to blame for Salka's unusual reaction – the alcohol and of course the trauma she had suffered. She was a changed person these days and, naturally, Una understood that.

'Help,' Salka said at last, slowly, the word sounding more like a question than a statement. 'Why would you want to help?'

Una didn't immediately answer.

Salka persisted: 'Are you from the police?'

The question left Una momentarily speechless.

'Do you know this man? This . . . what was his name again? Patrekur?'

Una shook her head. 'No, of course not.'

'Then I don't understand what would possess you to think of such a thing. To set the police on us, I mean.'

'But I'm not setting . . .' Una didn't bother to finish. There was no point arguing with Salka in this mood. It must be the wine. The bottle was empty and, although Una had drunk quite a bit, she suspected that Salka had put away the lion's share.

'This is a peaceful place, Una,' Salka said, composing herself with an effort. 'We're used to solving our own problems. That's the way it's always been. The villagers stick together and look out for one another. I know that, though I haven't lived here very long. It's in our blood.'

'Sorry, Salka, but I'm afraid I don't understand what you're talking about. I can't see how it would harm anyone to let the police know that we've seen a man who's been reported missing.'

Unless someone in the village is responsible for his disappearance, Una thought to herself, but didn't dare say it aloud. Instead, she said: 'It's, well, it's my duty as a good citizen . . .'

Salka laughed mockingly. 'Your duty as a good citizen? Next you'll be telling me we have to follow some unwritten code of behaviour? That everything in life has to be fair and just?' Her voice grew shrill: 'Was it fair that Edda had to . . . had to . . . die like that? Well, was it?'

'Salka, this has nothing to do with Edda. But I do see what you mean. This incident – this man's disappearance – doesn't necessarily have anything to do with us. I promise I'll think about it before I take any action.'

Salka nodded, looking appeased. 'Good. I'm glad to hear that. And I'm sorry . . .'

'No need to apologize,' Una said, but the conversation had only made her more determined to contact the police.

XXII

She got her chance to make the call the following evening.

It had been an unusually peaceful night, her dreams untroubled by visitations from Thrá, and she found herself hoping once again that the haunting had all been in her mind, a symptom of the stress she had been under.

Una had gone to Kolbeinn and Inga's house to give Kolbrún her lessons in the morning, but hadn't liked to ask to use their phone, since she didn't want to owe them any favours. Inga made no effort to hide her dislike for Una, whereas Kolbeinn went out of his way to be excessively charming, as if their awkward encounter earlier that winter had never taken place. Maybe hitting on other women was something he took for granted as his right.

When Una got back from teaching, Salka was at home; she didn't seem to have set foot outside all day, and Una hadn't dared to use the phone for fear that Salka would catch her in the act. Still, she comforted herself, at least there was only the one phone in the house, so there was no way of listening in on calls from an extension. Or rather, it was the only phone in the house *as far as Una was aware* . . .

Then, just after seven o'clock, Salka unexpectedly went out. She didn't call upstairs to say goodbye, but Una, hearing the front door closing, peered out of the attic window and saw Salka's figure receding into the gloom.

She would have to act fast; her landlady might only be going for a short walk.

Una raced downstairs, almost tripping in her haste, and thought what a ridiculous ending to the story it would be if she broke her neck running down a staircase. Maybe Salka was right and the whole thing really was none of their business.

Yet Una had got it into her head that she had to make the call, despite momentary qualms when she wondered if the solitude was affecting her judgement. When it came down to it, though, she knew it was the right thing to do. Sometimes you just had to have the courage of your convictions. Her father had taught her that. He always used to impress two things upon her: one was the importance of reading medicine, of studying 'the noble science', as he used to call it. She had failed him in that. The other was the need above all else to be a good person. Altruism had to take precedence over any self-interest. It was a lesson she had never forgotten. Perhaps that was why she was now standing by the telephone, the dog-eared phone book in her hands, leafing through it with trembling fingers to find the number of Reykjavík CID.

It didn't take her long to locate and learn the short,

memorable number before replacing the phone book. But next moment she heard the dining-room door slam. Una almost jumped out of her skin. Was Salka at home after all?

Damn it, Una had seen her go; she'd watched her from the window. Could she have been hallucinating?

Una looked round, then went into the sitting room. The door to the dining room was indeed closed. Could Salka be in there? There was no perceptible draught and, as far as Una was aware, none of the windows were open downstairs. She wanted to double-check that there was no one in the dining room but for some reason her legs wouldn't obey her and she just stood there, rooted to the spot.

Then she heard the faint tinkling of the piano.

It was so quiet that she couldn't be absolutely sure. Nor did she want to be sure.

Instead of going in to check, she retreated to the front door, opened it and went out on to the step, where she heaved a deep breath and tried to control her shaking knees.

She was safe out here, at least for now.

She strained her ears but couldn't hear the faint notes of the piano.

Why the hell didn't I move back to Reykjavík weeks ago? Una asked herself.

She waited a minute or two longer, staring out into the murk. There was a light on in Guffi's house, but apart from that the village was wrapped in gloom, darker even than usual.

Finally, she plucked up the courage to go back inside out of the cold, closed the front door behind her and walked with firm steps towards the dining room. She listened warily, then, hearing no noise from within, opened the door with infinite care. There was no one in the room, but the lid of the piano was open.

She felt her stomach constrict.

Closing the door behind her, she went back to the phone in the hall and dialled the number with frantic haste.

'Reykjavík CID, good evening.' Judging by his voice, the officer who answered was getting on in years.

'Good evening.' Having introduced herself, Una continued: 'I'm sorry to bother you, but I'm ringing in connection with a news story I read about a missing person.'

'A missing person, you say?' the policeman repeated with slow deliberation, apparently reserving judgement.

'The police reported him missing on New Year's Eve. His name's Patrekur Kristjánsson.'

'Ah, Patrekur. Yes, that's right, we're still looking for him. Have you seen him, Una?' His manner was still calm and reassuring, almost paternal.

'Yes, at least I think so.'

'You think so, I see. When was this?'

'Just before Christmas.' Una thought back. 'Yes, it was on 21 December.'

'And where did you see him?'

'Oh, sorry, I should have mentioned that before. I live in Skálar on Langanes.'

'On Langanes, you say?'

'Yes, he knocked on our door that evening.'

'Are you sure it was the same man?'

'Absolutely positive. I saw his photo in the paper.'

'I see.' The policeman was silent for a moment, then asked: 'Why are you only ringing us now? If I remember right, it's more than a week since we published a picture of him.'

'Yes, er . . . yes, that's right,' Una stammered, 'but the papers take a while to reach us out here.'

'I see.'

'Of course, I don't know if it has anything to do with his disappearance . . .'

'No, of course not. That remains to be seen. Look, there aren't many people in at this time of the evening, but I'll have a word with my colleague who's in charge of the investigation and he might come and pay you a visit. Would you be so good as to give me your address in Skálar?'

Una did so.

'Then we'll leave it at that for now,' said the policeman, and ended the call.

Una had been hoping for some kind of praise or at least thanks, some confirmation from the police that she had done the right thing. Sometimes, it seemed, selfless acts reaped nothing but ingratitude.

XXIII

Una was almost at the top of the attic stairs when she remembered Thrá. Turning round, she decided to take advantage of Salka's absence to make one more quick phone call.

This time she knew the number off by heart.

'Hello.'

'Hi, Sara. It's Una.'

'Una, well I never! This is becoming almost a daily occurrence. Did you get my letter?'

'Yes, I did. I just wanted to thank you. I'm incredibly grateful.'

'Did you find the man? The missing man?' Sara's tone was teasing. She never took anything seriously. It was one of her most attractive qualities and also one of her most infuriating faults.

'We'll see,' Una replied. 'Actually, I was wondering if I could persuade you to do me another favour.'

'Sure,' Sara replied after a brief hesitation. 'Within reason, of course.'

Una laughed. 'Of course. But it's slightly more complicated than the last one, so just say if it's too much trouble. I think it might be quite important, though.'

'OK, out with it.'

'It's an old incident I'm looking into – an incident that happened in Skálar.'

'What on earth are you up to over there, Una? I thought you were supposed to be teaching those two girls?'

Una was momentarily silent. Presumably news of Edda's death hadn't reached Reykjavík, or else Sara hadn't made the connection. 'I teach during the day,' she said eventually. 'But I have to keep myself amused somehow in the evenings.'

'OK, I'll look into it for you. How long ago did it happen?'

'In 1927.'

'In 1927? Are you joking?'

'No. It's connected to the house I'm living in and the woman I'm staying with. I really need to know more about it.'

'What happened?'

'A girl died – a little girl. Her name was Thrá.'

'How did she die?'

'I don't know, but I have the feeling it, er . . . that there might have been something suspicious about it.'

'And where exactly am I supposed to find that information, Una?'

'Well, I thought, you know, from old newspapers or something. If it ever made it into the news.'

'Did they even have newspapers in 1927?'

'Oh, come on, Sara! Of course they did. Would you be able to check it for me?'

Sara sighed. 'All right, I suppose so, but I'm not promising anything. I might be able to find it in the *Our Century* series. Mum and Dad have got all the volumes. I'll start there. Then I'll see if I can go down to the National Library and plough through the newspaper archives. I know we're friends, Una, but you have to draw the line somewhere.' This was said in a humorous tone, and Una smiled. Sara always managed to cheer her up.

'Thanks so much, Sara,' Una said, genuinely grateful. 'Give me a call as soon as you find anything.' She said goodbye.

Conscious of how few people she had on her side right now, Una felt all the more grateful for her friendship with Sara, as far as it went. Perhaps the separation had been good for their relationship, by giving them a chance to miss each other a bit.

Una found herself wondering yet again if she would be better off back in Reykjavík; whether her decision to leave had been a mistake. After all, she reasoned, if there was a risk of her becoming suicidal, as she had sometimes feared, there would be little to prevent her here in Skálar, where no one cared about her or kept an eye on her or bothered to come round and visit. Yet in spite of this she felt that the adversity had, if anything, made her stronger and more determined. And of course she couldn't be sure of finding work in Reykjavík at this time of year. She had taken a temporary break from her old job and without an income she wouldn't be able to survive. It wasn't as if she or her mother had any savings to live off. While they weren't exactly poor, they both lived pretty much from wage slip to wage slip, and couldn't afford any leeway. Here in Skálar, on the other hand, Una had finally been able to put a little aside from every pay cheque. Life was cheaper here than in the city, because there was virtually nothing to spend her money on and she got her accommodation for free.

She genuinely enjoyed teaching too, though she couldn't help wondering sometimes what it would have been like if she'd finished her medical studies and become a practising doctor, rather than an academic like her father. She certainly wouldn't have been short of money.

Her thoughts returned to the present. There was still no sign of Salka. Before Una went back up to the attic, she took a careful look around to make sure there was nothing to betray the fact that she had used the phone. She felt, absurdly, like a criminal hiding her tracks.

Once upstairs she lay down on the sofa. Her thoughts returned to Hjördís. Patrekur had been looking for her and had apparently found her, from what she herself had told Una when they met in church. Una hadn't mentioned this to the police; that could wait until an officer came out to the village. Her conscience was a little uneasy at the thought that she might be getting Hjördís into trouble, and even more so at the idea of causing any difficulties for Thór.

Hjördís was still a bit of an unknown quantity, though Una had got the feeling, the few times they had met, that there was something the other woman wasn't telling her.

She had been notably cool when Una went over there for dinner on New Year's Eve. It was as if she had a grudge against Una, though Una couldn't think what she had done to deserve it. The feeling was unpleasant; she wasn't used to being the object of someone's resentment. All she could think was that Hjördís's hostility must relate somehow to Thór.

In spite of that, or perhaps because of it, Una decided to go and see Hjördís to warn her that she'd spoken to the police and give her a chance to prepare herself. It was only fair, wasn't it?

Perhaps she was primarily motivated by a desire to protect Thór, but there was also a chance that on some level she genuinely wanted to improve her relationship with Hjördís. She simply couldn't tell. Glancing at her watch, she saw that it wasn't that late. Best get it over with now.

Una got up from the sofa, resisting the temptation to knock back a glass of wine first for some Dutch courage. She pulled on her boots and went outside into the darkness, leaving discreetly by the back door, though she was quite sure that Salka wasn't home yet. After going a few steps, she noticed that Salka's car was parked in its usual place, so she couldn't have gone far.

Una headed up the now familiar track to the farm. She took her time, mentally rehearsing her conversation with Hjördís as she walked, keen to explain her motives as clearly and concisely as possible.

And yet with every step her confidence dwindled and she had to keep reminding herself that if no one had anything to hide, there could be no harm done. No amount of insistence that the villagers preferred to solve their own problems could hold much weight in these circumstances. It would be impossible to follow this absurd rule in every situation, and in any case it didn't apply to her, as an outsider who had no interests to protect beyond her wish to do the right thing.

When she reached the front door of the farm, she paused a moment, going over what she intended to say one more time. Then she knocked and waited, but no one came to the door. She knocked again, louder, but there was still no response. Though the outside light was on, the windows were dark.

Stumped, she turned and walked over to the guest-house, thinking they might both be there – or Thór might, at any rate. But the lights were off, the curtains were drawn and there was no sign of life. She knocked anyway, diffidently. Thór had never invited her inside – or had any particular reason to do so – but there was something about the guesthouse that made her uneasy. Again, there was no response.

Where had they all gone? First Salka, now Hjördís and Thór? It occurred to Una that they might be together somewhere and she wondered what on earth was going on.

Her journey wasted, she set off back down the hill to the village. The place was eerily quiet. Entering among the dim shapes of the houses, she had the odd sensation that she was alone, that everyone else had left, deliberately abandoning her; as if she was marooned there and would never be rescued.

Then, her stomach tightening with fear, she saw figures materializing out of the night, coming from the direction of Guffi's house. As they drew nearer, she realized it was Hjördís and Thór, and behind them she made out Salka. Had they all been visiting Guffi?

Una was astonished. She couldn't decide whether to go over or to wait and see. In the end, she chose caution.

From where she was standing in the shadows, she noticed that they hadn't been the only ones visiting Guffi, because a short way behind Salka came Inga and Kolbeinn, and finally Gudrún and Gunnar. Apparently, the entire village had congregated at his house, yet no one had thought to tell her.

When they were close enough to see her in the faint gleam of Guffi's outside light, Thór bowed his head, but Hjördís looked straight at her, defiantly, as if she had nothing to hide or be ashamed of.

'Una, nice to see you,' she said, stopping right in front of her. 'Were you looking for us or just going for a walk?' Thór halted too but made no move to join in the conversation.

Una vacillated. This probably wasn't the time or place to discuss what she had been intending to say to them. Besides, she found Hjördís's manner so grating that it removed any desire she'd had to warn her. It would serve her right to receive a surprise visit from the police.

'Or was it Thór you were after?' Hjördís added, the sarcasm plain in her voice. 'I can make myself scarce if you two need to talk.'

'I wasn't looking for anyone,' Una retorted, sarcastic in

return. 'I see you've all been enjoying yourselves at Guffi's. He must have forgotten to invite me.'

Hjördís smiled. 'Guffi never forgets anything.'

'As it happens, I was on my way round to see him anyway,' Una announced, finally managing to disconcert the other woman.

Hjördís didn't answer straight away, just stared at Una, then turned to Thór, before eventually remarking: 'Well, I'm sure he'll give you a warm welcome.' She stalked off, with Thór following a few paces behind, not even casting a glance in Una's direction.

So much for his support. Yet again, Una found herself baffled by their relationship. One minute he was sitting hugging her on the sofa, listening to her most intimate secrets, the next he was totally ignoring her.

She stood there for a moment, at a loss. Having boasted that she was going round to see Guffi, she realized she had no choice, though it was the last thing she wanted to do. She dithered a while, not daring to look round. The villagers had all returned to their houses and the night seemed oppressively quiet again, but she had a horrible feeling that they were all peering out at her from their darkened windows.

The first steps she took towards the big house felt impossibly hard, but she couldn't back down now, couldn't let the others see that she'd been bluffing, that she was too much of a coward to confront the man who seemed to have the entire village in his grip.

XXIV

Una stood outside Guffi's imposing house, summoning up her courage, then rang the bell. She had been expecting to be kept waiting, but the door opened almost instantaneously, as if he had been waiting for her.

'Una, what an unexpected pleasure,' he said, meeting her eyes with an icy stare. 'Won't you come in? It's a long time since I've seen you.'

'Thank you. Yes, I've been busy.'

'Is that so? My wife's resting upstairs, as usual, so why don't you come down to my office?'

Una baulked at this, reluctant to re-live the claustrophobic fear she had experienced before in that cramped, windowless space. Then she reminded herself that this time she'd come here on her own initiative to confront him and it was vital not to let him wrongfoot her. Naturally, he had invited her downstairs since that was where he felt in control. And precisely because of this, because she could see through him, she nodded and said: 'Yes, sure. Let's talk there.'

He led her down the stairs and she took a seat in the office chair, the same as before, to show that she wasn't remotely intimidated by him. After all, why should she be afraid of this man? Other people in the village might owe their livelihoods to him, but she didn't. She wasn't intending to live in Skálar long term and, anyway, she had a signed teaching contract. He couldn't just sack her on a whim.

No, she told herself firmly, she wasn't frightened of him.

She waited for him to take the armchair, as he had last time, but, instead of sitting down he shut the door and positioned his imposing bulk in front of it. Despite her resolve not to be intimidated, Una felt unnerved. It was as if he had adopted the role of jailer.

Her heart began to pound and she drew a deep breath, trying not to let it show. She reminded herself that she had told Hjördís and Thór she was coming to see Guffi. It was just as well that someone knew . . . Perhaps she *was* a little afraid. But if anything happened, Hjördís and Thór would side with her, they'd fetch help . . . wouldn't they? Surely she could rely on them? Assailed by a sudden doubt, she felt her discomfort intensifying.

'Well, Una,' Guffi said after a weighty pause. 'I'm not convinced you understand the community you've moved into.'

It wasn't a question, but she felt compelled to answer anyway.

'Actually, I think I do.' Her voice emerged sounding shriller than she would have liked.

'I'm not so sure about that, Una no matter how often we've tried to explain to you how things work, *for your own good* . . .' He stressed the last words and she shivered at the implied threat.

The situation felt oddly nightmarish: the airless little basement room, the dim illumination of the single wall light and the greenish glow of the desk lamp that reminded her disturbingly of the lamp in her father's study; her exit blocked by this vile man in his dark-yellow jumper and worn jeans, with his rough hair and that nasty smirk on his face.

Briefly closing her eyes, she summoned up the image of her father. She remembered him so well, sitting at his desk, the complete opposite of Guffi: neat, polite, always well turned out, never raising his voice. If anything, he had been a little too placid sometimes, viewing the world with a dispassion that bordered on indifference. And she had loved him so dearly that not a day went by even now when she didn't think of him. In fact, she'd always been closer to him than to her mother, and losing him without any explanation like that had been a shattering blow from which she had never recovered.

Guffi broke the silence again, speaking in a loud, bullying tone: 'I hear you're claiming you saw a man in the village, a man you think the police are looking for.'

'Yes . . . yes, I think I did,' she faltered, cursing herself for not being bolder, more defiant, but she was feeling too cowed. He had succeeded in creating a menacing atmosphere that had got her seriously alarmed, as he had no doubt intended.

'And you've talked of ringing the police,' Guffi persisted.

'Why . . . why were you all holding a meeting this evening?' Una asked, unable to suppress the tremor in her voice.

'I'm the one asking the questions here!' Guffi roared, and she flinched. 'It's none of your business why I choose to invite people to my house.' After a brief pause to let his words sink in, he asked: 'Why were you going to call the police?'

She wondered if she should tell him that she had already gone ahead and done so, but didn't dare. 'Because the police need to know,' she said instead. 'The man's gone missing.'

'People are always going missing,' Guffi said scornfully. 'It's got nothing to do with us. We don't need any outside interference here – either from you or from the police. Do you understand? I'm not sure you do, Una.'

'Sometimes you . . . you just don't have a choice,' she stammered in a small voice. She wanted to say: *You don't have any power over me, Guffi. What I decide to do is none of your business.*

'You always have a choice.' He fixed her gaze with his. 'For example, I've got two alternatives this evening: I can let you go home or I can walk out of this room, lock the door behind me and leave you to think things over.'

Una couldn't believe her ears. Her muscles tensed and she had an urge to leap to her feet and dodge round him, but she knew her limbs couldn't be trusted to obey. 'What are you saying?' she asked at last, the tremor in her voice unmistakeable now. 'Are you threatening . . . are you . . . ?'

Guffi didn't answer. His face impassive, he stood there

rock-like, blocking the door, demonstrating that she wouldn't have a chance of getting past him. And she knew she couldn't take him on, in spite of the age difference. He was powerfully built; his shoulders and chest were strapped with muscle under his old fisherman's jersey.

He couldn't be serious. No sane man would dream of coming out with something like that except as a joke. But he didn't appear to be joking as he glowered at her from under his heavy brows.

'I'm not implying anything, Una. I just want you to understand how serious this is. We don't like your prying; don't appreciate the way you're . . . sticking your nose into our affairs. I was dead against your coming here in the first place, but Salka got her way. That won't happen again, I can tell you. My poor wife wanted me to give you the benefit of the doubt. She said it would be good to have fresh blood in the village, and I listened to her. We decided to let you take care of the Christmas concert.' He paused, then added heavily: 'And look how that turned out.'

Una gasped at the injustice of this. 'That . . . that wasn't my fault. There's no way I'm responsible for what happened to Edda.'

'That's irrelevant,' he snapped. 'Your presence here has brought us nothing but trouble. And now you want to call the police about something you think you saw — about some wretched lowlife who's disappeared. Well, I'm telling you, we've always taken care of our own affairs here in Skálar.'

Una rose to her feet. 'I think that'll do,' she said, anger

helping her to get her voice under control. 'I'm tired. I'm going home now.'

'I decide when this conversation is finished,' he said flatly. 'Sit down, Una.'

Instead of meekly obeying, she stood her ground, though she had no intention of getting into a physical struggle with this man if she could possibly avoid it. Her mind was racing. She suspected that he might actually be prepared to lock her in here to convince her not to ring the police. He must be confident that he could get away with it: his word against hers. He wielded the power in the village; he had the locals on his side. With a sudden sick feeling in the pit of her stomach, she wondered if he could have done something like this before? Or gone further, even? Was there a specific reason why he didn't want the police brought in?

'I've already made the call,' she said in a low voice. She had the feeling that this might just save her.

'You've made the call?' He sounded shocked. 'What are you talking about?'

'To the police. An officer's coming here tomorrow, to ask around about Patrekur.'

'You're not serious?'

'I swear it – I rang earlier. I grabbed the chance while Salka was out. Visiting you.'

'What did you tell them?'

'Does it matter?'

'Of course it damn well matters.' Spinning round, he opened the door and stormed out.

Una hurried out of the room after him, then hesitated

a moment before following him upstairs, relieved that he didn't look round or speak to her.

When she reached the top, she saw that he was waiting in the hall, but there was nothing in his body language to suggest that he meant to prevent her from leaving this time.

'It was nice of you to visit, Una,' he said in his deep voice. 'You must drop by more often.'

She gave him a look. Then, without a word, she opened the front door and fled back to Salka's house, never once glancing over her shoulder. Although she knew there was no one behind her, she felt as if there were eyes watching her from every side.

Never had she felt so alone, so frightened or so utterly defenceless.

XXV

Lullaby, my little Thrá,
may you sweetly sleep.

The voice was pure, low and hypnotic. It seemed to come from all directions at once. Una could feel the notes spreading through her body as if icy water were flowing through her veins, and sensed the words filtering in, seeping through her dream into her unconscious.

Lullaby . . .

Then she saw her.

The girl was standing there, staring at Una, in the same white dress as always, her eyes empty, her face pale, a vision in black and white, her lips moving in time to the words, only ever the one verse, never more; then her eyes closed and she stood quite still, as if watching Una through her eyelids, as if waiting for something, and Una waited too, listening to the silence. The girl didn't move, just remained perfectly still, waiting, her eyes closed, her face expressionless.

Then without warning her lids flicked open to reveal bloodshot eyes, and suddenly everything was red, and Una flinched as if someone had shaken her and sat bolt upright in bed, wide awake, confused about where the nightmare ended and reality began, unable to understand anything any more . . .

She had a splitting headache. At first she couldn't remember why, then she realized the wine was to blame. Better to blame the wine than herself. She'd had to open a bottle when she came home from Guffi's, shaking like a leaf, in desperate need of something to calm her nerves. The wine had done its job. She had almost finished the bottle before, succumbing to drowsiness, she had crawled into bed.

It was still night, she could tell by the silence, and she needed a few more hours' sleep before tackling the coming day. Although the girl had vanished, her image lingered, unnervingly vivid, and her song went on echoing in Una's head. She wondered why she was still sleeping up here, still putting herself through this hell. Why hadn't she moved out? Was it because she sensed that, in spite of everything, the girl didn't mean her any harm? Even if that were true, there was no hope of getting back to sleep with her nerves jangling like this. Perhaps one little glass of wine would help take the edge off her fear.

She groped on her bedside table but couldn't feel the bottle. Then she remembered that she had left it in her kitchen.

Una got out of bed, her eyes adjusting to the darkness, and walked slowly through to the other room, relieved that the song had fallen silent.

She was brought up short by the sound of breaking glass just as she reached the doorway and, fumbling for the light switch on the wall, pressed it. The living room leapt into view and she was met by the sight of the bottle lying smashed on the floor, the wine forming a dark pool among the broken glass, surrounded by splash marks that looked disturbingly like blood. The bottle had been on the kitchen table, only an arm's length from where Una was standing. And there was nobody else in the flat, no one who could have knocked the bottle on to the floor, before quickly making their exit.

But the kitchen window was open and air was blowing in, so it was possible the wind had swept the bottle off the table. Had it been standing that close to the edge? Una couldn't remember. Perhaps she had created a draught when she opened the bedroom door . . . She racked her brain for a rational explanation. The bottle couldn't have fallen on the floor for no reason, immediately after she'd had another nightmare about the girl who had died. The coincidence was too great.

XXVI

Next morning Una cancelled her classes. She had surfaced just before eight, to find herself curled up on the little sofa in the living room. Her headache was still there, though it had faded to a dull throbbing, but she had neither the willpower nor the energy to get up. She had crawled downstairs and rung Kolbrún's house, hoping to goodness that Kolbeinn wouldn't answer. Her wish was granted, as it was Inga who picked up the phone. Una explained that she was ill and couldn't teach today and Inga's reaction was cool, as it was to most things. Una was sure rumours would now start doing the rounds about how she'd started missing work because of her drinking. Well, so be it.

The situation could hardly get any worse. None of the villagers trusted her and she didn't trust any of them, feeling that they had ganged up on her. She asked herself if there was any point in continuing to take part in this deception and pretend she could do her job under these conditions; if she could carry on teaching one pupil. Was it worth it? It wasn't as if she even liked the child . . .

Una had returned to the sofa after speaking to Inga and managed to get a bit more sleep. Now a grey dawn was breaking outside, but Una had no particular desire to get up. All she really wanted was to ring Thór, but she wasn't even sure she could trust him any more. It crossed her mind to call Sara for a chat. But that would mean not only dragging herself off the sofa but going downstairs and taking the risk of bumping into Salka. Really, she couldn't go on like this; the situation was becoming intolerable. And to top it all, she'd finished all her wine again.

XXVII

Una was woken by the noise of the knocker. Someone had brought it crashing down on the door. She must have dozed off again on the sofa. She leapt up in a panic. As the fog of sleep cleared, she realized it must be the policeman, as no one else visited them. It wouldn't do to miss him.

She pulled on her dressing gown over her nightie and raced downstairs into the hall, only to find that Salka had got there first and opened the door. The man standing on the step was probably in his thirties, thickset and broad-faced, with slightly thinning hair that didn't suit him, but his smile when he saw Una suggested that he was a nice guy.

'Are you Una, by any chance?' he asked, his voice deeper than she had expected.

'Yes, that's me.'

'Hello, pleased to meet you.' He held out his hand and she approached and shook it. 'My name's Hjalti and I'm with the Thórshöfn police. Sorry it's taken me a while to get here. I got a call from Reykjavík yesterday evening,

277

asking me to check on something out here. I was going to come first thing, but, you know how it is – time flies, and all that.' He smiled again. 'You always have to prioritize and, to be honest, you can't always drop everything and jump to it every time that lot in Reykjavík call you up. I'm sure you understand.'

Una didn't know whether she was supposed to answer this, but Salka saved her the trouble: 'Oh, yes, I do.'

'It's ages since I was last over this way,' Hjalti continued. 'Shameful, I know, but it's just so rare that I have any business in these parts. I don't ever remember any crimes happening in Skálar, at least not since I joined the police. It's a peaceful spot, isn't it?' He was still standing on the doorstep.

'Very peaceful,' Salka replied, 'and that's the way we like to keep it. Won't you come in?'

'Thought you'd never ask!' he joked, and stepped into the hall.

'Let's go into the sitting room. Would you like a coffee?'

'I never say no to an offer like that.'

'Una, could you help me with the cups?'

Una obeyed, and they left the visitor alone in the sitting room. Una fetched the cups from the cupboard and waited while Salka put on the coffee. She avoided catching Salka's eye and neither of them said a word.

Once the coffee was ready, they went back in with it.

'This is good and strong,' Hjalti commented. Apparently, he was in no hurry to get down to business. Perhaps he needed to revive himself after the drive.

'Salka, wasn't it your daughter who . . . ?'

Salka nodded, her face tightening.

'My heartfelt condolences. It was terrible, terrible news.'

'Thank you,' Salka said.

'Were you both born and brought up here?' he asked, after a few moments when nobody spoke.

'Not in my case.' This time it was Una who answered first. 'I'm from Reykjavík and got a job here over the winter. I'm a teacher. Salka has more claim to be from here.'

Salka nodded. 'This is my home, my house. And this is where I intend to stay.' She sounded defiant.

Hjalti sipped his coffee. 'Thanks very much for the hospitality. It's a lovely house too, very handsome.' He smiled. 'It's good to get out of Thórshöfn once in a while, even in the middle of winter. But maybe I should get down to business – this bad business of the man who's gone missing, Patrekur . . . Patrekur . . .'

Una chipped in: 'Patrekur Kristjánsson.'

'That's the one. I don't know much about the case, to tell the truth; I was just asked to deal with this. They didn't give me much background. To be honest, I can't understand what on earth could have brought him out here.'

'Nor can I,' Una said.

'Yes, it was you who rang, I gather. Did you say you'd met him?'

'We both met him,' Una said firmly.

'And you're sure it was the same man?'

'Yes, positive. I saw the photo of him in *Morgunbladid*. It's the same man, definitely –'

'It . . .' Salka interrupted, then hesitated. Una turned to look at her.

'It wasn't him,' Salka said, after a brief pause.

Una felt as if she'd been kicked in the teeth. She couldn't believe her ears: Salka couldn't have said that.

'I beg your pardon? Are you saying it wasn't him?' Hjalti asked, evidently almost as astonished as Una was. 'It wasn't Patrekur?'

'No. We were both here when he knocked on the door, late in the evening. He was an Icelander, looking for somewhere to stay. He didn't introduce himself.'

'What do you mean, Salka?' Una cried. 'You've got to be joking?'

Hjalti stood up and laid a hand on Una's shoulder. 'Let's just take it easy. We'll get to the bottom of this. Maybe you both experienced it differently. I expect you've seen the photo, Salka?'

She nodded.

'Did the men look alike?'

'You mean you believe her?' Una asked, trying with an effort to compose herself. Salka had betrayed her; that's all there was to it.

'We'll see. There must be a simple explanation for this,' Hjalti said in a steadying voice. 'Salka, did the two men look alike?'

Una glared at Salka. Was she going to keep on lying?

Salka didn't immediately answer. There was a charged atmosphere in the small sitting room.

'No, actually,' she said at last. 'Not in the slightest. They looked nothing like each other. I just can't understand why Una's so obsessed with the idea. I've tried to make her see sense and I thought she was coming round, but it seems she went and rang the police after all. I'm . . . I'm only sorry you've had to drive all the way out here.'

Una was stunned. She didn't know how to react.

'Are you absolutely sure about that?' Hjalti asked Salka.

'Yes. I spoke to him and got a good look at him. I don't know where Una got this idea. I can't imagine . . . though, actually . . . Of course, it's been difficult for her. Being so isolated here, you understand? It's a bit of a shock to the system after Reykjavík.'

Hjalti smiled. 'You can say that again. I lived in Reykjavík for several years. Thórshöfn and the city are worlds apart, so I can just imagine what a big change it would be to move here to Skálar.'

Una couldn't speak.

'It's all been a bit of a strain,' Salka went on, lowering her voice. 'She's also . . . well, she also claims the house is haunted.'

'It *is* haunted!' Una intervened desperately, realizing as she did so that this was doing nothing to help her cause.

'A beautiful house like this, haunted?' Hjalti asked, looking at Una with his eyebrows raised, and she could see from his expression that he didn't believe her. That he felt sorry for her.

She wondered whether to withdraw her claim, but that might make matters worse. 'Well . . . well, I don't know . . . A girl died in the house more than half a century ago and people say she haunts the place. I think I've sensed her up in the attic – in the flat up there. Which is where I live.'

Hjalti studied her, frowning slightly. 'And what form does it take? The haunting?'

'There's this lullaby she sometimes sings in the night, and I've heard the piano playing too . . . and I've seen her, or at least I think I have . . . And then last night, a wine bottle broke for no reason and . . .' None of this sounded very convincing when she said it out loud.

Salka glanced at Una, then back at Hjalti. She smiled indulgently as if to say: *Be gentle with her; she's not in a good way.*

'I've heard stories like that before,' Hjalti said. 'And a broken bottle, you say?'

He caught Salka's eye, then turned his gaze back to Una.

'What kind of wine?'

'What?'

'What kind of wine? White? Red? Something stronger?'

'Just red wine.'

'Of course, it can help to wile away the long winter nights when you're on your own. Drink a fair bit, do you, Una?'

'No, only the occasional glass,' she replied, suddenly feeling as if she was in the middle of an interrogation, suspected of committing a crime. 'Just every now and then.' She didn't dare lie outright, though she tried to make the situation sound better than it was.

'Sometimes have a drop to drink in the evenings, do you, Una? A nightcap before you go to bed? Before you see the girl?'

'Sometimes, yes, but definitely not always. I've seen

her when I haven't been drinking as well,' she insisted, trying to remember if this was true. But she couldn't be entirely sure. She hadn't connected the two things until now. After all, she'd often had a drink when living in Reykjavík and had never seen a ghost or heard creepy lullabies in the night. But could there be an element of truth in it? Had the alcohol made her see things that weren't there? She felt a sudden twinge of doubt.

'What about when the man knocked on the door, Una? Had you been drinking then?'

'I don't remember,' she said, which was true. She genuinely couldn't recall. Perhaps that was a sign that her drinking wasn't as under control as she liked to think.

'So, a man came round,' Hjalti said kindly. Una thought again what a nice person he seemed, despite the unpleasantness of the situation. 'And you both saw him. He was looking for somewhere to stay.'

'That's right,' said Una.

'I see. And neither of you knew him. Then a photo of Patrekur appeared in the papers and you believed you recognized him, Una. Is it possible that you just wanted it to be the same man, to liven things up a bit? Could that be what happened, Una?'

Una felt sure it wasn't possible, and yet a seed of doubt had been sown in her mind. Surely she had seen Patrekur? Why wasn't Salka backing her up? She wondered if she could really have started imagining things, unhinged by the isolation.

A silence had fallen. Hjalti waited patiently, apparently in no hurry for her answer. She had to say something, and preferably something that they could all agree on. Was it possible that she hadn't heard any lullaby? Could the man she met have been different from the one in the newspaper?

'Una, could that be what happened?' Hjalti repeated, without the faintest hint of accusation in his voice. As if they were just old friends having a chat.

'Er, yes, maybe,' she faltered, not knowing what to think any more.

'I see,' Hjalti said. 'That would shed some light on the matter – provide us with a natural explanation for the whole thing.' He smiled good-naturedly. 'The most obvious explanation is often the right one, in my experience. There's no reason to complicate things unnecessarily.'

Una nodded, then immediately regretted it, and regretted the fact she'd said yes to Hjalti's question. Of course she was sure. Of course she'd seen Patrekur. She couldn't have got so badly confused about something as important as that, could she? The doubts came crowding in again. She couldn't bring herself to contradict Salka outright, though she gave her an accusing look. Salka averted her gaze.

'Never mind, it was still a pleasure to meet you both,' Hjalti said. 'It breaks up the week, you know.'

'It was nice to meet you too,' Salka replied politely. 'Won't you have another cup?'

'I think I'd better leave it at that,' he said. 'Best get back in good time.' Then, as an afterthought, he added: 'It would certainly have made things interesting for us if the blessed man had turned up here before he vanished, but

I'm guessing the truth is simpler. He's quite an ugly customer, from what I've heard, who's been mixing in some bad company over the years.'

'Well,' Salka said, rising to her feet to signal that the visit was over.

Hjalti followed suit.

Only Una remained sitting there, left numb by the conversation. She didn't feel anything except an insidious craving for just one quick drink.

XXVIII

Una had gone straight upstairs after Hjalti left. She had barely exchanged a word with Salka, but then it appeared that neither of them had any desire for further conversation.

Una was feeling shell-shocked. She couldn't understand what had happened or why Salka had lied like that. What's more, the conversation had undermined her confidence to such an extent that she was no longer even sure that she was right about the man being Patrekur.

She suspected that Salka wanted to avoid talking because she was guilty about the lies she had told. At least, Una hoped that she had a scrap of conscience left.

She didn't feel she could go on teaching, not now. In fact, she could hardly see how she could stay on in the village now that everyone had turned against her; even Salka, who had been responsible for getting her the job here. It would probably be better if she just headed back to Reykjavík, resigned herself to being unemployed for a while, and moved in with her mother. She could try to make ends meet in the short term with the rent she was earning on her flat. It would be an admission of defeat, but she supposed that was unavoidable in the circumstances.

Right now she couldn't care less about that wretched Patrekur. She had only tried to do the right thing, as her father had taught her, but it had backfired on her. She no longer gave a damn why the man had come to Skálar or why he had gone missing. People were forever going missing.

Hannes and Hilmar haunted her nightmares every night, their life-less bodies lying side by side in a fissure in the lava-field. She didn't know where, but her dream always conformed more or less to the scenario the police had described for her. It wasn't something she could remember and, despite her confession, she wasn't at all con-vinced that she had been present at the scene.

And now she had been charged, along with a couple of other people, with murder.

The days in court passed by in a blur. She didn't experience any guilt or regret, but nor did she have the feeling she was innocent. The police officers' description had been too persuasive for that.

She tried to detach herself from what was happening, as a way of preserving her sanity.

She had even stopped missing Hannes, for the most part, having long ago reconciled herself to the knowledge that he was gone. Besides, if she had been involved in his murder, she had no right to miss him. Her time with him seemed hazy now, as if it had been a dream. If only it had never happened, she thought; if only they had never met and he had never vanished. He and his mate Hilmar.

She had regular meetings with her lawyer, at which he assured her that she had a good chance of being found innocent. The police had no evidence to base their case on, apart from her confession.

There was a certain comfort in this thought, though she could hardly imagine what the newspaper coverage must have been like. Even if she was found innocent, to the public she would always be guilty. Was there any way out of this?

Subconsciously, she knew she would be found guilty of the murders. She stood no chance against the system . . . against the police, the judges. She was nobody, a nonentity who could conveniently be sacrificed to tie up the case in a simple, tidy manner.

So it didn't really matter any more whether she had been involved in murdering the two men or not. No one was on her side. She was alone, and when you're alone in the world, concepts like guilt or innocence cease to have any meaning.

XXIX

Una was woken by the phone. The jangling resounded around the whole house, as usual. She glanced automatically at the clock, saw that it was midday and realized she must have dozed off on the sofa. Well, she had needed the rest.

The phone kept up its peremptory ringing and it occurred to her to run downstairs and answer, but she knew – or believed – that Salka was home and she didn't want to jump in ahead of her. Quite apart from which, she had absolutely no desire to bump into her after what had happened.

The noise stopped abruptly mid-ring. No doubt Salka had picked up.

Una wondered who it could be. Salka didn't get many phone calls. Someone from the village, perhaps? Were they planning another meeting from which Una would be excluded . . . ?

She was startled to hear a knock at her door.

'Una?' The door opened and Salka put her head round. 'Were you asleep? Sorry. There's someone on the phone, asking for you.'

'What? For me?' Una sat up, rubbing her eyes, and realized how tired she was. She could happily have gone on sleeping.

'Yes, some woman.'

'OK, thanks, I'm just coming.'

Salka disappeared.

Una hurried downstairs and into the hall.

'Hello?'

'Una? Hi. Did I wake you this time?' It was Sara at the other end of the line.

'What? Oh, no, not at all. But there's only one phone in the house and I was upstairs.'

'Aha. I'll see for myself when I come and visit.'

Yeah, right. Una refrained from asking exactly when this visit was supposed to take place, not least because she wasn't sure how much longer she would be able to stick it out there herself.

'What's up?' she asked sleepily, not really in the mood for a chat, though she realized it would probably do her good to talk to someone who didn't live in the village.

'Oh, I just wanted to let you know that I looked it up for you, that business of the girl who died.'

Una perked up a little and her tiredness temporarily receded.

'Oh? Did you find something?'

'Yes, just in *Our Century*, you know, at Mum and Dad's house. I didn't have to search long, but I think I've seen enough.' She paused: 'Unless you need to write a whole essay about it.'

'Oh no, nothing like that. So what happened?'

'From what I read, it sounds like quite a gruesome story. The girl drank poison.'

'She drank poison?' Una whispered.

'Yes, can you imagine? She was only young.'

'Was it an accident?'

'Nobody knew, as far as I can tell. Which makes it all the more horrible, if you ask me – wondering if someone poisoned her deliberately. You never know what living in such an isolated spot can do to people. But you'd know more about that than me.'

Una was shaken by the story. It wasn't what she had been expecting at all. And Salka hadn't bothered to tell her, though she must know about it.

'Well, what do you think?' Sara repeated, when Una didn't answer.

'I'm speechless,' Una replied. 'I wasn't prepared for that at all. It sounds pretty gruesome, as you said. The poor child must have suffered terribly.' She was fairly sure of that after her years studying medicine. 'What kind of poison was it?'

Not that this was the most important aspect.

'Rat poison, according to the book. I should think people in the countryside would have needed to have it to hand in those days.'

'When you read about the incident, how did it strike you?' Una asked. 'Did you feel there was any suggestion that she might have been murdered?'

'Hard to say, but, yes, maybe.'

No wonder the poor girl can't find any peace, Una thought to herself.

'Does this help you at all?' Sara asked.

'Yes, thank you. It was important for me to know. It'll help me learn to understand this place a bit better.'

'How are you coping?' Sara asked unexpectedly.

Una hesitated. She wanted to lie to avoid any further discussion, and say that it was an absolute dream, that it was fantastic living in the heart of nature, in such a tranquil spot. That would be the easiest answer.

'Actually, it's pretty grim,' she said instead. 'I don't get on with the locals and I don't think they like me. It's a weird place. There's a lot of sadness. And too many secrets. To tell the truth, I'm not sure I'll last the whole winter here.'

This time it was Sara's turn to be silent for a while before replying. 'Oh God, I . . . I wasn't expecting that. I thought you were happy there.'

'Not any more. I probably never was.'

'I'm sorry.'

'It's not your fault, Sara.'

'I feel partly to blame . . . I mean, I was the one who showed you the advertisement.'

'But it was my decision to take the job. I wasn't happy in Reykjavík either and I needed a change of scene. I just chose the wrong place.'

'Of course, it's terribly far away. You know I'll come and visit you as soon as I can.'

'There's no rush.'

'No, I'm serious . . . I'm going to check what the weather forecast is like for the next few days and see if I might be able to make a quick trip up to see you either next weekend or the weekend after. It all depends on the weather and the state of the roads.'

'That would be great, if I'm still here then.'

'Have you got room for me?'

'More than enough. I've got a whole flat to myself.' Thinking of the ghost, Una qualified this: 'Sort of.'

'What happened about that man who disappeared?' Sara asked. 'I heard on the news that he's still missing. Did the picture help at all?'

'No. It seems it may not have been him after all.'

'Oh, I see.'

'By the way . . .' Una suddenly recalled a remark the policeman had made. 'Someone mentioned that the man – Patrekur – was mixed up in bad company. Has there been anything about that in the news? Was he some sort of criminal?'

'Yes, hadn't you heard? There was a front-page article about him at the weekend in *Helgarpósturinn*.'

'The papers get here late and irregularly,' Una said. 'If at all.'

'It was quite a dramatic story. He was a suspect in the Hannes and Hilmar murders, before the trio confessed. Apparently, he was high on the police's list. I had no idea and don't remember his name being released at the time.'

'And now he's vanished too.'

'Exactly. Of course, it's mostly just the press being sensationalist, but the journalist was suggesting there might be a link between the cases. That the person who bumped off Hannes and Hilmar might have been responsible for Patrekur's disappearance too. In which case, the trio who are in prison can't be guilty.'

'There were always stories doing the rounds, claiming they weren't necessarily responsible,' Una pointed out.

'So I've heard.' After a brief silence, Sara continued: 'So, in other words, you don't think Patrekur was in Skálar after all?' The article in the paper had obviously aroused Sara's interest in the mystery.

'I doubt it. It's hard to tell from the picture.'

'Yes, I suppose. It would have been a good story, though. You could have sent it to the papers. Perhaps even got a reward for the tip-off.'

'Yes, well, I'll bear that in mind.' It occurred to Una that this was still an option.

'Anyway, I'll be in touch, Una,' Sara said, sounding unusually affectionate. 'Look after yourself. And if you're unhappy there, just come back to town. There's no reason to hang on in a miserable situation.'

'Thanks. Either way, hopefully we'll see each other soon,' Una said. 'If you do come, could you bring me some bottles of red wine?'

'You bet.'

After they had rung off, Una peered into the dining room. Salka was sitting very still at the table, her head bowed.

Now might be as good an opportunity as any to sit down with her and have a talk; try to get at the truth for a change.

The verdict hadn't come as a surprise to her.

She was now a convicted murderer.

It wasn't as big a shock as she had thought it would be. She had mentally prepared herself for the news. According to her defence council, the case would now go to the Supreme Court and they would have a better chance there. She wasn't sure how realistic this was, but then she had long ago given up the fight.

Maybe she had been there and taken part in killing Hannes and Hilmar. Or maybe she was innocent and the other members of the group were guilty. They had all been convicted and given prison sentences of varying lengths.

She herself had got the full sixteen years.

She avoided calculating how old she would be when she got out. Her lawyer had tried to keep her spirits up by saying that the Supreme Court verdict would be more lenient and that in any case she wouldn't have to serve the whole sentence. Eight years max. And she had already spent nearly a year in custody. 'So, of course, they'll take that off,' her lawyer had said, with a forced smile.

It was easy to look on the bright side when it wasn't you who was going to be locked up for years.

By now she had got into a routine of sorts in prison and she tried to take it one day at a time. She wouldn't start counting down the days yet, not until there was a shorter time left.

And, of course, there was always the Supreme Court.

XXX

'Salka?'

She jerked her head round. Evidently, she hadn't heard Una enter the dining room.

'Yes?' She spoke quietly, looking in Una's direction without meeting her eye.

'Salka, can I talk to you? Shall I make us some coffee?'

'I don't want any coffee, thanks. Not now.'

Una sat down at the table facing her.

There was a deathly hush in the old house.

Salka lowered her eyes, staring at the table as if it held the answers to all the world's riddles.

'I've been reading about Thrá,' Una said, tweaking the truth a little.

Salka raised her eyes. 'Have you? Why?'

'I know you don't want me sticking my nose in, but I hope you'll forgive me. I was just curious because I feel kind of invested in what happens here.'

'No need to apologize, Una,' Salka replied dully.

'I read that she'd . . . well, that she'd drunk poison.'

'Thrá?'

'Yes.'

'Yes, I suppose you could put it like that. I was told the story made it into the papers at the time. It was horrific, of course. Utterly horrific.' Her voice had grown a little stronger, but her tone was sombre.

'Do they know what actually happened?'

Salka didn't answer.

'Was it an accident?'

Salka met and held Una's gaze. 'It wasn't an accident. It wasn't a bloody *accident*,' she said, with sudden vehemence.

After a long pause, Una asked: 'What happened?'

'Thrá was my mother's sister, did I tell you that?'

Una shook her head, though she should have guessed.

'My mother's older sister. Born in 1920. My mother was two when it happened. Naturally, she couldn't remember anything herself, but she learned the whole story later. Like I did. People knew what had happened. I first heard the story when I was older. My mother never talked about it.'

Una waited patiently, wanting to give Salka space to tell the tale since it was obviously a painful subject.

'It was rat poison, bloody horrible stuff. The little girl drank it mixed into her milk. No one ever knew why my grandmother did it. There just . . . there just wasn't any explanation . . .'

'Your *grandmother*? She poisoned her own daughter?'

Salka nodded, with such sadness in her eyes that it was as if she were describing recent events, not something that had happened nearly sixty years ago.

'Are you sure?' Una asked.

'Yes, I believe she admitted it when they questioned her. She claimed she couldn't stop herself, but she didn't know why she'd done it. She was just seized by a fit of madness.'

'Was she convicted for it?' Una asked. Sara hadn't mentioned any details like this after reading the summary in *Our Century*. But surely the woman couldn't have got away with her crime?

'No, she wasn't convicted. Because the police were never informed. The village stood by my grandmother and hushed it up.'

'Stood by your grandmother? What about the child? Did no one stand up for her?' Una was stunned.

'Apparently not.'

'Was she allowed to raise your mother after that?'

'Yes. It's quite incredible when you think about it, but that's how it was. I suppose the locals didn't want the village to get a bad reputation. Just like now. There are so many things that can't be talked about.'

'Like what?'

'People look out for each other.'

Una seized this opportunity to up the pressure: 'What are you all keeping from me, Salka?'

Salka was silent, but now at least she was prepared to meet Una's gaze.

'There *is* something, isn't there?' Una insisted.

'I wasn't going to tell you about my grandmother. Not everyone knows — not outside the village. She died at a ripe old age and went on living in this house right up until near the end.'

'That's shocking, Salka. I can hardly believe it.'

'I stopped coming to see her after I learned what she'd done. I couldn't look her in the eye any more. I didn't come back here for years, not until I inherited the house. Then I felt it was time. My family has such strong roots in Skálar, and I was happy here, until . . . you know . . .' Grief had banished every other emotion from her face.

'Are you going to stay on here?'

'I need to stay with Edda. I feel she's still here, like Thrá.'

'Have you seen Thrá too?' Una asked. 'Have you heard her?'

Salka nodded. 'Yes . . . at least I think so. She's always haunted the house, from what I've heard. It's impossible to get rid of her. And perhaps there's no reason to. I believe that people who die in traumatic circumstances always come back. But not necessarily because they've got unfinished business – unless you count lost opportunities, I suppose. Things just didn't end the way they were supposed to and that's why she makes her presence known.'

Una didn't say anything.

'Just like Edda,' Salka added after a long interval, in a choked voice. 'Sorry, it's just so hard to talk about.'

'I understand,' Una said. 'Do you have any idea what happened?'

Salka shook her head. 'No, they can't explain it,' she said, her voice still thick with tears. 'She'd been in such good spirits – there was nothing to suggest she had anything wrong with her. The doctor couldn't give me any explanation.'

'It's . . . It's just so awful.'

'It won't change anything now, of course, but I . . . I . . .' Salka's voice gave way. After a moment, she recovered enough to go on: 'I've sometimes wondered if I might have done something . . .' She didn't finish.

'Done what?' Una asked. 'What do you mean? She was just taken ill.'

'No, I mean . . . You know, like my grandmother. If I could have given her something but blocked out the memory. I'd begun to think the house might have this effect on people, that there might be some evil spirit here or . . .' She broke down in tears again and continued through her sobs: 'Or something in our blood. My grandmother killed her daughter . . . Would I be capable of that? Could I have done it without remembering?' She slumped forward on the table, her body heaving, and began to howl.

Una got up and went over to place a wary hand on her shoulder. 'Of course you didn't, Salka. Don't be ridiculous. That sort of thing can't be inherited,' she said, though she wasn't sure this was right. 'Of course you'd never have harmed Edda. That's an absurd idea. You mustn't let yourself think like that, Salka.'

'No, I know,' the other woman said through her gasps. 'I know.'

This was her chance, Una thought, unfair though it was to exploit the situation like this: 'Salka, the man who came here before Christmas. Are you sure it wasn't the man in the papers? That it wasn't Patrekur, the man who's vanished?'

Salka sat up but didn't look round. 'I think I need to go and lie down, Una.' She rose to her feet and left the dining room without another word.

Una stood there without moving. Her thoughts returned to Edda's death. She wasn't sure what to think. Was it conceivable that Salka could have done something crazy and suppressed the memory? Could she have poisoned her daughter in a fit of insanity, just as her grandmother had done long ago?

Una knew from her medical studies that there were drugs, easily available drugs, that could damage the liver but leave no trace in the body afterwards. Perhaps . . . perhaps . . .

She was no longer sure of anything.

'The accused, Björg Helgadóttir, is hereby sentenced to sixteen years in prison. The time she has already spent in pre-trial detention will be deducted from . . .'

The wording of the Supreme Court verdict was etched on her memory. She had let herself hope, and that had been a mistake. Hope had made her disappointment all the keener. It seemed she wasn't to receive any justice in this life.

She sat in her cell, and now she had started counting down the days. There were years left, of course, but now the verdict had been passed and couldn't be undone she had to reconcile herself to it and try to focus on the future. It wasn't easy, though; it was so far from being easy.

She had been sober for so long now that she had got used to the condition. The alcohol and drugs that had cast such dark shadows over her life were now nothing but a hazy memory from another world. And the more she thought about the case – she had no shortage of time to think these days – the more certain she became in her own mind. If she'd been involved in a murder – let alone two murders – she would have remembered it, however drunk or out of *it she had been at the time. In spite of her confession, she couldn't for the life of her recall having taken part in killing Hannes and Hilmar.*

Yet here she sat, unable to do anything about her situation.

All the escape routes were closed.

She met her lawyer from time to time, though increasingly less often with the passing of the years, and he still claimed he believed her; that he knew she was innocent.

Perhaps he was lying; perhaps not. It wasn't important.

He promised not to forget her. Promised he would fight for the case to be reopened if any new evidence came to light; anything that could suggest she was innocent.

The problem was that, so far, there was no sign of any such evidence.

XXXI

Una was sure about one thing: the man, who she still believed was Patrekur, had been looking for Hjördís.

Which meant Hjördís might hold the key to the whole mystery, assuming Una hadn't lost all touch with reality.

For once, she was stone-cold sober. She could picture it clearly: Patrekur's visit, the fact he had asked where to find Hjördís. Damn it, of course she remembered what he looked like. She wasn't going to let Salka deliberately confuse her.

It *was* the same man.

It was nearly midnight, but Una didn't feel at all tired. Rather, she was filled with determination to get to the bottom of the mystery. So what if it was none of her business? The fact was that she had been threatened by Guffi, whether directly or by implication. Salka had lied to her and to the police. The villagers had closed ranks against her. A little girl had died and a man connected to a notorious criminal case had come to Skálar and was now missing.

She had to know the truth.

XXXII

Una headed up the track towards the farm, regretting the fact she hadn't put on warmer clothes but trying to ignore the cold.

Despite the late hour, there was a light on in the farmhouse.

As she drew near, she could make out the shapes of two people through the windows: Hjördís and Thór. They didn't notice her, cloaked as she was by the darkness, until she approached the front door and entered the circle of light, at which point she saw the quick lift of Thór's chin as he caught sight of her.

Their eyes met for an instant and he shook his head, almost imperceptibly, conveying the message that she should go away and avoid causing any more trouble than she already had.

The moment reminded her, oddly, of that first evening in Skálar when the girl had watched her from Salka's window. Had it been Edda . . . or Thrá? Had she been trying to warn Una? To tell her to turn back before it was too late? And now the same thing was happening again.

She halted, unsure what to do. But she couldn't back down now. She took another step forward and knocked on the door. Despite Thór's silent warning, she had no intention of giving up. She'd had enough. Out of the corner of her eye she caught a movement as Hjördís rose to her feet. Then the door opened and Hjördís was standing there.

'Una,' she said, her voice emotionless, betraying neither surprise nor anger, fear nor pleasure.

'Can I come in?' Una asked, dispensing with all small talk. The time for that was over.

Hjördís gave a curt nod and stood aside. 'Take a seat.'

Thór was still sitting at the kitchen table. He seemed keen to avoid eye contact now and the thick beard obscuring his features made his expression impossible to read.

She took a seat at a discreet distance from him, and Hjördís joined them, pushing a mug and the thermos of coffee across the table to Una.

'So, Una, what can we do for you?' she asked, a note of exasperation breaking through.

'I had a visit from the police,' Una said. 'About the man who came and stayed with you.'

'So we heard,' Hjördís said drily.

'He went away again. Salka made sure of that.'

Hjördís nodded. 'Quite. What did he want here anyway? This is . . . this must be the quietest spot in the country.'

'The stranger who visited – I know who he was. His name was Patrekur, wasn't it?'

Hjördís shook her head. 'He wasn't called Patrekur.'

'Was he an old schoolfriend of yours? That's what you told me in church.'

'Yes, that's right. He was at school with me.'

Una darted a glance at Thór, who lowered his gaze, clearly intending to stay out of it. 'I saw a photo of him in the paper,' she said. 'He's the man they're looking for in Reykjavík. He's been missing for quite some time. Then I heard that he was linked to the Hannes and Hilmar case. As a suspect.'

Hjördís didn't say anything.

'Haven't you seen a picture of him?' Una persisted.

'Yes. It's not the same man. I should know,' Hjördís said, then added, with an edge to her voice: 'I expect you were drunk.'

So her drinking was common knowledge now. With a horrible sinking feeling, Una realized that there was a conspiracy in the village to blame the alcohol for her 'confusion'. They had all turned against her. But she wasn't giving up; she couldn't give up now.

Not when it was blatantly obvious from Hjördís's evasive eyes that she was lying.

XXXIII

'Did he leave straight away the following morning?'

'What does that matter?' Hjördís asked angrily. 'What does it matter what some old schoolfriend of mine did or didn't do? I don't even know what he wanted out here.'

'I can always ring the police again and tell them to talk to you this time.'

'Why don't you go ahead?' Hjördís fired back, even angrier than before.

'Did something happen? While he was visiting you? Something that might explain why he disappeared?'

'What the hell has it got to do with you, Una?'

It was Una's turn to raise her voice: 'Everybody's lying to me! A little girl is dead, a man has vanished. Perhaps the two things are linked – who knows?'

'Of course they're not linked!' Hjördís shouted.

'Then tell me the truth!' Una shouted back.

'There's nothing to tell,' Hjördís said, the heat going out of her voice.

At this point Thór looked up, straight into Una's eyes,

then turned to Hjördís. 'Just tell her,' he said in a quiet, level voice. 'Just tell her.'

'What? What do you mean? We can't,' Hjördís retorted.

'Of course we can. It's our secret, for Christ's sake.'

Hjördís leapt to her feet. 'Stop it, before you say too much.'

'It's our secret and I trust her.' He looked back at Una, his eyes suddenly bright with despair. 'I can trust you, Una, can't I?' Then he corrected himself: '*We* can trust you?'

Una was momentarily lost for words. She stared at Thór, knowing perfectly well what her answer would be. She was dying to hear more. 'Yes, of course,' she said at last.

'Fuck this,' Hjördís said. 'You've got to be fucking joking.'

'It's all right, Hjördís. Una's one of us now. The whole village shares our secret and now Una does too. There's no point keeping it from her any longer. We've tried, but it didn't work. And I have no desire to see the police back here.'

Nineteen eighty-six.

Björg would be thirty this year. When she was younger, she used to dread this landmark, seeing it as the year when she would be properly grown up. But never in her worst nightmares could she have imagined that she would be spending it in a prison cell.

It was five years since she had been convicted.

She had been told that she could probably apply for parole in three years. That wasn't such a long time in the great scheme of things. She'd missed out on so much already; the best years of her life had passed her by. She had long ago given up the fight to get her case reopened, as it seemed hopeless, so now the most she had to look forward to was getting out of prison in three years or so, burdened with a murder conviction, alone, uneducated and destitute. After that she would have to try somehow to get back on her feet and build a life for herself.

She had long ago stopped believing that she had murdered Hannes and Hilmar. The police's lies had lost their power of persuasion now that she was no longer locked up in solitary confinement.

It was too late to do anything about that now. And clearly there was no white knight coming to rescue her.

There was nothing to do but count down the days.

For three more long years.

XXXIV

'You mentioned the Hannes and Hilmar affair,' Thór began.

'Yes?'

'Presumably you're familiar with what happened?'

Una nodded.

When Thór didn't continue, she felt compelled to fill the gap: 'Three young people murdered two men called Hannes and Hilmar. About six or seven years ago. The bodies were never found but they all confessed to the killings.'

'That's right,' Thór said.

'And, er, the girlfriend of one of them was among the killers, as far as I can remember. It was all very shocking.'

'Yes, Hannes's girlfriend,' Thór said. 'Her name's Björg. She confessed, like the others. Hannes and Hilmar were mixed up in a drugs ring — a big-scale operation, with some extremely dangerous men behind it.'

Una couldn't remember the details, but she did recall the furore surrounding it and the way it had dominated the headlines. Even politicians had been drawn into the debate and had put pressure on the police to solve the case. Nevertheless, it had been some time before the three young people had been arrested and had finally confessed.

'Una,' Thór said gravely. 'Una, you remember your promise. What we tell you now must never, ever, go any further.'

She nodded, doubtfully though.

'The thing is, Una, I know that the people concerned, Hannes's girlfriend and the two men . . . I know that they're all innocent. And that's not all. I know who really did it –'

XXXV

Una had a horrible feeling she knew where this conversation was heading.

She braced herself during the pause that followed Thór's words. *I know who really did it* . . . She waited, her body tense, for him to come out and say it, to confess to murder, even double murder. The man she was so attracted to. Could she really have fallen for a killer? Swift on the heels of this question followed another: did she even want to know the truth? And would she be able to keep her promise of secrecy?

'Thór . . .' she interrupted, when she saw that he was about to carry on. 'I don't . . . I don't think . . .'

I don't think I want to hear any more, was what she had been about to say, but she couldn't finish the sentence. Her curiosity was too strong. She needed an explanation for the mysterious goings-on in the village, and she wouldn't have been human if she hadn't wanted to know the truth about the most notorious murder case in Iceland's recent history.

Thór looked at her, his brows raised: 'Are you all right?'

She nodded. 'Are they really innocent?' she asked. 'And locked up in spite of that?'

'Yes. Patrekur . . . the man you met . . . he's the one who should have been convicted for the killing, not them. The sick bastard. The murdering piece of scum.'

Una was utterly wrongfooted. Was Thór innocent after all? She experienced a rush of relief but didn't want to celebrate too soon. 'How do you know?' she asked. 'Were you . . . Were you involved in the murders?' She immediately regretted having phrased the question like that.

Thór shook his head. 'No, but it's hardly surprising you should ask. I knew Patrekur, though – knew what an evil bastard he was. I'm all too aware what he was capable of.'

She noticed that he spoke of Patrekur in the past tense. 'In that case, why's he still a free man?' she asked.

'Because the police buggered up the investigation. They arrested a bunch of innocent people and the courts played along.'

'If that's really true, Thór . . . If . . . Why haven't you told people? Can't you prove it? Can't you help those poor people get out of prison?'

He hesitated, his eyes flicking shiftily away from hers.

Una glanced at Hjördís, but she was sitting very still, her face grim, staying well out of it.

'Una, there's nothing I can do,' Thór said.

'Why not?' she asked, her voice coming out harsher than she had intended. 'For God's sake, Thór, why not?'

'Because they'd kill me, Una. Those bastards are unbelievably dangerous.'

'Who are you talking about?'

'The men who were – still are – behind the smuggling ring. We were disposable, you know – just the little guys. But we decided to get out while we could and go to the police. They'd gone too far, way too far. But somehow they got wind of the fact we were planning to betray them.'

'Who's we?'

'Me and Hannes.'

'Hannes? The man who was killed? Did you know him?'

'Yes. We were going to pull out and go to the police together. But then they unleashed Patrekur on us.'

'To do what?'

'To kill us, Una.'

'What? You said he killed Hannes and Hilmar. Was he supposed to kill you too? But you got away . . .'

'Una, you don't understand,' he said, lowering his voice, then reached across the table and took her hand. 'Una, he only got to Hannes. Although his body's never been found, I understand it's somewhere in the lava-fields on Reykjanes. But Hilmar . . . Hilmar vanished without trace. He not only survived but he's sitting in front of you now.'

XXXVI

'What are . . . what are you saying?' Una's heart was pounding. She felt faint. She couldn't have heard right. Had Thór really said that Hilmar was sitting in front of her? Hilmar, the man who had vanished at the same time as Hannes . . . The man for whose murder three young people had been sent to prison?

'Hilmar Thór,' he said. 'My name's Hilmar Thór.' Letting go of her hand, he stood up, went over to Hjördís and put his arm round her shoulders. 'And Hjördís here, is my sister, or half-sister, rather. The farm belonged to our father.'

Hilmar Thór.

'You mean . . . You mean you've been here since . . . ever since you went missing . . . or deliberately disappeared?' She could hardly take it in. Was it possible that she was sitting in front of the man whose fate had been a mystery all these years? Then, following hard on that came the thought that he had watched without saying a word while three innocent people went to prison because of him.

'Yes,' he said, in a matter-of-fact tone. 'I fled out here as soon as I guessed what was coming. I knew my sister would take me in. I'd never lived here myself or had much contact with Hjördís, so I thought it was unlikely it would occur to them to look for me here. As you've probably worked out by now, I live here in the main house with my sister, not in the guesthouse. I lied to you about that. Sorry. I never thought I'd end up staying here all these years or that the case would blow up like that. The whole thing just escalated until, in the end, I felt it was too late for me to come forward. And all this time I've been living with the knowledge that my life is in danger. That's why I grew the beard, just to be on the safe side.' He stroked his thick facial hair. 'The truth is, I'm still frightened – scared to death of the guys behind it all. You don't know what they're like, Una; what they're capable of. But they never thought to come looking for me here, not until Patrekur showed up.'

Una frowned as she tried to recall the photos of Hannes and Hilmar, which had long been familiar to everyone in Iceland after being splashed all over the papers for years on end, but the beard made it hard to fit Thór's face with that of the man who had disappeared. At least she understood now why he had struck her as oddly familiar the first time they met.

As if reading her mind, Thór went on: 'That's why I was a bit pissed off the first time we bumped into each other. I didn't know if it was a good idea to get to know you, in the circumstances . . .'

'Was Patrekur searching for you?' she asked.

'Yes, well . . . actually, it was Hjördís he was looking for. Those men have kept up the hunt for me all these years. They wanted to finish the job. And somehow they finally got wind of the fact I had a half-sister living on Langanes. I don't think Patrekur *knew* I was hiding out here, but he may have had his suspicions.'

'Salka rang and warned me,' Hjördís chipped in, suddenly finding her tongue.

Una, remembering that phone call, saw it in a completely new light. Salka hadn't been ringing just to let Hjördís know about the visitor. She had been warning her. And this begged another question:

'Does Salka know?' she asked Hjördís. Then she raised her eyes to Thór, who was still standing with his hands on his sister's shoulders: 'Does she know who you are?'

It was Hjördís who answered: 'Everyone in the village knows . . . everyone except you, that is. There was no way of hiding it and we sometimes needed their help in protecting my brother, like when the TV film crew turned up here. You see, Una, they grew up together, the four friends: our dad, Guffi, Gunnar and Kolbeinn's dad. It was their village, as you might say, and people take care of their own here. We stick together. Salka stood by us too because her grandparents were from Skálar, and they say the villagers covered for her grandmother back when her daughter died.' She paused: 'That's why Guffi . . . all of us . . . were against you coming here. It was Salka who forced it through. She wanted the kids to have a proper teacher and felt it was worth taking the risk. She didn't see why you should ever find out the truth about Thór . . .

My main hope was that you two would never meet but, of course, that was unrealistic of me, and anyway, that hope was dashed the very first evening, wasn't it? When you ran into each other . . .'

Una nodded. She took a mouthful of coffee, feeling in need of fortification. It was almost cold.

'I . . . I can still hardly believe it,' she said, with a catch in her voice. 'None of you wanted me here and . . . and now it turns out you were all lying to me the whole time.'

'I wouldn't put it quite like that,' Hjördís replied grimly, 'but we didn't trust you.'

'It would have been better if you hadn't put two and two together in connection with Patrekur, Una,' Thór said, and although his tone didn't change, she shivered. She found herself wondering if she was safe there with these two. They had revealed a terrible secret to her, and if she kept quiet about it she would be complicit in keeping innocent people behind bars. Could she live with that? No wonder Thór and Hjördís weren't confident that they could trust her.

'Yes, that bloody picture in *Morgunbladid*,' Hjördís said.

'I almost didn't see it,' Una said in a small voice. 'The papers didn't come.'

Hjördís's expression betrayed all that needed to be said and Una realized that her suspicions had been correct; it hadn't been a coincidence at all. '*Morgunbladid* . . .' she said slowly. 'The paper that never arrived . . .'

Hjördís and Thór exchanged glances and, in the end, it was Hjördís who answered: 'Gunna got rid of the papers for us. You'd told her your suspicion and she warned us and Guffi too. We hoped you'd leave it at that.'

'Then Salka lied,' Una said, more to herself than them. 'She lied to the police that the visitor hadn't been Patrekur.'

'Naturally,' Hjördís said coldly.

'I don't understand how you've got away with it all these years. Somebody must know he's here. In a village of only ten people . . .'

And then it struck her – the fact that had completely passed her by. She counted them up in her head: *Salka and Edda, Guffi and Erika, Gunni and Gunna, Kolbeinn, Inga and Kolbrún . . . then Hjördís and Thór.* Eleven people. There were eleven people living in the village, not the official ten. Damn it, how could she have missed that?

'Quite easily,' Hjördís said. 'Or at least it *was* quite easy, until that murdering bastard turned up here, searching for my brother to kill him.'

Patrekur.

The question hung in the air. Una hesitated, drew a deep breath, listened to the silence for a moment, then asked: 'So where is he? Where *is* Patrekur?'

XXXVII

Una's only answer was more silence.

'Where's Patrekur? I *know* you two know what happened to him. If you don't want me to report you, you'll have to tell me the whole truth.' In her heart of hearts, Una already knew she wasn't going to betray Thór. Her best course of action would be to throw in her lot with him and the villagers. She liked him, maybe she was even a little in love with him. The brother and sister had entrusted her with a potentially deadly secret. If she informed on him, she could be putting his life in danger. If he was murdered as a result, how would she be able to live with herself?

'He had an accident,' Hjördís said at last.

'He's dead?'

Hjördís nodded.

'What happened?'

'I was going to deal with him myself,' Hjördís said. 'When Salka rang, we couldn't be sure it was him, of course, but Thór took the precaution of going into hiding.

But the moment he turned up at the door I guessed who he was. He asked if he could stay and I said I could give him supper and a room for the night. His manner wasn't at all threatening at first; I expect he wanted to scope out the place before he did anything.' Hjördís paused to take a deep breath, then continued: 'I decided it would be best to get rid of him permanently and just hope that no one outside the village knew he'd come here. But my plan went wrong, and that night he pulled up a chair where you're sitting now and put his cards on the table. He said he was looking for Hilmar Thór. He said he knew I was his sister and threatened to kill me if I didn't tell him where my brother was. I managed to grab a knife and hold him off for long enough to escape from the house, and that was when Thór took over . . .'

'Really it was self-defence,' Thór said, speaking up for the first time. 'I had to protect myself and my sister. The bastard deserved to die and that's all there is to it.'

'What happened?' Una repeated.

'I was listening from the cellar. When I heard him threatening Hjördís, I grabbed a piece of wood, ran upstairs and hit him. Things couldn't go on like that. And once he'd seen me, that was it. After that there was no hope that we'd be left in peace.'

Una was finding it hard to breathe. Thór had more or less admitted to murder, yet behaved as if it was no big deal. Justified it by claiming he'd been saving himself and his sister and that the dead man had had no right to live . . .

Una tried to put herself in his shoes; in the situation of

a man who had been on the run, in hiding, for all these years . . . Who'd finally been cornered and struck out in self-defence. Who was she to judge what was right and wrong when it came to the shadowy underworld he was mixed up in?

She took stock of what she had learned. Patrekur was dead. He'd been murdered the night before the Christmas concert. After which the brother and sister had coolly turned up to church as if nothing had happened.

'What did you do with him?' Una asked, swallowing.

Hjördís glanced at Thór.

'I put him in his car and . . . and drove it to the edge of the cliff in the middle of the night, then pushed it over. Hjördís followed me so she could give me a lift back. As you know, you can reach the main road from our farm without being seen from the houses down by the sea.'

'And . . . are you confident they won't find him?'

'Well, fortunately no one's looking for him up here. The sea will take care of the rest. All we can do is hope for the best.'

Another silence fell. Una felt a growing disquiet. The events the brother and sister had described seemed so unbelievable and yet were so terrifyingly real. A man had been killed, but somehow Una hardly cared. She was merely glad that the reckoning had resulted in Patrekur dying and not Thór. How she regretted now that she had ever called the police.

'I don't know what to say.' She let out a long breath. 'I have to go now. I need time to think about all this.' She got shakily to her feet.

'You won't betray us,' Hjördís said, half rising, with a look of sudden menace.

'No, I won't,' Una reassured her, realizing, as she said it, that this was the way it would have to be. She looked Hjördís steadily in the eye, sensing that there was almost nothing this woman wouldn't do to protect her brother. And then Una remembered what Hjördís had said: *I was going to deal with him myself.*

'Hjördís,' she said. 'What were you going to do? How were you planning to deal with him? You said you'd had a plan that didn't work out . . .'

Hjördís hesitated. 'I . . . I was going to poison him.'

'What?'

'Yes. I didn't know quite what effect it would have but I made a strongly seasoned stew for supper and left it on the table. I laid a place for him, then made myself scarce. Thór was hiding in the cellar. I'd told Patrekur that supper was included in the price of the room. But I didn't want to be there in case he got suspicious because I wasn't having any stew myself.'

'So . . . what went wrong?'

Hjördís faltered. 'I just don't know. I think he ate the food. At least, the plate was dirty when I came back later. But he seemed fine, as if it hadn't affected him at all.'

'What did you give him? What kind of poison? It wouldn't necessarily have worked straight away.' Una had a flashback to her medical lectures.

'Paracetamol. It was the strongest thing I could find in the cupboard. A hell of a lot of pills, crushed up in the stew. I'd heard somewhere that it's dangerous in large quantities.'

Una nodded and took a sip of the cold, bitter coffee. 'Yes, that's right. But I don't think it would take effect immediately. I'm fairly sure it would take . . .' She broke off in mid-sentence.

She felt hot and cold, then faint, as if the whole room was spinning.

As the days passed, one after another, in the monotony of prison life, Björg had come to recognize the importance of hope.

Days, months, years . . .

A faint spark of hope could keep a person alive even when it seemed certain that there was no way out.

That's what made days like this one so difficult; when the despair was there waiting to ambush her the moment she opened her eyes in the morning, when she felt so crushed by futility that she couldn't move, couldn't get out of her hard bed, couldn't eat, couldn't speak. On those days the isolation seemed all the more oppressive, her loss of freedom impossible to bear.

She was overwhelmed by the urge to give up; she didn't have the energy to keep fighting, to keep tilting at those windmills, at those people who had locked her up, against their better judgement.

Yet, through all her despair, she knew, or rather trusted, that things had to get better.

That maybe tomorrow would be a better day.

XXXVIII

Una closed her eyes and waited for the spell of dizziness to pass. She felt sick.

When she opened her eyes again, the faintness was gone. The half-siblings were still sitting there, in the kitchen of their family farm. Everything appeared depressingly old and shabby: the screamingly yellow kitchen units, the table, the chairs, the chipped white coffee mug on the table in front of her.

The faces of brother and sister were grave. They both had murder on their conscience, and yet, Una thought, the act had been, to some extent, excusable. And from their demeanour she sensed that Patrekur's death didn't weigh that heavily on them; they felt they'd been justified in defending themselves. She studied them, first Hjördís, who stared stonily back at her, then Thór, whose gaze slid away from hers.

They haven't a clue what they've done, Una thought, a chill suddenly running through her flesh. She would have to break it to them. There was no question of sparing them, even though she thought that Thór at least would be devastated.

They haven't a clue what they've done . . .

XXXIX

Neither Hjördís nor Thór spoke. They seemed to be waiting for Una to finish what she had begun saying. She was still standing there, her words hanging in the air.

'I . . . I think,' she said carefully, 'it could be quite a while before an overdose of paracetamol would take effect. I'm not sure, but I'd guess, um, about twenty-four hours.'

'Twenty-four hours?' Hjördís obviously hadn't made the connection. 'So if we'd waited, he might have died after all?'

'That's not the point, Hjördís. It wasn't Patrekur I was thinking of.'

'Oh, then what are you talking about?'

Una didn't speak. She reached for her mug and finished the cold coffee, bracing herself for what had to be said. 'It was . . . It was Edda I was thinking about.'

'Edda?' And then she saw the blow fall as first Hjördís, then her half-brother, cottoned on. Hjördís exploded to her feet, shrieking: 'No, not Edda . . . no, no . . . no!' She subsided into her chair again and buried her face in her hands, her shoulders shaking, utterly distraught.

'I learned enough during my medical studies to remember that paracetamol poisoning causes damage to the liver. And it was liver damage that caused Edda's death.'

Hjördís's face was frozen. 'It's not possible . . .'

'The incident in the church happened about twenty-four hours after you made the meat stew, Hjördís. And you told me you thought he'd eaten some, didn't you? That there had been a dirty plate on the table.'

'Yes, I just assumed – I didn't ask – but, now I come to think of it, he said he'd gone for a lie-down in his room. He didn't mention the food at all . . . didn't thank me . . .'

'Edda used to eat with you sometimes, didn't she?' Una asked, although she already knew the answer. She had a clear memory of her first evening in Skálar and Salka telling her that Edda was never home but always off somewhere, helping herself to food at their neighbours' houses. Even up at the farm, Salka had said.

Una now remembered that the evening before the concert in the church, the evening Patrekur had knocked at the door, it had been just the two of them, Una and Salka, at supper. Edda had been out somewhere, as so often, but they hadn't found it in any way odd.

Hjördís nodded and raised her eyes, her face ashen. 'Yes, she was always round here, coming and going as she liked, eating with us. We usually knew she was here, but sometimes . . . sometimes she used to help herself to food from the fridge . . . coming round without us even being aware . . .'

'So that's what happened,' Una said, speaking more to herself than to them. 'A terrible mistake, an accident – and Edda paid the price.' She felt suddenly sorry for Hjördís.

All life was sacred, that's what Una had been taught, but the reality wasn't always quite so clear cut. Things were rarely black and white; they were much more likely to be shades of grey. In the great scheme of things, Edda's life had been worth so much more than Patrekur's.

He could stay in his watery grave – that was nothing to her – and she was already sure in her own mind that she wouldn't do Thór and Hjördís the disservice of betraying them to the police.

She asked herself again if she could keep quiet about the other secret, the secret of Thór's real identity. In that case there were three innocent victims, the three people who were still locked up in prison for their supposed role in murdering Hilmar. She knew what her father would have wanted her to do, what her conscience was telling her to do – the right thing, which meant going to the police. But for once Una resisted. She would delay making a decision until she'd had a little more time to think. After all, she told herself, she didn't want to do anything to endanger Thór.

Finally, there was Edda – or rather, Salka. Wouldn't she have to tell Salka the truth about Edda's death? Even if it meant destroying the solidarity of the village? For good or ill, Salka had to know. Maybe not immediately, but sooner or later.

Neither Hjördís nor Thór said a word. Feeling it would

be better to leave them in peace to let what they had done sink in, Una quietly slipped outside, without saying good-bye, into the darkness, and walked down the track, her shoulders bowed as though she were weighed down with all the world's secrets.

PART THREE

Four Weeks Later

I

There hadn't been any sight or sound of Thrá for a whole month now.

Una had almost succeeded in convincing herself that she had imagined the whole thing and that the alcohol had been to blame. She couldn't actually remember if she'd been drinking every time she had been aware of Thrá, but perhaps it was no coincidence that she'd been sober for four weeks now, ever since that fateful evening in the farmhouse kitchen with Hjördís and Thór.

She had come to two momentous decisions. The first was to try to make a go of things with Thór. The second was to give up drinking, temporarily at least. Their relationship had got off to a promising start. It was still early days. They were taking their time and avoiding talking too much about the future and all the practical problems that would eventually rear their heads if she were to move in with or even marry a 'dead man' . . . But they would solve those when they came to them. He couldn't stay in hiding for ever.

Una was still living in the attic flat but hadn't yet found the right moment to tell Salka the truth about Edda's death. She couldn't bring herself to do it. But she had every intention of doing so, sooner or later.

Una hadn't exposed Thór's secret cither. She had promised to keep quiet about it and had no intention of breaking her word. Nevertheless, she had the odd bad night when she was tormented by images of the innocent people languishing behind bars for his sake. But the village had got a hold on her: she was trusted now, and it was a good feeling. They had accepted her. And it wasn't as if she bore the responsibility alone: they were all complicit in hiding the truth. Her teaching was going well too, but then a single pupil hardly presented much of a challenge. It was more like a private tutoring job. And Kolbrún seemed to be coming out of her shell and even thriving, now that she was the centre of attention, without Edda there to steal the limelight. There had even been talk of Una carrying on for another winter. It wasn't such an unwelcome prospect.

In spite of Thrá's continued absence from her dreams, Una often found herself thinking about the little girl who had died in such a horrific manner that her spirit might never have been able to find peace. She was glad she had finally got to hear her story.

Yet although Una had tried to convince herself that the haunting had all been in her mind, she couldn't shake off the lullaby. The fact was that she hadn't recognized Thrá's song, and this troubled her. She could hardly have started composing songs in her sleep. There could only be one logical explanation: that she had heard the lullaby as a child and later forgotten it.

That had to be the answer.

II

The verse was the key to the mystery.

Una rang her mother for the first time in ages.

'Una, darling, how are you?'

'Oh, fine, Mum. How are you both?'

'We're both very well. But we miss you. We'll come and see you as soon as spring arrives.'

'Please do, Mum. I might pop down to Reykjavík too, when I get a chance.'

'That would be lovely.'

'Mum . . .'

'Yes, dear?'

'There's something I wanted to ask you. It's about a little rhyme I heard, a lullaby. Can I sing it to you?'

'Of course, darling,' said her mother, though she sounded a little doubtful, as if she wasn't sure why Una was asking this.

The words of the lullaby were etched in Una's memory. She couldn't forget them, however much she wanted to.

Lullaby, my little Thrá,
may you sweetly sleep,
dreaming of the sunny lands
beyond the ocean deep.

'Oh yes, I remember that,' her mother said.

Una gasped. She had never been so relieved in all her life. 'Really, Mum? You remember it? Did I know it when I was small?'

'Yes, I should think so. I often used to sing it to you. It was one of my favourites.'

'It's a pretty verse,' Una said.

'Very pretty. By Davíd Stefánsson, if I remember right.'

III

Later that evening the phone rang.

Salka answered it, then called up to Una: 'It's your mother.'

Una was a little taken aback, since she hadn't expected to hear from her again so soon.

'Hello, Una, you weren't asleep, were you?'

'No, Mum. I haven't started going to bed early just because I've moved to the countryside,' Una joked. She was in a good mood; it had made such a difference to have it confirmed that the haunting had all been in her imagination, as if a weight had been lifted off her chest.

'Una, about that lullaby . . .'

'Yes . . .' Her heart began to thud ominously.

'It *was* by Davíd Stefánsson, as I thought,' her mother said. 'I remember I always used to read his poems to you. But you didn't get it quite right.'

'Oh?'

'No, I looked it up. The poem I used to read to you is different.'

Her mother read, and as the words flew from one end of the country to the other over the crackly phone line, they struck an icy chill through Una's flesh.

Lullaby, lullaby baby,
may you sweetly sleep,
shutting those pretty blue eyes,
with never a single peep . . .

Una interrupted: 'Mum, that's a completely different verse.'

'Yes, it is actually, but it sounded familiar. That's why I got muddled.'

'What about the other lullaby, Mum? Don't you remember that? Don't you remember it at all?'

'I'm sorry, darling. It was the poem by Davíd Stefánsson I was thinking of. Does it matter?'

After a brief pause, Una answered: 'No, Mum, it doesn't matter. Thanks for checking for me.'

'My pleasure, darling.'

Una said goodbye and hung up. As she did so, she had a sudden, overwhelming sense of Thrá's presence. The feeling was so strong that she was almost afraid. As if in a daze, she went into the sitting room. There was no sign of Salka; she must have gone to her room. Una walked over to the bookcase. She wanted to find the photo of Thrá. She had to find the picture.

It didn't take her long to locate the book and take it down from the shelf. She had never touched it herself, only seen the photo briefly when Salka had shown it to her. She sat down at the dining table with the old volume in front of her and opened it carefully. The picture was in its place. Thrá stared out at her, and Una felt the hairs rising on the back of her neck, as if the girl were standing right behind her. She didn't dare look round.

Then her eye happened to fall on the text of the page where the photo was kept. It was a poem, a familiar poem.

> Lullaby, my little Thrá,
> may you sweetly sleep,
> dreaming of the sunny lands
> beyond the ocean deep.

A lullaby by Thorsteinn Th. Thorsteinsson.

Above the title, someone had written in elegant pencil, the lettering a little faded:

The favourite poem of my little girl Thrá.

IV

Somehow Una made her way into the hall and to the foot of the stairs, hardly knowing what she was doing, so great was her shock. Thrá's favourite poem had come to her in a dream. It was a poem she hadn't heard before, as far as she knew. She couldn't see any natural or logical explanation for that . . .

Darkness had fallen outside and the staircase lay in shadow.

She mounted the first step and reached for the light switch as she did so. There was a deathly hush in the old house, not even broken by the usual moaning of the wind or creaking of the timbers.

As Una pressed the light switch, they appeared at the top of the stairs: the figures of two little girls, Edda and Thrá, standing side by side.

Both dressed in white, their faces blank, their eyes boring into her.

Once again Una felt the chill spreading through her nerves and flesh.

She stood frozen to the spot, her gaze fixed on theirs, until gradually it came home to her that she was no longer afraid.

Neither figure spoke, they just went on staring at her in the weak glow of the low-watt light bulb, only now she knew exactly what their silence was meant to convey:

Welcome to the village, Una.

Lullu-bía litla Þrá

Lyrics by Þorsteinn Þ. Þorsteinsson
(1879-1955)

Music by Evan Fein

Lull - u - bí - a litl - a Þrá, lát - tu þig fag - urt dreym - a.

Fyr - ir ut - an æg - i blá, át - tu sól-skins - heim - a.

English translation:

Lullaby, my little Thrá,
may you sweetly sleep,
dreaming of the sunny lands
beyond the ocean deep.

Read on for a preview of
Ragnar Jónasson's heart-pounding
new novel . . .

OUTSIDE

Coming in 2022

The snow,
mother soft,
enfolds me,
for a moment
I am saved.
I hear
a loud whisper
– are you here?
It's so cold,
hold me tight.

Fill,
fair snowdrift,
so gentle,
the emptiness
inside me,
but not quite yet . . .
. . . let me live
just a little while longer –

It was mind-numbingly cold.

Although Daníel was well wrapped up in layer upon layer of wool, with a thick down jacket over the top, it didn't help: the cold still found its way inside, piercing him to the bone.

He wondered if his travelling companions were suffering similar torments but didn't dare ask, just kept his head down and ploughed on, buffeted by the wind and driving snow. He couldn't see the surrounding landscape; couldn't tell what kind of terrain they were crossing. His whole world was reduced to a swirling whiteness and the vague shapes of figures moving ahead.

No one had said anything for a while now. They were all doing their best to keep going, trying to stick close together and follow Ármann's lead. Since he knew the area better than any of them, all they could do was trust him when he said there was an old hut 'not too far away'.

The way he put it didn't exactly inspire confidence.

Although Daníel had grown up in Iceland, he'd been

living in Britain for a number of years, first as a student at drama school, then trying to make a living from the stage.

This reunion trip with his old friends had been on the cards for a while. Ármann had offered to organize it, then, at the last minute, suggested they swap their planned visit to a summer house for a ptarmigan hunt on the moors instead. He was from the east of Iceland and assured them that he'd been on countless hunting trips in the highlands there, and that there could be few better ways of cementing their friendship. When the message arrived, Daníel had been extremely busy with rehearsals in London and simply hadn't had time to raise any objections. He didn't have a gun licence but Ármann had offered to teach him to shoot. 'There'll be no one there to see us, so you'll get a chance to bag a few birds, don't worry.'

Then everything had gone wrong.

They didn't even have all their luggage with them, only provisions for that day, though they had their shotguns, of course, since that was the whole point of the exercise. Daníel had suggested leaving the guns somewhere and coming back for them later, but this had not gone down well.

He tried to soldier on, reminding himself that he must on no account lose his concentration. There was a tacit agreement among them to put their faith in Ármann and trust that he would get them to shelter.

Sure, Daníel was freezing, but hopefully the worst of the chill would be banished once he was safely indoors, out of the elements. He tried not to dwell on the thought that they didn't even have their sleeping bags with them, and that the wretched hut they were trying to find apparently didn't have any form of heating. No electricity; no way of getting warm.

As if the cold wasn't bad enough, deep down the fear was growing that they were lost; that Ármann's sense of direction wasn't all it was cracked up to be. If this turned out to be true, Daníel wouldn't just be worried, he'd be literally scared to death. There was no chance of their finding their way back. If the storm continued with the same violence, they would have no choice but to stop somewhere and wait it out.

He couldn't see a bloody thing.

Of course, Daníel remembered storms from his youth, but nothing like this, and his years in Britain's gentler climate had softened the memories, making him forget what the cold was really like. The blizzard they were experiencing now was more brutal than he would have believed possible. And that it could be pitch black in the midst of all this whirling white snow was incomprehensible.

He was terrified he would lose sight of the person immediately in front of him. They were walking in more or less single file, with him bringing up the rear, and it was taking all his strength to keep up. He could tell that the others were more experienced at coping with conditions like these, or at least Ármann and Helena were. They had been eager for the hunt, not just eager but excited. Daníel had never shot a ptarmigan before and now it didn't look as if the weather gods were going to give him the chance to do so, not today, anyway. He wasn't even sure he'd ever tasted ptarmigan. When he was younger, perhaps.

All of a sudden, he noticed that Helena, who was second to last in the line, had stopped just in front of him. Then Daníel saw through the thickly falling flakes that the whole group had come to a halt. Had something happened?

Ármann called back to them but Daníel couldn't catch a word through his woollen hat and the thick hood of his down jacket.

Helena turned to him and said something but he still couldn't make out a word. He loosened the knot on his hood and pushed it back from his face.

'What did you say?' he shouted.

'Ármann says it's here, just around the corner. At least, he's pretty sure,' she said. *Pretty sure* was not what Daníel wanted to hear right now, and for the first time it came home to him that they could die of exposure out here. He could quite simply die, tonight, in this snowy waste. His thoughts flew to his girlfriend in London. For all she knew he was on a harmless adventure tour with his Icelandic friends. To be fair, she had warned him against it, asking whether it wouldn't be more sensible to go on a trip like that in summer rather than in the depths of winter. She'd had a better instinct for the potential hazards in his native country than he had.

No, he mustn't think like that. He was with a good group of people and together they'd find a solution. He had to keep these negative thoughts at bay. They never did any good, as he knew from bitter experience.

He had been staring into the void, into the falling snow, but now he glanced back at Helena. She smiled at him and seemed to be waiting for him to start moving again.

'Ready?' she called.

He nodded and put his hood back up.

The group set off again and Daníel waded through the drifts, thankful that he was wearing a good pair of boots.

If anything happened, if anyone got ill, they would be completely helpless. No one in the group had any medical experience.

They had each trodden their own path in life. Helena was an engineer and worked for some start-up that was making waves – according to her, anyway. Gunnlaugur was a lawyer and Ármann a guide. Well, he didn't actually want to call himself a guide any more, not since he'd set up his tour company. These days he was probably richer than all of them put together. There seemed to be no let-up in the growth in tourism, and, if you believed Ármann's tall stories, he was making money off every single visitor who came to Iceland.

Daníel liked them all well enough, that wasn't the issue. He was even fond of them, in spite of their flaws. The problem was simply that whenever they met up it was generally to celebrate something – a birthday, a wedding – and on those occasions the booze always flowed freely. But he hadn't been sure he'd be able to cope with spending a whole weekend with them, especially with no alcohol to smooth things over. He was certainly stone-cold sober now. Which was just as well, of course. But he remembered that Helena had stuck a bottle of whisky in her backpack, so at least they'd have something to warm themselves with and help calm their shattered nerves once they'd finally made it to the hut.

If they made it . . .

At that moment he saw a dim shape ahead.

Had they arrived?

His friends seemed to be slowing down and he felt briefly relieved.

Yes, it looked as if they'd found some sort of hut, however inadequate, out here in the wilderness.

Ármann had kept his word.

Daníel felt a rush of relief, as though he'd been saved from certain death. He pushed back his hood again to try to hear what the others were saying.

They each had a torch and the beams darted here and there, competing to light up the hut through the driving snow. It looked to Daníel as if it was painted red, but it was hard to be sure in these conditions. Anyway, it was at least shelter from the wind and weather, which was all that mattered now.

Gunnlaugur was standing by the door and appeared to be trying to open it, but it was taking its time and Daníel could feel the cold biting harder with every second that passed.

'The door – uh – it's sticking,' Gunnlaugur called in a despairing voice. He seemed completely out of place out here, battered by the savage elements.

'Let me try.' Helena pushed him aside. 'It's only locked.' Her voice was calm. It took a good deal to throw Helena off balance.

'What, locked?' Daníel exclaimed. 'Isn't it supposed to be an emergency refuge?'

'Some huts are kept locked,' Ármann replied. 'There should be a key box here somewhere.' He directed his torch at the wall beside the door and, sure enough, there was the box.

'Can we open it?' Daníel could feel his heart pounding. He had to get inside, into shelter.

'I don't have the code,' Ármann said. 'I didn't know we'd be coming here. Let me think for a minute . . .'

Daníel moved closer. 'Shit. We must be able to break it open?' He took off one glove and attempted to tear the box off the wall. But it wouldn't budge and now he was more aware than ever of the merciless cold. Hastily he pulled his glove back on but he'd already lost most of the feeling in his fingers. 'We need a tool of some sort.'

'Can't we just break a window?' Gunnlaugur asked, his teeth chattering.

Ármann gave him a look. 'Break a window? And try to sleep in sub-zero temperatures tonight? Good luck with that . . .' His tone was acid.

'We must be able –' Gunnlaugur began, but Daníel interrupted:

'Why the hell's the hut locked? Aren't these refuges supposed to be for people in our situation? We'll die of exposure if we can't get in!'

'Calm down, Daníel,' Helena said. 'No one's going to die of exposure.'

Once again, tensions were rising among the group.

From the moment he'd stepped off the plane Daníel

had started regretting his decision to take part in this weekend trip, and the feeling had grown steadily worse. He would have given anything to be at home in his little flat in London with his new girlfriend. She was an actress too, fifteen years younger than him, and already more successful than he was, though he wouldn't admit to the fact in anyone else's hearing.

'Should we try calling – try the phone?' Gunnlaugur asked.

'We're in the highlands, Gunnlaugur,' Ármann said flatly. 'We're alone here. Miles from the nearest house – the nearest person. We just need to face up to the fact and sort this out ourselves. No one's coming to rescue us – or not any time soon . . .'

'It's a bloody pain that there's no phone signal here,' Daníel muttered, more to himself than the others.

But Ármann heard and replied, 'We were aware of that. I mean, wasn't that the plan? To be in the middle of nowhere together and try to switch off for a while? That was the whole idea, wasn't it?'

Helena intervened: 'Just leave it, guys. Look, we need to get this door open, make ourselves comfortable and get some whisky down our throats before bed. So can we concentrate, please?'

'It's a pretty flimsy door,' Gunnlaugur pointed out. 'We could probably . . .'

'We'll break open the key box. We won't do anything stupid. Then we'll buy a new box to replace it. End of story.' Ármann took the shotgun off his back.

Daníel jumped. It wasn't that he was actually expecting

Ármann to shoot anyone; it was just an involuntary reaction.

'No need to worry, mate,' Ármann said, with a grin, but in this strange situation Daníel had the feeling that his words were charged with meaning. There was an indefinable smell of fear in the air, among the thickly falling flakes.

Ármann raised the barrel of the gun and started hammering at the box, again and again, until it came loose, then kept on bashing at it until he could finally extract the key.

'Right,' he said firmly. 'It worked. Now we can relax a bit.'

He put the key in the lock and after a brief struggle to turn it, opened the door. They were met by pitch darkness.

'Well, let's get inside.'

Helena didn't wait to be told twice and almost pushed past Ármann.

Gunnlaugur followed behind, in no apparent hurry. Daníel patiently waited his turn. At times he wondered if Gunnlaugur was only half alive, he was so placid.

Daníel directed his torch in front of him as he entered. It was hard to work out the size and layout of the hut with his friends' torch beams flashing this way and that, crisscrossing the room.

He put down his backpack in the corner and drew a deep breath. It was chilly in here, but a little warmer than it had been outside, and Daníel felt as if he could finally get enough oxygen in his lungs, finally catch his breath and relax a little . . .

It was then that Gunnlaugur gave a yell.

It was a piercing yell, so disturbing in the darkness and the quiet, that Daníel felt an icy shiver running down his spine. There was a confused noise and it took him a moment or two to work out that Gunnlaugur had cannoned into Ármann, sending them both flying.

After that there was dead silence.

Daníel stood rigid with fear for a moment or two, trying to work out what had happened. Gunnlaugur had seen something, that much was obvious.

Daníel walked a little further towards the back of the hut, peering to both sides and illuminating the interior with his torch, but couldn't see anything out of the ordinary. Then he shone the beam straight ahead, at the wall facing the front door.

The sight that met his eyes was so unexpected, so horrifying in its simplicity, that he felt as if his heart had missed a beat.

Daníel tried to cry out but couldn't utter a word, couldn't move, just stood there, staring.

He felt suddenly cold all over and the shivering spread through his body with terrifying speed.

He had never been so afraid in his life.